Of Wood, Metal and Glass

David Reynolds-Moreton

sci-fi-cafe.com

Of Wood, Metal and Glass
David Reynolds-Moreton

ISBN 978-1-910779-30-9 (Paperback)
ISBN 978-1-908387-44-8 (ePUB)
ASIN B005MEKR2U (Kindle)

sci-fi-cafe.com

One:
A Leader born

THE SOFT DRUMMING of wooden wheels on hard wooden rails, plus the occasional creak of the rigging as the wind changed direction slightly were the only sounds to be heard as the truck swept smoothly along the track towards Brent's home settlement.

He felt pleased with himself after a good day's trading, exchanging coils of their twine and rope for the hard metal needles and other items they so badly needed.

As the truck approached a slight curve in the track he let the boom rope out a little, so taking full advantage of the apparent change in wind direction, speeding him on his way to more familiar surroundings and relative cool comfort of his hut.

Wiping a trace of thickened spittle from the corners of his lips, Brent took a slug of water from his drinking flask and swirled it around his mouth, gargled, and then spat the foul tasting mixture over the side of the speeding truck, cursing the hot arid air of the barren lands and the ingested metallic tasting dust which had lined his mouth and throat. A long drink from the flask put him in a better frame of mind, and he settled down to the task of squeezing every last drop of energy from the constant blast of hot air from the North.

Although he had done this and countless other journeys many times, he always felt vulnerable and very much alone out here in the desolate wastes between the settlements.

The land around him consisted of sand, gravel, and monstrous outcrops of dark menacing rock formations, towering over him like hideous monsters from the legends of old.

The rails curved around the base of these up thrusts of the planet's rocky mantle and around the seemingly bottomless pits which dotted the landscape.

The mountainous rock piles he could understand, but the unfathomable holes in the earth's surface were something which even the elders of the settlement could not explain.

They had an almost hypnotic fascination for him, not just because they were so dangerous, but because there seemed to be no rational explanation for them. Most were inverted cone shaped pits, several hundred metres across, and once an unfortunate had lost their footing on the crumbling edge they were gone for good. Not only that, but the pits seemed to slowly grow in size, eating into the surrounding land.

One such hole lay beside the track up ahead, and Brent let the sail out a little, slowing the truck down to half its normal speed. Because of a natural dip in the terrain, the rails were raised up on a long embankment of stone, and on the way out he had noticed that some of the ballast between the tracks had slipped away, and the rails were no longer firmly held in place.

As the truck approached the loosened section of track, the rumbling tone of the wheels took on a hollow sound, which had alerted him to the fault on the outward journey. A repair team would have to be sent out, and before long the track would have to be re-routed as the gaping hole in the earth's surface crept ever nearer to the works of man.

An involuntary shudder ran through him as he looked over the side of the slowly moving truck at the yawning chasm below. At that moment, a huge section of the ground gave way, cascading several hundred tonnes of rock, gravel and sand to the inky depths below. The ripping rumbling sound of the landslide ended as quickly as it had begun, with no sound of it having hit anything below, and only a wisp of dust drifting away on the wind to indicate that anything had happened at all.

As soon as the yawning hole had safely receded behind him, Brent trimmed the sail and the truck sped up accordingly. There was still a long way to go before he would reach the haven of his settlement, and he spent the time mulling over the various mysteries of life, most of which remained as elusive in their solving as ever.

There were three settlements in total, the last one only being found some fifty or so years ago, each one differing according to the circumstances which surrounded it. Brent's settlement was most fortunate in that it was situated beside a huge lake, with a plentiful supply of timber and other materials, and abundant food obtainable from the vast forest which stretched to the far horizon.

Even so, it was not the paradise it could have been, as the forest only yielded up its bounty reluctantly, and many lives had been lost before a rigid regime had been established to circumvent most of the dangers it held.

The first few hundred metres of the forest's edge supplied most of their needs, and was reasonably safe during the hours of daylight. At night it was quite a different matter.

Although very few had witnessed the beasts of the forest and lived to tell the tale, the remembered noises which emanated from the tangled mass of greenery during the hours of darkness was quite enough to cause a hasty retreat at the first signs of twilight.

In his youth, Brent and a few foolhardy teenagers had ventured beyond what was considered to be the safe limits of travel, hacking a tunnel through the tangle of creepers which hung down in vast festoons from the trees above.

Eventually they broke through to the main forest where giant trees grew to unimaginable heights, shutting out the light from above, leaving a dim and damp twilight world.

The ground between the giant trunks was totally clear of live vegetation, but was carpeted in a deep layer of dead and decaying leaves. A dank musty smell pervaded the air, and one member momentarily wanted to turn back and head for the light until a fusillade of derisive comments from the others shut him up.

The further they penetrated into the forest, the larger the tree trunks grew, until they stopped in awe at one massive trunk which was estimated to be some fifteen metres in diameter. Looking up, they could see huge branches reaching out to other giant trees some distance away, seemingly joining into their trunks to form a vast solid interlaced network of living wood extending into the far distance.

It was while they were standing there, trying to assimilate the wonder of it all that a rustling of the leaf litter drew their attention to things more pertinent. Some twenty metres away the ground seemed to heave itself up into a continuously growing ridge, and it was advancing towards them at a good walking pace.

Once they had got over the initial shock of the seemingly impossible, they turned tail and ran, except for one, who, either from bravery or sheer terror, stood his ground until a large pallid grey white head reared up from the advancing ridge. Once the jaws opened, exposing a set of very workman like teeth and a cavernous gullet behind, he too turned and ran, joining the others in a mad scramble through the tunnel they had previously cut in the thick undergrowth.

Returning to the sanctuary of the settlement in a state of shock and dishevelment, one of the Elders had enquired as to the reason for their appearance. The story was blurted out as they tried to explain what had happened and get their breath back at the same time.

Several other Elders were called, and the story retold a little more coherently; they were none too pleased.

'That is one good reason why we only go so far into the forest,' commented one Elder, 'the other is that we don't want any of those things in the deep forest to follow you out and into the settlement. We've had problems with them before, according to the old legends, and we don't want that to start all over again.

'I didn't know about that,' one of the youths replied contritely, 'or we wouldn't have gone in so deep.'

'That's why we build the huts up against the cliff face on stilts, some of the more adventurous forest beasts used to come out at night and attack us.' another Elder added, not wanting to be left out of the conversation.

'But there's no sign of the forest animals coming out now, so why do we still build up so high?' queried another lad.

'Mainly because that's the way things are done, and it also offers us some degree of protection should any of them try,' came back the tart reply, 'anyway, if you get into trouble in the deep forest, no one is going to come to your aid, so don't do it.' The Elders left, feeling they had delivered their reprimand, and done their duty to the young and inexperienced members of the settlement.

This was not the last time they ventured into the deep forest, as Brent well remembered, but they were a lot more careful next time, and he recalled the adventure with a grin.

The track had swung around to the South again to avoid another outcrop of rocks, so he adjusted the sail to take maximum advantage of the steadily blowing wind. All being well, he should be home by evening, so he drank the last of his water supply, rinsing his mouth out first to get rid of the ever present dust.

The truck picked up speed again, the wooden wheels drumming away on the hardwood rails, adding a comforting sound to the otherwise silent journey.

Brent looked out over the barren landscape, a gently undulating field of sand and gravel punctuated by the ubiquitous rocky outcrops and the massive towering peaks of igneous rock which had once been the core of molten outpourings from deep within the planet. The dreaded funnel pits dotted the area like great open wounds, sucking the surrounding ground into their cavernous throats, and slowly growing larger. 'What the hell's going to happen when they all join up?' Brent mused, as the truck rumbled on towards the settlement and the comforts of home.

He had once put this question to one of the Elders, and was told to 'Just get on with life today, and don't worry about the future, it will take care of itself.' He remained unconvinced.

The track curved away from a mass of shattered black scintillating rock with a central column which rose up into the sky like some hideous accusing finger of doom, a cold shiver ran down Brent's back as he adjusted the sail again for the new direction.

A thin high pitched screech rent the otherwise still air, echoing back and forth among the rocks for a few seconds before being swallowed up by the desert's all absorbing silence.

'What the hell was that?' Brent said out loud, knowing full well that nothing lived out here in the barren lands. It was well known that plants would not grow anywhere other than in the forest, or the carefully cultivated gardens the settlement had nurtured into being over several generations.

He had never seen any life forms on his journeys.

He nervously scanned the rock mass for any sign of motion, half hoping not to see the slightest flicker of movement. Thankfully all was as still as the rest of the terrain.

The jumble of rocks at the base of the giant finger was unusual in that they seemed to suck in any light which fell upon them. They were a dull matt black colour, but tiny sparkling pinpoints of fire dotted their surfaces. He put it down to the possibility of small crystals of clear quartz embedded in the matrix, but there was no way he would stop the truck to prove his theory one way or the other.

As rocks do not make noises, Brent was left with the uneasy growing probability that something lived there, and had just had an unfortunate mishap, so he decided to report this to the Elders when he reached the settlement. No plant or animal could live out here according to them.

In the past, so he had been told, there had been many attempts to grow produce in the sandy area outside the settlement, but everything just withered up and died, despite copious watering. The Elders put this down to there being something indefinable in the ground which growing things could not tolerate.

As the forest seemed to flourish so abundantly, they cleared an area of gravel and stones until they hit bed rock, and then over the years transported huge quantities of leaf mould from the forest edge to be mixed with sand from the lake's shore, so making a growing medium. This worked, and now they had all the vegetables and fruits they needed, the excess being exchanged with other settlements for those things they could not produce themselves.

This of course, left the perplexing question as to why the forest could grow so voraciously in the first place. No one had an answer to that either.

As the ominous rock mass and its possible occupant fell behind the speeding truck, Brent relaxed a little, he would soon be coming up to one of the sections of track which had a gentle down slope, so he would have to reduce the pull of the sail or the truck might jump the rails.

He always enjoyed this section of the journey as it was the fastest part of the track, the shallow gully through which the track ran giving the illusion of travelling much faster than it really was.

The truck was really a simple affair, just a large wooden box with four flanged wheels on Ironwood axles.

The mast supported a single sail of cloth woven from the fibres of one of the forest's strange variety of vines, the rigging being spun from another more flexible type.

The rails were also made from Ironwood, which itself had some odd properties. When freshly cut, and still green, it could easily be shaped with simple tools, but once the moisture had dried out of it, the resins within the fibres under went some strange chemical change, turning the wood into something more like the rare material called metal, and almost impossible to cut or machine. Because of its hardwearing properties, they had made the track rails from it, although in time of course, it had to be replaced.

At the front end of the truck, just before the mast, was the windmill. Now it looked more like the closed bud of an enormous flower, but when needed, the petals of the mill could be opened out by the pull of a lever.

The only time he needed to use the mill was when the truck was facing directly into the wind, as the sail was then of no use. The speeding blades of the mill drove a set of Ironwood gears which in turn fed power to the front axle, driving the truck forward at a good walking pace.

Brent now wished he had saved a little water, as his mouth and throat were dry from the metallic tasting dust he had inadvertently inhaled through quickened breathing during the incident at the black rocks. Thinking there might be something succulent left to eat in his carry bag, he rummaged about on the floor of the truck trying to retrieve the bag from the overlay of items he had exchanged for the ropes.

His searching fingers soon found the needles as one of them sank deeply into the base of his thumb, causing an involuntary jerk of his arm. This reaction unfortunately sent the needle pack sailing over the side of the truck.

The enormity of loosing the needles, the most precious items of the exchange, hit him in the stomach like a physical blow. With one hand he hit the cleat holding the sail boom rope to release the sail and pulled hard on the brake lever with the other.

The brake blocks squealed as he now increased the pressure using both hands, wisps of acrid smoke swirling up from the protesting blocks making his eyes water. The truck eventually screeched to a shuddering stop, and Brent then lashed the brake lever in the full on position with a spare piece of rope.

Climbing over the side he looked around for suitable rocks to put under the front wheels, just as a precautionary measure. To be left out here without the truck would be certain death. It took a few minutes walkabout to locate two suitable wedge shaped rocks, which he then jammed under the front wheels. With the truck now secured, he tried to apply a little logic. A close scrutiny of the rails showed some faint markings from the braking action, and although they were only just visible, he managed to followed them up the track, still not certain where the needle pack had actually fallen.

He tried to reason out how far the truck would have travelled from the moment the needles went over the side to the application of the brakes, reckoning this to be about ten metres based on the speed of the truck. So five metres back up the track from where the scuff marks began he made a mark in the ground beside the rails.

A quick look around at this point failed to reveal the missing needle pack, so he began walking out in ever increasing circles from the mark, thereby covering the whole area in which the pack could have fallen. He was about to give up the search when he nearly trod on the missing pack.

It was far out on the periphery of the circle, and looking back towards the track he could not understand how it could have travelled so far from just a simple jerk of his arm.

Again that uneasy feeling swept over him, nothing he could identify specifically, but uncomfortable nonetheless.

It was when he looked back down the track towards the truck that his blood ran cold. There was no truck, just a cloud of dust or fog, and that was drifting slowly away from him. Nothing had moved in the barren lands for several millennia as fast as Brent as he sprinted after the drifting cloud, hoping against hope that it contained his only means of transport back to civilization.

As he drew nearer, the cloud dissipated, thinning out into a multitude of twisting grey wisps which were then carried away on the wind, the truck slowly coming back into view.

Reaching the now stationary truck, he clung desperately onto the side, partly in an unconscious effort to prevent it being spirited away again, but mainly to remain ambulant.

His leg muscles ached unmercifully from the vicious sprint and the breath rattled in his throat as he tried to get some oxygen into his lungs from the hot dust laden air.

Once his breathing had returned to normal, he tried to make some sense out of what had happened. Why were the needles so far away from the track? He felt sure he could not have thrown them that far, even if he had tried, so had something moved them? Why had the tuck moved? The two stones he had wedged under the front wheels were now cast aside some way from the track, much further than if they had been dislodged due to a vagrant blast of wind putting the truck in motion. And what the hell was the grey cloud? Why had it disappeared as he approached? Somehow it had moved the truck against the tied on brake lever, so some physical force must have been at work. Brent shivered again at what that force might be. He quickly looked around at the ground for any telltale marks which might have been left, but there were none.

Rather than risk another threat to his existence, he heaved himself over the edge of the truck, thankful that the needles had been recovered and the truck was still in his possession. With the brake off and the sail set, he was on his way again, only then did he notice the thick layer of dust which had adhered to his sweating body. Where had that come from?

He would have expected a little dust, which was always in the atmosphere, but this looked as if it had been applied with a trowel, and it was beginning to itch.

In a state of renewed panic he began scraping it off with the piece of wood he normally used to wedge his seat with, the soft muddy coating falling to the floor of the truck in a succession of plops. With most of the mucky coating scraped away, the rest quickly dried and flaked off, and then he noticed the lumps which had fallen to the floor of the truck had coalesced into one lump of slimy goo, and that was almost in contact with his left foot.

This was too much for Brent, as a new flush of sweat oozed from his body. Without thinking, he quickly scooped up the blob of goo in a series of panic driven movements and flung it over the side. The last few traces of goo on the floor of the truck dried out as he watched, turned to tiny flakes and were whisked away by the ever present wind.

As he settled back into his seat, his body still tense and trembling slightly, his thirst returned with a vengeance, and he ached for a long cool drink. His mind was momentarily taken off the subject of refreshment as the truck entered the long gully with the down slope. Brent released the sail boom from its normal position, allowing it to flap freely and ineffectually in the wind as the truck gathered speed at the top of the slope.

The normal soft drumming of the wheels soon turned into a vibrant rattle as the truck raced down the gully, the low banks of rock and gravel flashing by ever faster, giving the illusion of fearful speed. Brent would have enjoyed this part of the journey if it had not been for the earlier unpleasant and frightening incident, but his one thought now was to get home safely and tell his tale.

The truck shot out of the end of the gully like a cork from a well shaken drinking flask, and Brent quickly pulled the sail boom in tightly to keep the momentum up.

After ten minutes of careering along the track, one of the yawning holes in the earth's surface loomed up ahead, and the track curved sharply away from its hungry maw to head directly into the wind. The sail was now useless; it was time to deploy the windmill.

With the sail boom left to flap freely in the wind, Brent pulled the lever to release the mill vanes which then sprang out like a giant flower does to greet the morning sun.

Although the gears creaked and rattled like a demented rope winding mill, it was a comforting sound, in fact the only sound, as the drumming of the wheels on the rails had disappeared at this much reduced rate of motion.

Brent always felt a little uneasy as he passed this particular hazard, but even more so today. Although he had no real inclination to investigate the hole, it always imbued in him the urge to stop the truck and go to its edge, daring the hideous rupture in the earth's surface to tempt him onto its deadly slippery slope to oblivion. He shuddered at the thought of what might happen if he did.

The truck slowed down to a crawl as it rounded the bend at the end of the diversion, the mill vanes now being at an oblique angle to the constant wind and providing little drive power. With the sail billowing out once more and the mill vanes collapsed into their bud like form, the truck soon gathered speed, the drumming of the wheels taking over from the rattle and clatter of the wooden gears of the mill.

Brent settled back again into his hard wooden seat, its firm unforgiving nature keeping him in touch with reality. He was now on the 'home run' as he liked to think of it, no more natural hazards to speak of except one short run between two towering cliffs of stone, a fortunate split in a long ridge like barrier which extended to either side for as far as the eye could see. Without this natural break in the massive ridge, there would be no way the two settlements could contact each other.

He had tried many times to find out how the different groups had established contact in the first place, but the Elders had always been either evasive as if they were holding back some dreadful secret, or had dismissed his queries as though they were of little importance.

This seemingly unreasonable resistance to his enquiries only made him more determined to find out more. He had made one such possible contact on this goods exchange visit, it being a very old man with a kindly face who seemed to take a shine to him during the bargaining process.

Several times he had seen the old man grinning in his direction as he bartered his settlement's goods for the best possible exchange, feigning little interest for those things he really wanted, and adding to or deleting from little piles of items to gain the best value. When all had been settled, and both parties thought they had got the best deal, the old man had invited him back to his home for refreshments.

It was a cosy mud brick two roomed structure, comfortably furnished with padded wooden chairs and a highly polished table in one corner of the main room. A selection of strange objects was carefully arranged on a series of shelves which clung to one wall, while the opposite wall sported a picture of breathtaking beauty.

A deep sided valley covered in trees, the like of which Brent had never seen before, swept down to a vast spread of sparkling water, small waves gently breaking on a sandy beach. Opening up on each side of a path which led down the valley, small clearings were bursting with flowering plants of such rich and vibrant colours that Brent thought they could not possibly have been painted from a real scene.

'Yes it is real, or was once,' the old man said, with a grin, 'and I wouldn't mind betting you would like to go there.'

The old man was an affable conversationalist, talking in soft musical tones which Brent found both soothing and pleasant to listen to. He had freely answered any questions Brent asked, although common courtesy decreed the exclusion of anything personal, or of too deep a nature.

Taking a chance, he ignoring the accepted protocol, and expressed an interest in some of the artefacts on the shelves.

The old man seemed not to mind this disregard of formal politeness and talked freely about his collection, but not in great detail. One item in particular had taken Brent's interest, a shiny collection of beautifully cut gears, all intermeshing with each other without any seeming purpose, the whole mounted in a sturdy frame.

'What is this?' asked Brent, 'I recognize that they are gears, but what do they do and what do they belong to?'

'I have no idea what they were for, but they must have been part of something larger I would suspect, possibly controlling a motion of some sort. You are going to ask where I obtained them next. That's all right. I found them on one of my expeditions when I was a much younger man, as I did most of what you see on the shelves. They belong to a bygone age, a very very long time ago.'

'According to the Elders in my settlement,' Brent responded, hoping to keep the conversation going, 'many generations ago, we came from the forest. Simple creatures, knowing little of what we now know and do, and before that I would assume we were little more than the animals of the forest, with regard to skills and knowledge.'

'Is that what you believe?' the old man had asked with a smile, 'so where do you think things like this came from?'

'I don't know, but I would certainly like to find out.'

'Perhaps you will one day. You seem to be an inquisitive young man, and you have youth on your side. I could tell you much, but this is not the time for such. There are many things most people are not aware of, some in the barren lands, some in the great tree areas, one of which is close to your home. There is plenty to find if you but look.'

Brent's interest had now fully awakened, and he would have liked to carry on the conversation deep into the night.

Unfortunately it was time for him to be leaving, otherwise he would not get back to the settlement before the hours of darkness, and no one ever went out very far in the dark, especially into the barren lands.

'I sense you would like to stay longer,' the old man said smiling, 'but I'm sure you will be this way again before long, and we can then continue our conversation.'

The truck rumbled up a slight rise in the terrain, slowly losing speed, the billowing sail straining against the wind.

Brent took a chance, and pulled the sail in even tighter, the truck struggled up the last few metres of the slope, and then he was in sight of the settlement. There was just the first hint of the dusk as the truck coasted the last stretch.

'Glad to see you back,' one of the store men said, touching palm to palm with Brent, as was the custom after a long journey, 'looks like you had a tough time.'

'That's putting it mildly.' Brent retorted, dusting down.

'Are they getting better at bargaining, at long last?' the store man asked, looking just a little worried.

'No, nothing like that, we did very well. Got a great exchange with the needles, twice as many as I'd expected, and six really good knives plus a long saw among other things.'

'OK, you've earned a good rest, leave the rest to us, we'll take care of the old truck, you go get something to eat and drink.' With that, the store man turned his back and put his not inconsiderable shoulder to the back of the truck, pushing it into the main store shed. Brent left the store area and headed for the ladder which would lead him up to his hut perched half way up the cliff. It was good to be home.

Brent's dwelling was much like the many others which clung to the cliff face, though perhaps a little smaller than most. It suited him well enough, although he would have to move to a larger one if he took a mate.

The huts were all of the same basic design; a sphere with the bottom quarter cut away, much like a Quin fruit which had slumped a little through being over ripe. It was generally agreed that they no longer needed to live at this elevated level, but did so by tradition more than anything else.

In the long and distant past, those living on the ground were prone to disappear at night when creatures of the forest came a-prowling, but those days were long gone, and they no longer had night visitors.

The construction of the huts was simplicity itself. A platform was made in the form of a circle from logs bound together with creeper strands. Around the edge of the circle, but leaving enough room for a walkway, vertical poles were attached which were later bent over to form the familiar sphere shape. Once all had been tightened into place with more bindings, a mixture of volcanic ash, sand and burnt lime was made into a mud-like mixture and plastered on the outside and then the inside. This set to a hard waterproof finish, and lasted for as long as anyone could remember.

Window holes with wooden shutters and a door completed the abode, a small fireplace often being added for those who preferred to cook their food.

Ladders and walkways were constructed to connect the huts into a community, and the view out across the lake was far better than that which could be had from a ground based dwelling. Brent's home had a comforting spicy warm log fire smell about it, and he relaxed in his long chair for a while before preparing a long awaited meal.

Brent's eyelids slowly drooped as he lay there, and soon he was recalling the extraordinary events of the day in an almost dreamlike state. An involuntary shudder ran through him as he again realized the truck had disappeared into the strange cloud of dust, and then he nearly jumped out of the chair as someone banged on the door.

A bright cheery face peered in through the half open door.

'Just heard you got back and thought you might like a bite to eat. Don't see why a chap should have to prepare his own food after a day like yours. Hear you did really well again.'

Brent followed his friend down two ladders to the lower level and into a somewhat larger hut than his own, to be greeted by two boisterous children and their smiling mother.

'Did you see any monsters today?' asked the elder one, jumping up and down with anticipation and excitement.

'No, not today. I did have a good look as I promised, but I think they must have all been hiding in their holes when they heard the truck coming.'

'Why did you just shudder then,' asked the bright youngster, 'you don't normally do that. Come on, tell me what you saw, did it have big teeth like the forest monsters?'

'No, I really didn't see any monsters.' said Brent without lying, but strongly tempted to say what he had experienced.

They sat down, and all thoughts of monsters faded as a large steaming cooking pot was brought to the table.

'One of your favourites.' Eslie said, as she removed the lid, the steaming vapours tantalizingly promising the culinary delights which would soon be portioned out.

'Good thing you found her first,' said Brent, grinning at his friend, 'I'll bet I'll never find anyone else who can cook like her.' Soon the rattle of wooden spoons on wooden bowls took the place of conversation.

Once the main course was finished, a large bowl of forest fruits was brought to the table along with some sweet flat cakes, a speciality of Eslie's.

When all had had their fill, which left very little unconsumed food, the platters were whisked away and a dark battered gourd with two small cups was produced by Eslie.

'I'll leave you two to do what men do best, talk,' she said with a grin, 'I'll put the little ones to bed.'

With that, the men were left alone, Eslie and the two children disappearing into an alcove which contained their sleeping quarters. As their dwelling was bigger than Brent's, there was space to partition it off for the various needs of a family, which left the main area clear for entertaining and general living.

The gourd contained a liquor made from one of the rare forest fruits. They were difficult to find, and hazardous to collect, so the juice they contained was looked upon as something rather special, as was the effect it had upon those who consumed it. Three small portions was enough to put one into a deep sleep for several hours, two portions rendered the legs incapable of a predictable performance and did little for coherent speech, while one small cup imbued the recipient with a feeling of well-being, a somewhat loosened tongue and few inhibitions.

Macie reached up to a shelf behind him and produced an ornate crystal lamp. The central burner was fed with vegetable oil, and the light from the wick flame was collected and then spread out by a series of scintillating crystals which surrounded it, giving a soft but widespread glow.

The lamp was lit as the sun finally dipped below the horizon, plunging the whole cliff face into a mass of distorted shadows and twinkling lights, as others lit their lamps.

A soft plop as Macie gently pulled the cork from the neck of the gourd brought Brent back to present time. His thoughts had been drifting back to the unnerving journey he had experienced earlier, and wondered whether to tell his friend about it.

Looking back on it, there seemed little point in relating the details to the Elders who generally dismissed anything which did not fit into their safe and stable world.

'You look somewhat preoccupied,' Macie said as he carefully poured out the thick yellow liquid, 'what really did happen today? You're not your usual jolly self.'

'Don't quite know how to explain it,' Brent began, 'it seems so silly and unreal when I look back on it, but at the time it was real enough,' a shudder ran down his spine, nearly causing him to spill the well filled cup of precious liquid. 'I really don't know what to make of it.'

'Why don't you tell me about it? Perhaps between us we can sort out what really happened, it can't be that bad or you wouldn't be here now.'

Brent began with his feeling of unusual unease when passing the funnel holes, the screech when passing the black rocks and finished with a good description of the disappearing truck. Macie followed every word intently, breaking in occasionally to question anything he didn't understand.

'Well, that sounds real enough,' Macie said, sitting back in his chair, 'I think I'd have felt a bit disturbed if I'd gone through that. There's one bit I don't like the sound of in particular, and that's the strange coating you seemed to pick up. Are you sure it pulled itself together into one lump after you scraped it off and then advanced towards your foot?' Momentarily Brent looked doubtful, then nodded his head vigorously, answering with an emphatic 'Yes.'

Macie looked pensive for a while.

'That would imply a living thing, or a life force?'

'Yes, I know, that's the worrying bit, just what are we up against out there? It's never happened before, so why now?'

'Maybe something has crept out of the forest and taken on a new form in the barren lands, which would explain the shriek you heard, although I must admit it doesn't fit in with everything else we know.' Macie replied, sounding doubtful.

'That's the problem, just how much do we actually know? The Elders are next to useless when it comes to asking questions, either they don't know, or would prefer not to find out.'

'Or both.' Macie said, trying to ease the tension.

There was a long silence, apart from the shuffling of the children, and then Macie raised the flask and his eyebrows.

'Better not,' Brent said, shaking his head, 'I'm going to the forest tomorrow, they've found something odd and want me to look at it before they try to move it back here.'

'You know, I've never been very far out of the settlement, never needed to,' Macie said after another silence, 'how about I join you on your next trip. Two of us together would be much stronger, and perhaps two heads seeing things differently might solve some of these strange happenings?'

'Sounds good to me,' Brent replied enthusiastically, 'but I don't think Eslie would be too happy about it. You could sound her out I suppose, it's certainly worth a try.'

'I don't expect she'd mind if I joined you tomorrow, that would get her used to the idea of us doing things together.'

The scheming went on until Eslie joined them, and then the conversation took on a lighter note until it was time for them all to retire. Brent went back to his hut, his mind working overtime, so sleep evaded him for quite a while.

After a hearty breakfast of sweetbread and fruit, Brent called in to see if his friend would be joining him on the forest expedition.

'She's all for it.' Macie said quietly as he closed the door gently, and nearly trod on Brent's head in his enthusiasm to get down the ladder.

They joined four others by the storage sheds, who were armed with spears and bows and arrows, and then set off along the lake shore towards the dark green mass of the forest. A few reeds and other small plants grew along the water's edge, where the gently lapping waves had leached whatever it was plants could not tolerate from the ground, but it was a narrow band of growth.

To their right, punctuated here and there by massive rock formations and the occasional solid spear of unbroken rock pointing skyward like a finger of doom, the barren lands stretched off into the distance until they merged with the distant horizon in an indistinct blur.

As the forest grew closer, it was easy to see the way in which various plants and trees had stratified into distinct bands, each type growing taller as they approached the main forest giants, a few hundred metres in. It began with a few grasses, some of which had been cross bred a long time ago to produce the grain grasses they now used for food. After them, small fruit and berry bearing bushes eventually gave way to taller trees, most of which could be relied on to produce succulent fruit, although one or two proved to be quite obnoxious to the taste. After that came a general mixture, among which the Ironwood tree was most highly prized for its hard wearing qualities. Creepers and vines adorned the last band of tall trees in great profusion, and then the forest proper began, but that was something else.

The little party swung away from the lakeside onto the well worn main path into the beginning of the forest.

Progress was slowed somewhat as they stopped to pick handfuls of ripe berries every now and again, and then they entered the tunnel which had been cut through the taller growth leading to the vine laden trees at the edge of the permitted area. Beyond this was a thick mass of creepers, forming a solid green wall as if to keep all intruders out, or possibly something in.

No one ventured further than this normally, but two days ago a couple of youngsters had broken the rules and made their way into the cathedral like space between the giant trees, reminding Brent of his own adventure long ago.

They had stumbled across what one of them described as, 'A large metal log, with a knob on one end.' When one of them had tried to turn the knob, it hissed at them, and they ran for their lives. Fortunately, it transpired, the 'knob twister' instinctively turned the knob back before running off, so whatever was in the 'log' should still be there, according to the Elder who ordered the investigation.

They soon found the hole cut in the creeper wall by the adventurers, but some of the quicker growing strands had already begun to fill the gap, and these had to be cut back.

It was a slow job as some of the creepers had a juice in their strands which was quite corrosive to the skin, and they had to wait for it to drain away.

Eventually they were in the great open spaces under the forest giants, and stood still for a few minutes while their eyes got used to the unaccustomed gloom. The trail left by the hurriedly exiting youngsters was plain to see, the leaf litter being disturbed by their fleeing feet, exposing the darker decomposing material below the surface.

They were now advancing with spears and bows in the attack position, just in case anything aggressive made an appearance, but all was quiet apart from the soft swish swish of their feet in the leaf litter.

The trail grew fainter as they followed it deeper into the forest further than any of them had ever been, and nerves were beginning to show. A twig snapped under someone's foot and they all jumped as if they had been simultaneously stung by something very unpleasant.

'What worries me,' said Macie in hushed tones, 'is that it looks as if something has been putting the disturbed leaves back in place, you can only just about see the trail now.'

'Don't worry,' Brent replied in an equally quiet voice from a few steps ahead, 'I think we've found it.'

The stub end of a gas cylinder complete with its control valve was just visible poking up from the decomposing leaf litter. Brent quietly asked for a spear, and gently scraped away the damp clinging leaves from its otherwise shiny surface. The others took several respectful steps backwards.

'It won't hurt you,' Brent said cajolingly, 'it's only a metal thing, it's not alive.' No one was very convinced until Macie stepped forward to stand beside his friend.

'What about the hiss?' one of the others enquired nervously, 'they said it hissed at them, snakes hiss.'

'So does a boiling pot with a tight lid,' Brent replied derisively, 'but I've never been bitten by one.'

Brent wrapped both hands around the end of the cylinder, and heaved. Slowly and reluctantly, the forest floor gave up its hidden treasure, and the gas cylinder lay before them in almost as pristine a condition as when it had first been manufactured, so very long ago.

'Don't turn the knob!' one of them called out in panic.

Brent ignored the plaintive plea and continued to clear the last few leaves from the cylinder before standing up to admire his handiwork, and that of a bygone age.

'We'll need some vines so we can pull it back to the settlement,' Macie suggested, 'it's far too heavy to carry.'

His real motive being that he did not want to actually get his hands on it just yet. Two spear carriers hurried off to the vine barrier, having simultaneously worked out that this was probably the quickest way to get out of the forest, although it entailed a bit of running about.

With two bowmen standing guard and four vines attached to the cylinder, the other four eagerly put their weight to pulling, and so began the long journey back to full daylight.

As they approached the vine barrier, several pairs of eyes followed their every movement, while one pair of jaws salivated copiously, but no one heard the drip drip of saliva on the leaves below as they heaved their prize along.

As they cleared the last of the bushes they were in for a pleasant surprise. A small flat bed truck with wide wheels awaited them, its attendant raising his hand apologetically.

'Thought this might come in handy if you found anything heavy,' the little man said, sounding as if he expected a reprimand for daring to suggest they needed help, 'it's not very big, but the wheels are wide to spread the load.'

'That's damn thoughtful of you,' Brent said, smiling his widest smile and slapping palms with the hesitant trucker, 'I'm certainly pleased to see you. We had no idea what size of object we'd find, so didn't think to bring any transport. This will do just fine.'

They heaved the cylinder onto the truck, which was only just big enough, wedging it safely in place with flat stones and set off in cheerful mood for the settlement.

With two pushing and the rest pulling, the truck made wobbly progress until it reached the harder pathway alongside the lake, and then things became a little easier.

'What do you think it is?' asked Macie, wiping the sweat from his brow, 'and how can it make a noise if it isn't alive?'

'Water makes a noise when it falls from a height and this truck is making a noise as it hits a rough patch, so I don't think that's a problem. What's in the damn thing is more likely to be the danger.' Brent raised his hand to halt the group so they could take a rest. 'The hissing sound could be air or something like that inside trying to get out, and the knob on the end could be the release device. We'll have to be careful when we turn it, but turn it we must.'

'Why?' asked a puzzled Macie, 'why not just leave it in there? Surely it can't harm us if we leave it inside.'

'That's not the point,' replied Brent impatiently, 'one, we need to know what's inside so that we can understand what it's all about, so adding to our knowledge, and two, we can't trade it to the metalworkers if it isn't safe, they'd never do an exchange with us again.'

At a signal from Brent they began to haul their prize towards the settlement again, Brent being the only one eager to find out what the gleaming metal cylinder contained.

A small group of Elders greeted them as they heaved the truck up the slope and into an empty store shed. All stood respectfully back from the truck except Brent, who remained beside it with one hand nonchalantly resting on the shiny surface, mentally defying all to take it away from him.

'Firstly, we must expunge any evil spirits that may be present.' One of the Elders pronounced, which got a few embarrassed looks from the other Elders and a scowl of contempt from Brent.

The 'evil spirit' Elder had been trying unsuccessfully for some time to start up a religious group, no doubt to some hidden agenda of his own, but so far none of the others would have anything to do with it. Brent felt fairly safe to deride the attempt to add a little mysticism to the proceedings, and increased the depth of his scowl.

'This is a scientific investigation, not a prayer meeting,' he announced with venom, 'so let's cut the nonsense and get on with finding out what this thing is.' Fortunately the other Elders all nodded their assent, and Brent took that to mean they were at least in agreement, and on his side.

'Could someone please find the lad who twiddled the knob when they found this thing in the forest?' he asked, 'I want all information possible before I turn the knob again.'

'Why do you want to make it hiss again?' someone asked, not fully cognizant of the importance of their find.

'So I can find out what's in the damn thing,' an irritated Brent replied, a little testily, 'otherwise we'll be none the wiser what it's supposed to be or do.'

A few minutes later the youth who had begun the whole incident was ushered in panting, to join many other members of the settlement who, having heard about the fun and games taking place, had crowded into the shed.

'Tell me exactly what happened when you turned this knob.' Brent asked, his hand moving towards the offending item. Everyone drew back a few paces, those at the back being squashed unceremoniously against the shed wall.

'It's all right,' Brent yelled out, 'I'm not going to do anything, yet.' The youth explained he had seen the knob, and instinctively turned it without thinking, and it had hissed viciously at him. He then turned and ran, not remembering turning it off.

'Don't look so worried,' Brent said to the youth, soothingly, 'you didn't do anything wrong. You weren't to know it would hiss. Anyway, the hiss is harmless, it's only a sound.' he added, hopefully. There were many present who did not believe him, despite his bravado.

'I'm going to turn the knob just a little, to see if it will hiss for me.' he announced. As if by magic, the shed almost emptied in the next few seconds, only some of the Elders and the original hunting party remaining, and they were evenly spread out against the walls of the shed.

Brent put his hand on the control knob of the gas cylinder and a few more watchers slipped out of the doorway, glancing back nervously. His fingers tightened, his pulse rate shot up, and his wrist turned, just a little.

A gentle hiss came from the end of the cylinder, but nothing was visible as the compressed gas escaped.

'Something is coming out of this thing,' he announced to a much reduced audience, 'but I can't see it. I think we should submerge the knob end in water, that way we should be able to see what's happening.'

After a lot of persuading and a little coercion, they dragged the cylinder out of the shed and over to a small inlet from the lake, and with a bit of manoeuvring they got the knob end of the cylinder safely under the water. Brent turned the knob, and a steady stream of bubbles rose to the surface.

'There you are,' he said triumphantly, 'it must be a vapour, like steam or even air maybe. There's something else I want to try,' he added, 'fetch me a small pot or something like that, and a flame.'

'What are you going to do?' asked Macie quietly in Brent's ear, his curiosity getting the better of his caution.

'Learn a bit more about what's coming out of this thing.'

Moments later someone threw a large ceramic pot to Macie, which was the nearest they were going to get to the threatening cylinder, while another stood by with an oil soaked rush taper and a flint fire maker.

Brent took the pot, dipped it into the water and while still under the surface upturned it over the knob.

'OK, light the taper please and hold it nearby.' Brent's words were a bit muffled as he contorted himself over the cylinder, holding the pot with one hand, gripping the knob with the other and trying to see what he was doing at the same time without falling over into the water.

A faint gurgling sound indicated that the knob had been turned and whatever was in the cylinder was now bubbling into the upturned pot. When a few bubbles slipped around the side of the pot, Brent shut the valve off, slowly withdrew the pot from the water and reached a hand out for the taper.

As he returned the pot to the vertical position, he brought the flaming taper up to the rim, and a loud plop accompanied a jet of blue flame tinged with orange which leapt skywards.

Those who were not already at a respectful distance from the experiment immediately took a few paces backwards, bumping into those who had been a bit more circumspect.

'You knew it would do that.' said Macie accusingly, being the only one to have held his ground beside Brent.

'I had a fair idea it would contain something other than ordinary air,' Brent replied with a satisfied smile on his face, 'it just needed proving.' Brent sniffed the rim of the pot as if looking for further clues as to what it had contained, and as there were no further explosions, the others gradually drew nearer.

'That silver thing holds a strong evil force which must not be released, or we may all go up in a sheet of flames.'

All heads turned to the Elder who had earlier tried to interfere with the proceedings, and a tangible silence ensued.

'What the hell are you on about?' asked an angry Brent, as he turned to face the would be terminator of the experiment, 'what's all this mumbo jumbo about evil forces? It's only a container full of burning air, I've proved that.'

'Wait a moment, Brent,' one of the other Elders stepped forward, 'I'm not sure you're qualified to judge what that thing contains or what might happen if we keep fiddling with it. You are only a truck sailor and negotiator. I sense a hidden danger here, and I think it should be left alone until we know a little more about it.'

By now a small crowd had gathered and were listening intently as a lone settlement member took on the might of the Elders.

'No. You wait a moment.' Brent's face had darkened with fury at the interference with his experiment, as he saw it, and he had no intentions of anyone stopping it.

'You Elders are all the same. You don't produce anything, you don't do anything useful for the settlement, and when we come to you for advice or to get a question answered, we are treated as if we're idiots and the query is dismissed as being of no importance.' He stopped to draw breath in the stunned silence which followed his outburst.

'And furthermore, I may be only a truck sailor, as you so derisively put it, but I am at least out in the real world, observing things, solving real world problems and trying to improve the lot of the settlement. What do you do? Wander around in your long white gowns, trying to looking dignified and aloof from everyone else, but what do you actually know, what helpful advice do you give us? What actual use are you to the settlement?' He ran out of breath again.

Macie gently put his hand on Brent's trembling arm.

'I think you've said enough for now, let things calm down a bit, I don't think they'll stop you now.'

The Elders just stood there in stunned silence; no one had ever spoken to them like this before, especially before an audience of other settlement members.

After a low murmur of subdued voices, one of the Elders drew himself up to his full height, and hesitatingly said,

'As you retrieved the silver container and have taken the risk involved in examining it, we have decided that you may continue to explore its potentials, but this must be done well away from the confines of the settlement in case anything goes wrong, and must involve the least number of people possible. We have one question we would like to ask of you, how did you know about the existence of burning air, as we have never heard of it?'

Brent relaxed a little, and tried to smile before replying, but this only produced a distorted grimace as he was still tensed up within himself.

'When I visited the northern settlement where they make glass and the hard earthen pots we use, I saw the black flame stones they use to make their furnaces hot. They heat these stones in a big container and the stones give off a burning air which smells foul but gives them heat and light. The stuff in this thing is just the same, only it doesn't smell.'

The Elders looked suitably impressed at Brent's explanation, as did most of the quite large crowd which had now collected to watch the goings on.

At some unseen signal, the Elders moved off as one, leaving the rest of the crowd to see what would happen next.

'Well, you got away with it this time, but don't push your luck too far with the Elders.' Macie said quietly.

Having still got a captive audience, Brent decided to capitalize on it to see if there were any more who were of a like mind to Macie and himself.

'I'm going to demonstrate the burning air again, just to show you that it is harmless if handled properly.' And with that he plunged the pot back into the water, and turned on the valve. Macie, despite his misgivings, obligingly put the still burning taper to the upturned pot and a gasp of amazement went around the assembled group as a tongue of flame leapt skywards.

'What would happen if we put a hollow vine tube on the end of that little pipe next to the knob, and then lit the burning air which came out of the end?' asked Macie, his curiosity now raised.

'Let's try it,' Brent replied. 'I expect it will just burn like one of our oil lamps if we only let a little of the burning air out at a time.'

By now, the crowd had dissipated somewhat, leaving just eight curious souls clustered around the shining cylinder, waiting to see what would now transpire.

After a while, someone produced a two metre length of hollow vine tube and offered it to Brent, who then pushed it onto the stub of metal pipe protruding beside the control valve. Everyone took a couple of paces backwards, Macie produced the taper, Brent turned the control valve, waited a few seconds and then nodded his head.

As Macie put the taper to the end of the hollow vine, a thin blue flame leapt from its end, the tip tinged with yellow.

Brent turned the valve a little more, and the quiet flame leapt out to about a third of a metre, accompanied by a deep throated roar. Brent looked up at his admirers with a very satisfied smile on his face. No one had moved.

They dragged the cylinder back into the shed, making sure the valve was fully closed, safe in the knowledge that no one was likely to interfere with it until it was needed again.

'Where do you think it came from, and what will you do with it now?' someone asked.

'I think it is something from the very distant past, like the other bits of metal we sometimes find. Such things must have belonged to another race of people, far more advanced than us, and from a very long time ago. I don't suppose there's a lot of burning air in it now, so we'll let the rest out to make it really safe and then it can be exchanged with the metal workers for something useful.'

'What do you think happened to those other people? I asked an Elder once, and he pretended to know nothing about them.' Brent smiled one of his knowing smiles.

'I don't know much about them, but they could work metal much better than the metalworkers we know can, and they made many other things too. I once saw part of a big shed made from artificial stone, it was all in one piece, not built up with blocks like ours, and it went deep down into the ground with many rooms. We had to use torches to see our way it was so dark, and we nearly got lost in the labyrinth of passages down there.'

'Where was this?' someone asked in disbelief, 'I've never heard of anything like that.'

'When I visited the glass makers once,' Brent replied, recalling the memory clearly, 'they asked me if I would like to see something very strange from a distant age. It was some way out in the barren lands, but well worth the long journey we had to do on foot.'

'The Elders must know about these things, so why don't they tell us about them?'

'You know what the Elders are like,' Brent replied knowingly, reinforcing the points he had made earlier to their faces, 'they don't know as much as they would like you to think, and what they do know, which doesn't amount to very much, they keep to themselves.' All nodded their heads in agreement, confirming what Brent had often thought.

The group broke up, but not before Brent had made a careful note of who was present, in case he wanted a willing group for further ventures.

Macie suggested they go to his dwelling for refreshments, and to tell Eslie what had happened. As they made their way up the ladders, Brent asked Macie if he thought Eslie would be willing to let him go on his next journey. Either Macie failed to hear him, or chose not to answer as they scrambled up to the walkway above.

Eslie must have sensed their intentions, or seen them coming, as she had a supply of sweet meal cakes and fruit juice ready on the table as they came in.

'Heard you two were having a bit of fun down by the store sheds, and upsetting the Elders.' she added with a chuckle.

This was obviously an invitation to relate what had taken place, and they did so, surprised not to receive a respectful reprimand from Eslie for their audacity towards the Elders.

She seemed to agree with most of what they said, especially the fact that the settlement had made little improvement in the last few generations, and that things needed a good kick start if they were to improve.

'The other two settlements are far more able to make things of use than we are, although they can't make ropes and cords like us,' Macie stated, 'so if we can increase our knowledge of these arts, and perhaps discover new ones, it could make life better for all of us.'

It was agreed that Macie should go on the next journey which was due in two days time. Brent intended to leave the gas in the cylinder and show the metalworkers how to control the flame. His reasoning being that they may be able to use the heat in their work, and thereby increase the trading value of the cylinder before it was broken for its metal.

Metal was one of the most useful materials left behind by the ancients, in fact just about the only thing so far discovered that could be used to make tools. Any pieces of this precious material, no matter how small, were traded with the metal workers for tools, thus each of the settlements made things for the benefit of themselves and the other two through trading.

It was Brent's intention to visit the metalworkers first, trade the cylinder, or accrue tokens to its value, and then go on to the glass makers, where he had his own special project hopefully under way. He had asked them to cast flat sheets of glass so that he could set them in his window openings, replacing the shutters that they all used. That way, he could have light coming in, even when the wind tried to blow rain in through the opening, and so would not need to light his lamps. They had never tried this before, and he was eager to see if they had succeeded.

A smaller truck would be added to carry the cylinder and the other items he had to trade, leaving more space for the two of them in the main unit. It would be a tight squeeze, and they would have to take extra rations with them as towing the extra truck would slow them down and so increase the total journey time. The damaged track Brent had found on his last trip had been reported to the Elders, who would see to its repair in their own good time, he hoped.

Both men eagerly awaited the departure, checking their equipment over very carefully, as a mistake or breakdown in the barren lands could be fatal. A spare wheel for the main truck was added as a precaution to an already overflowing load in the smaller unit, and extra water flasks were squeezed into every gap that remained.

A somewhat sleepy group pushed the trucks out from the shelter of the storage buildings and onto the open plain in the grey early light of dawn, a well wrapped Eslie joining the entourage to see her man off on what could be a dangerous enterprise, as no one really knew what the barren lands were capable of.

Both men climbed aboard, Brent handling the sail as Macie had had little experience with sails trucks, and Brent wanted a professional looking departure to mitigate the results of the overall event in case there was a disaster later on.

The sail slapped and cracked against the mast until Brent set it just right, and then they were off, gradually gathering speed as they rumbled out into the colourless gloom of the barren lands, Eslie waving goodbye long after they were out of sight.

'Hell, it's cold out here.' Macie commented over the thrumming sound of the wheels, his hot meal of crushed grain having lost its heat giving properties long ago.

'Won't be for long,' Brent responded cheerfully, 'you wait 'till the sun comes up, you'll glad of a little cool then.'

It was a long crawl up the sloping gully, and they wondered if one of them would have to get out and augment the sail with a push, but the pair of trucks just made it to the top of the rise, and then they were on their way again at a respectable speed just as the deep red sun broke the horizon, bathing everything in a sinister blood stained glow.

As they approached the immense cleft in the rock formation which separated the two vast areas of the barren lands, Macie sat staring at it open mouthed.

'It looks as if someone has cut a great vertical slice out of the ridge,' he commented, 'is it really a natural break?'

''Spose so,' Macie answered, 'unless the ancients did it for some reason, from what I can understand they could do some pretty impressive things.'

As the trucks rumbled through the cleft, the noise echoed back and forth in an ever rising cacophony of sound until Macie found himself instinctively crouching down, at least, until he found Brent grinning down at him.

Once clear of the rock barrier, it seemed strangely quiet, except for the constant rumble of the wheels, but that too soon faded from their attention as the constancy of it was accepted. The track suddenly curved into a direction which was more favourable to the wind, and the trucks came alive, rocking from side to side as they gathered speed until Brent eased the sail out a little for fear of them being derailed.

By the time the sun was fully up and had changed to its normal white yellow colour, they were approaching the area where the needles had been lost, and Macie noticed that Brent had tensed up a little.

'This is about where...'

'I guessed that,' said Macie, cutting in, 'you look as if you've seen a ghost. Whereabouts was it exactly?'

Brent scanned around, but was unable to pinpoint any particular spot until Macie pointed to a pile of rocks some two hundred metres to one side of the track.

'No, it was on the track.' Brent said. At that moment they both saw what looked like a cloud of dust slowly glide behind the rocks Macie had pointed out.

'Did you see that?' they both chorused together, as the cloud slipped out of sight.

'Perhaps it was an ordinary dust cloud,' Macie suggested, unconvincingly, 'although it was moving across the direction of the wind, and it couldn't do that, normally.'

Both men looked back as the trucks rattled on, reluctant to take their eyes off the rock pile in case the cloud of whatever it was crept up on them unawares.

They were still occasionally looking nervously over their shoulders when the big funnel pit hove into view. The track curved around the northern edge of the vast hole and from their angle of approach it looked as if the track was on the actual rim of the hideous void. Macie went quite white as the trucks picked up speed due to the slight change in direction on the beginning of the curve, and Brent adjusted the sail to slow them down a little.

'It looks worse than it really is,' Brent said encouragingly, 'the track is actually some way back from the rim and we go around it at a reduced speed anyway.'

The words of comfort did little to convince Macie that all was well until half way around the curving track, and then he seemed to relax a little, leaning out of the truck to gaze hypnotically down into the enormous funnel shaped cavity.

A deep grinding sound made them both jump as a section of the funnel wall just beside the track suddenly fell away, adding another great scar to the landscape. The grinding sound developed into a deep throated roar as the ground each side of the main slide was ripped away until it seemed the whole world would soon disappear down the ever enlarging hole. Even the dust stirred up by the landslide was sucked down, and that was against the laws of nature Brent pointed out, and then the track straightened out again.

With the sail tightened in again, the trucks picked up speed on the next section of straight track, and the perils of the funnel hole soon receded to the backs of their minds as the conversation turned to how the tracks came into being, and what the glass makers settlement was like.

'The tracks have been down for several generations, so I'm told, although no one seems to know exactly when they were begun,' Brent said casually, trying to ease the tension they were both feeling, 'we are responsible for new tracks and maintenance, although there haven't been any new ones in my lifetime.'

'How did the settlements find each other in the first place?' Macie enquired, 'there's no way they could have discovered another settlement on foot, the distance between is far too great, and how would they know which direction to go in the first place?'

'That's something else no one seems to know,' Brent replied, 'the damn Elders don't keep records, or if they do, they keep 'em to themselves, and that's something else I don't agree with.'

'After we have visited the metalworkers, we swing north and go on to the glass makers, they make all sorts of other things beside glass, like the pots we cook in and drink from. They dig out some special earth which if you heat it enough it goes hard, and then they coat it with some glass-like stuff.'

'Do they have forests like us then, for firewood?'

'No, they have a hole in a cliff face which they go into, quite some way according to what I've heard, and then they dig out the black flame rocks. When you heat them, they burst into flame and get very hot. They use it to heat the pots and make their glass.'

'Why don't we make our own pots, if it's known how it's done?' asked Macie.

'We don't have the flame rocks or the special earth. Anyway, if we all made everything we needed, there would be no need to trade, and the settlements would remain isolated. That would stop the spread of new ideas and skills, also it's good for people to take mates from another group, it's supposed to make us healthier somehow.'

Brent swung his arm out, pointing towards a cluster of dull black rocks they were approaching.

'That is where I heard that awful scream,' he said, shaking at the memory, 'listen out to see if you can hear it.'

They strained their ears over the rumble of the wheels and the sigh of the wind in the sail, but to no avail, whatever it was that had screamed before had decided not to repeat the performance, or was unable to.

The conversation took off again and the kilometres flew by, until Brent eased the sail out to reduce their speed.

'This is where the track needs a little maintenance,' he said, 'the ballast between the rails has shifted and the rails are a bit loose. I told the Elders, but as they don't have to use the tracks, I don't suppose they'll put much importance on it.'

The ties between the rails held them together, but the trucks swayed alarmingly as the track way moved up and down under the weight, and then they were speeding off towards the metalworker's settlement again.

'I've made a good friend in the settlement,' said Brent, once they had picked up speed again, 'and I'd like you to meet him. He's an old man now, but like us, in his youth he went exploring and found some very strange things. We'll get him to talk about them, that'll whet your appetite.'

Two:
Something Down Below

JUST AFTER MIDDAY the trucks with their two weary travellers trundled into the ironworker's settlement, the sail flapping against the mast as Brent coasted down the last bit of track to the terminus, the buildings shielding them from the ever present wind.

Eager hands unloaded the coils of rope and twine and when the silver cylinder was offered, they were unable to suppress their excitement at such a large piece of metal.

After some refreshments, they had to explain how they had acquired the trophy, and Brent went into detail about the burning air it contained and how they might use it to their advantage. After a prolonged period of haggling, a huge amount of credit was allocated to Brent's settlement, enough to keep them in metal tools for quite a long time.

Macie was highly amused at Brent's bargaining skills, seeing a new side to his friend's already unusual talents.

It was decided to go on to the glassmakers early next morning, as there would not be enough daylight left to complete the journey in safety, especially as they would be heading almost into the wind most of the time.

Macie wanted to see the metalworkers actually making something, and with the agreement of the foreman, they were given a conducted tour of the various processes employed to manufacture a wide range of tools.

Flame rocks, which had all the burning gas removed from them by some mysterious process the glassmakers did, powered the furnaces, air being forced into the grey pumice-like fuel by a series of bellows manned by a team of sweat soaked pumpers. Once the fragments of metal had been made glowing hot, they were hammered into shape by the most skilled members of the group, the forgers.

There were many other processes employed to change the qualities of the metal according to its final use, but details of these were quite understandably a little sparse, having been learned over many years of trial and much error.

After seeing how knives and other blades were sharpened on water soaked rotating stones, the tour was completed with a visit to a small display of finished goods, the purpose of most items being a complete mystery to the visitors, but they preferred not to show their ignorance on such matters by asking questions as to what one did with them.

As they left the main works area, the old man Brent had met on his last visit was waiting for them.

'Heard you were here and thought you may like to take a little refreshment, it's hot and drying to the throat in there,' he said, waving his thin brown arm in the general direction from which they had come, 'and I have some chilled fruit juice I'm sure you will find enjoyable.'

Brent smiled; he always found the quaint method of speech employed by the old man a delight to his ears, plus the soothing musical tones of his voice. 'Something left over from a more genteel age.' he mused, as they followed the bent old figure down between busy workshops, accompanied by the scraping of files or banging of metal on metal.

With the exchange of names and palm touching completed, which such occasions required, they were invited to sit down.

A large jug and three cups appeared, and the old man poured out a generous portion of the chilled juice for each.

'How do you get it so cold?' enquired Macie, politely, 'by this time of day everything in our place is warm.'

'By the application of a very simple principle.' said the old man, failing to hide his grin of pleasure at being able to supply a cold drink at this time of day.'

'The jug is stood in a shallow bowl of water, a cloth is draped over it so that the ends dip into the water, and the whole is placed in the window opening. The drift of air evaporates the water, and in so doing drops its temperature, cooling it and the jug. Very simple really, it just needs a little thought about what you want to achieve,' he added.

Macie was impressed, while Brent just saw the logic of it and accepted the facts, wishing he had thought of it first.

'I understand you are travelling on to the glassmakers,' the old man said, 'and I wish to ask a favour of you. Could you please bring back some glass pieces they are making for me, that's if they are ready. I am making something you may find interesting.' A square piece of wood with a tube held in a vertical frame was placed on the table, and the two travellers were invited to look down the end.

Brent applied his eye to the tube, jumped back in disbelief, and looked again. He then peered under the bottom end of the tube, shook his head and returned his eye to the top.

'That is the damnedest thing I have ever seen,' he exclaimed in wonderment, 'how does it work?'

Macie was a little more cautious in his approach to the crude magnifier, and so jumped a little less.

'When light travels through a piece of glass which has a curved surface, the light, and therefore what you see, is bent or distorted from its true size,' the old man said gleefully, 'and so things look much bigger or smaller, depending on which way you view them.'

'How on earth did you work that out?' asked Brent, his estimation of the old man's abilities going up several notches.

'I did not work it out, I got the idea from this old artefact,' he said, reaching over to his shelves of things he had collected over the years, 'and that got me thinking.'

'It must have been made by the ancients, I do not think we have ever had the skills to make such a fine thing.'

Brent took the offered spectacle lens with a reverence reserved for things most holy, turning it this way and that, trying to understand the mysterious principles upon which it worked.

'I ground a piece of glass with a sharper curve to it,' the old man said, 'but it took a very long time, so I have asked the glass makers to cast me some pieces with curves on them, so I can then finish them off to my own requirements.'

Brent returned the lens to its place on the shelf, while Macie took another look through the crude microscope.

'Hey, there are other tiny insects on the bigger insect's back, I wonder if the little ones also have even smaller ones on their backs?'

'That is something I shall be able to determine when I make the new magnifier,' the old man said, 'but that will be sometime in the future.'

'You may be able to help us with something we were discussing on the way over,' Brent broke in, changing the subject, 'and that's how the settlements ever found each other, and why this settlement is stuck out in the middle of the barren lands, all on its own. How did you all get here in the first place and why here?'

'I do not know if I can answer all your questions,' the old man replied, 'but I will do my best.

'Your settlement is close to a forest, and I think ours was, a very long time ago. From what little I can gather from the old stories, we all lived in the forest, but then moved out for some reason. If you look to the south of here, you will see a deep depression, which I am told, leads back to the forest, a very long way away.'

'Most of our burning wood for the fires comes from that big gully, the stumps of giant trees are buried beneath the sands, and we dig them up when needed. Nowadays, of course, we have to travel some way down the gully to get the wood, but there are masses of it below the ground, so I think flowing water must have filled the gully at one time, and the forest grew either side of it. I suppose we must have travelled up through the strip of forest when it was still green, and then the forest died out for some reason.'

'Maybe the water stopped flowing,' Macie suggested, getting interested in the tale, 'that would cause a die back.'

'It may well have,' the old man continued, 'we still have water nearby, but deep wells have had to be sunk in order to reach it. There is enough for our needs now, but the wells get deeper as the years go by.'

'What about the glassmakers?' Brent asked, 'they're way out in the middle of the barren lands, there's no sign of a forest out there.'

'I do not know much about them, except for their flame rocks. I was once given a piece of one, and when I split it open, there was the imprint of a fern like leaf inside. I can only suppose that the flame rocks came into being within a forest of some sort, the leaf somehow being trapped inside the rocks when they were made.'

'How about the tracks which join our settlements together?' Macie asked, 'what do you know of them?'

'Your people built them a very long time ago, as they had access to plenty of the correct type of wood. I can only suppose that an expedition set out from each of our settlements at about the same time, and met in the middle, although it seems a bit far fetched when you consider the vast area of the barren lands.'

'As for how the glassworkers ever joined us, I have no idea at all.' The old man paused to pour out more fruit juice.

'Where did you find all those interesting things on your shelves?' Brent asked, now eager to find some himself.

'I found some here in the settlement, just by digging about in the ground, and some were given me by those who put little value on their finds. My father began the collection, and as a boy, I helped him in his searches.'

'I wonder why so little of the ancient's things have survived? They must have lived in dwellings like us and have had great skills and workshops.' Brent offered, to keep the conversation going.

'I have heard of the remains of an old building belonging to the ancients, somewhere out in the barren lands, but I'm much too old to make the journey, even if I knew where it was. But you two are young enough,' the old man added wistfully, raising his eyebrows as an invitation to take up the challenge.

The two younger men looked at each other, and nodded.

'It certainly sounds interesting, and we'll give it some thought,' Brent responded, 'there must be more to life than just sailing a truck across the barren lands and doing the occasional bit of bargaining. Don't know what our Elders will think of it, but I don't suppose they've thought much about anything, really. What are your lot like?'

'Much the same, I would think,' the old man replied, sadly, 'I don't have much to do with them after I put in my request for the special glass pieces, and that was quite a while ago. They could see no reason for the request, and in the end I had to contact the glassworkers personally, and the Elders were not amused by such impertinence.'

'We can expect much the same.' Macie added quietly.

'They're a pretty useless bunch, really,' added Brent, wishing to stress the point, 'but if we get enough people on our side, I don't see how they can stop us doing what we want, as long as it doesn't actually harm the settlement.'

The conversation went on well into the night, until the old man was visibly tired. Fortunately for Brent and Macie, he had arranged accommodation quite close by, somehow sensing their needs long before they had arrived.

Early next morning the two were up, well fed, their stocks of food and water replenished, a payload of metal tools for the glassmakers carefully stacked up along with several packages for individuals at the other end of the track way.

Each time a truck went between settlements, apart from the main load for exchange, there was always a small collection of personal items destined for those who had left their birth settlement, and had taken up residence elsewhere. There was no charge for this service, it being of a reciprocal nature, and it kept the bond between settlements strong.

As the early morning mist cleared, they were surprised to see that the old man had come to see them off. Brent sensed there was something a little more than just a new friendship going on, but he was unable to reason out what it was.

The extra small truck was left behind, and as a team of six sleepy individuals pushed the loaded truck out onto the main line heading north, the wind caught the extended sail, and they were off.

'We shall be quite busy on this leg of the journey,' Brent announced, 'as the sail needs to be swung from side to side quite a lot due to the fact we are sailing close to the wind.'

'What do you mean?' Macie asked, looking puzzled.

'The wind is mainly coming towards us, and to get the sail to work, it needs to be a little bit to one side.'

The builders of the track had fortunately understood the art of sailing very well, and the track had accordingly been laid in a series of sweeping loops so that the trucks could take advantage of the almost constant head wind, the tricky bit being the changeover of the sail as the loops turned back on themselves. This wriggling layout of the track meant an increase in the distance travelled, but it at least made the journey possible by sail truck. To cover this distance on foot was not worth even contemplating.

Although the windmill enabled the truck to progress into a head wind, the much reduced speed made this a very inefficient mode of travel, and it was only used in short bursts when absolutely necessary.

By midmorning, the two of them had settled down to a smooth routine, and the truck rumbled on its way towards the glassmakers and a cool drink, their own drinking water now being lukewarm, despite it being covered up from the direct glare of the almost overhead sun.

'I'd better warn you of the track up ahead,' Brent said as nonchalantly as he could, 'it looks much worse than it really is, so there's nothing to worry about.'

'OK, what's there not to worry about?' a startled Macie asked, 'and how little do I need to worry about it?'

'It's just that the track goes over a deep ravine, and there's not much each side of it. In fact there's nothing either side of it, but it's quite safe, I've done it no end of times.'

Macie rather wished he did not have to see.

The truck creaked and rattled its way up a gentle slope, and then the ravine was before them. A vast gash in the earth's surface separated the two halves of the barren lands as if some giant knife had made a deep cut to remove one of them, and then decided to leave it where it was.

Macie went a dirty grey colour, and his mouth dropped open as he pointed to the huge gap between the two land masses, joined by a flimsy looking bridge of poles and ropes, the track running along the middle of what looked like a spiders web, and a delicate one at that.

'It's all right really,' Brent called out as he dropped the sail, 'we don't use the sail on this bit, in case the wind veers and we go over the side, so we just pick up speed on the down slope and coast across, much safer.'

The colour had now completely left Macie's face, but he did manage a little squeak of terror when the drumming of the wheels on the track turned into a distinct rumble as the truck picked up speed and headed for what he felt sure was total oblivion.

The ragged edge of the ravine raced towards them at an ever increasing speed, the goods they were carrying now adding to the noise of the truck which was quickly acquiring a life of its own.

'Best keep your head down if you don't like the look of it.' Brent yelled out over the rising rattles and squeals of protesting wood, and pushed Macie's head down between his knees.

Suddenly the deep rumbling of the wheels took on a much thinner note as they shot onto the suspended track way, and the sounds slowly diminished to a mere ear shattering level as the vehicle gradually lost speed.

They were still doing at a fair speed as the truck bounced up onto the firmer rails on the other side of the ravine, and Brent quickly hoisted the sail again to keep up the momentum. A little colour had now returned to Macie's ashen face.

'There you are, not too bad, was it?'

There was no reply from the shattered Macie for a while.

Eventually, Macie got his breath and speech back.

'You could have warned me a little earlier, you rotten sod.'

'And what would you have done? Got out and walked? I can't see you walking over that lot, I know I wouldn't like to. Much better in the truck and it's over quicker, too.' Brent said calmly, trimming the sail in a little tighter.

Macie suddenly lent over the side of the truck and was violently sick, several times. Luckily on the leeward side.

'Easy on,' Brent said cheerfully, 'or your shoes'll be next.'

Soon the experience was put to one side, but not forgotten, as they ploughed on into the barren landscape, the occasional clump of rocks or a funnel hole breaking up the monotony as the track wound back and forth, but always in the general direction of the glassmakers.

'I've noticed that odd looking lump of rock several times,' Brent announced, as the truck swept closer to the dark mass, 'often wondered why it's so different.'

The lump in question had a certain symmetry about it, as though it had been something else at one time, and then changed its mind. What little of it protruded above the surface was flat and smooth, the corners distinct, but the top was rough and jagged as if it had been snapped off by some giant angry hand.

'Wouldn't mind a closer look at that one day.' said Brent, almost as though he was talking out loud to himself.

'How do we do that?' Macie asked, dreading the answer.

'Simple enough.' replied Brent. 'We just stop the truck, get out and walk. It's not that far, and we could take extra rations and water just in case if you wish.'

'In case of what?' queried Macie, this time intending to be fully prepared for all contingencies.

'Anything really.' was Brent's non-committal reply.

The truck, following the rails faithfully, swung around to head back towards the West, leaving the enigmatic rock mass behind, and with it, the real or imagined problems of getting to it. Weaving back and forth across the barren landscape, they headed ever northwards, Brent explaining that the return journey was much more pleasurable, the wind being behind them, so all they had to do was sit back and make sure they didn't go too fast and derail themselves.

Just before they reached the glass makers settlement, they passed another of the huge funnel pits. This one was the biggest they had yet seen, and Brent slowed the truck down a little so they could have a good look at it.

Nearly three kilometres across, its distant rim was only just discernible against the hazy horizon. Even as they watched, a section of the funnel wall slipped, paused a moment, and then slithered down to the unfathomable depths below. The writhing cloud of dust generated by the landslide twirled around a few times, and then that too went down the cavernous hole, as if sucked in by some invisible force.

'There's something really frightening about those holes,' Macie said as they watched, fascinated, 'it's almost as if something is eating the world away beneath our feet.'

'You may have got something there,' Brent replied, thoughtfully, 'I remember some old chap at the glassmakers saying he had seen something falling from the sky one evening, and where it hit the ground a hole appeared some days later, and it then continued to grow into one of the funnel shapes. When I asked some of the others about it, they dismissed the whole idea as a figment of his imagination, probably brought on by imbibing a potent brew he was known to make. There may well be something in it, but I doubt we'll ever know for sure.'

'We could always find the old man and see if we can get any more details from him.' Macie suggested.

'Unfortunately it's a bit late for that, the last thing I heard was the old fool had been seen walking out into the wilderness decked out in a flowing white gown, a glass crown on his head, waving an elaborately carved stick and chanting himself hoarse. Never been seen since. I reckon one of the holes got fed up with the racket, and swallowed him up.'

'Did no one go looking for the poor old sod?' asked Macie, a touch of concern in his voice.

'I doubt it, anyway, where would you look. It's just kilometres of sand, gravel and the odd clump of rock out here, Oh, and the damned holes of course. He could have been anywhere. Once you leave a known path, or this track, you've had it if something goes wrong, no one will find you. That's why we have strict rules about travelling.'

Both men went silent for a while, and then, just as they were leaving the vicinity of the funnel hole, another huge lump became detached, and slid off into oblivion with an earth shaking roar.

The glassmakers settlement was a welcome sight as the truck with its two weary travellers careered down the last section of track and into the huddle of buildings which formed the main manufacturing area.

Two columns of black smoke and sparks belched out from a pair of tall chimneys in the centre of the complex, while dotted around them were the smaller workshops of the artisans, manufacturing glass objects and containers from the strange earth which set hard in the fire of their ovens.

The truck was pushed the last few metres into the main store and transfer shed, where goods were received or awaited collection.

Brent had received a request to visit one of the Elders of the settlement, and taking Macie with him, set off to find the illustrious person. He had a little more respect for the glass-maker's Elders, as they seemed to take their work seriously, organizing the inflow of materials which the settlement could not provide and scheduling the flow of trucks for transporting the required goods.

The main hall was where the Elders held their meetings with visitors or attended to settlement matters, and as the two entered they were offered the customary refreshments afforded to all travellers before meeting the elite of the settlement.

With thirsts slaked and bellies full of spicy tasting hot cakes, they were ushered into the hallowed inner sanctum of the Elders. An elegant tall thin man with white hair arose from his seat at a table, and extended his palm for touching.

'I trust you had a pleasant journey, Brent.' It was a formality statement rather than a question, and needed no answer. Macie was introduced, and all three then sat down to discuss the business of the day.

'I noticed the big funnel hole near here is getting very close to the track,' Brent began, 'the track will have to be moved and extended soon, I wondered if it had been planned for the near future?'

'That is the first matter for us to discuss,' the Elder replied, 'if you have a stock of rails to hand, I will arrange the schedule for collection, we have already worked out the quantity needed and our men can carry out the work. I will make sure you have the details before you leave.'

Knowing who was travelling when and where was of paramount importance to those travelling, as the system joining the settlements was only a single track.

If two trucks met, either one had to go back or be derailed to allow the other to pass, and a goods transport needed six men to put it back on the rails. Derailing was not an option, so careful scheduling was needed to keep the system running smoothly, which it did.

Someone had once come up with a system whereby a portable section of rail was carried, and when the inevitable meeting took place, the rails were set up so that one truck could be rolled off the main track, allowing the other to pass. The idea was a good one, but totally impracticable due to the extra mass which had to be carried, and so the scheme was abandoned.

'The special glass sheets you ordered last time have proved troublesome to make, so may I suggest you visit the makers and see if there is another way to overcome their difficulties,' the Elder stated. 'But they were successful in making the round blobs of glass required by someone in the metal workers settlement. Do you know what they are required for? It seemed a strange request, as they are not containers of any sort.' Brent gave a few details of magnifying device which seemed to satisfy the Elder's curiosity.

The meeting continued, requests from both sides being made and exchange values placed on the required goods until a balance had been reached to the satisfaction of both parties, and then they left for the workshops.

'I can see why they got you to do the trading bit,' Macie stated, 'you're a cunning old sod when it comes to a swap of goods, the poor old Elder didn't stand a chance.' Brent just grinned, he knew he was good at his job, but it was nice to be told so once in a while.

The air got hotter and smellier as they made their way into the maze of workshops in the centre of the complex.

They located the required glass workshop, announced themselves and walked in. One of the men came over, touched palms, and immediately went into a long explanation of why he was unable to make the flat sheets of glass as requested.

'I've tried pouring the glass onto metal surfaces, but it cracks as it cools, I've tried dusting the metal with fine sand to allow the glass to move as it cools, but that leaves a gritty surface, and you can't see through it. We've all had a go, but can't do it, sorry.' And he looked sorry, so Brent didn't deliver his usual tirade of derision reserved for those who had failed to make the effort.

'I've got one idea we could try,' Brent said, thinking on his feet, 'do you have a flat sheet of metal the edge of which we could dip into the molten glass, and then withdraw it slowly. The glass should stick to the metal edge and set as it is slowly withdrawn, pulling up more glass as it goes.'

They hunted around, found a suitable piece of metal, erected a simple wooden frame with two pulleys and some rope, and they were ready to try the experiment.

Sure enough, as the metal was withdrawn, a crude clear sheet of glass was being drawn up from the molten mass below, which was then left to cool, the rope sending up curls of acrid smoke from the close proximity of the heat.

The glass workers were just as pleased at the result as Brent was, and a request was made to complete the order for the two of them to collect the following day, when they would return home.

Macie expressed a wish to see how the fired earth pots were made, and after the usual polite request had been made and assent given, the tour began, passing the time interestingly, as there was little else to do.

They were shown the great piles of special earth which had been dragged up from tunnels deep within the earth, the heavy spinning wheels of stone which were spun up, a lump of the special earth thrown onto the middle, and a pot formed by skilled hands as it slowly spun round. Unless the pot was very big, one spin up of the huge stone wheel was usually enough to finish forming a single pot, when it was cut off from the wheel and left to dry.

Some pots had patterns cut into their surfaces; some were painted with strange powders which then changed colour when exposed to the heat of the furnaces, while others were left plain. When the furnace was hot enough, a plug was withdrawn, and salt thrown in, causing a shiny surface to form on the pots, which was only evident when the pots had cooled and been removed from the furnace.

Just outside the settlement, a tunnel had been dug deep into the hillside, and it was from this that the flame rocks were extracted. Black, shiny, and very hard, they burnt with a black smoky flame once they had been heated up enough, and it was this material which was used to fire the pot making furnaces.

A long time ago, someone had discovered that if the flame rocks were heated in an enclosed vessel, a gas which would burn was driven off, and this could be used to provide light.

The leftover porous grey rock which remained in the vessel after extracting all the gas, also burnt, if heated high enough first, and it did so with no smoke to speak of.

This was a commodity much sought after by the metal workers, who used its intense heat to form their tools from the scraps of metal which turned up from time to time. Stories were told of the ancients who had mountains of the precious metal, and they valued it little. Quite unbelievable.

That evening, both men were invited to a special meeting with the Elders, and a meal they were to talk about for some time to come.

Word had reached the Elders of the new method of producing flat glass, and they had decided to make a special occasion of the event, waiving any charge for Brent's flat sheets, and a promise of more should he require them.

The glass workers had brewed their own special concoction for such occasions, and after imbibing liberally, everyone was in a very relaxed mood, some taking time out to lie prone on the floor long after the rest had retired to bed.

A couple of speeches were made by the Elders, while they still had some degree of control over their vocal cords, extolling Brent's virtues in solving the flat glass problem, as this would now increase the items they could trade with and so bring even more prosperity to the settlement.

Next day, everyone agreed it had been a very good evening, except for a few who could remember very little of it after the meal and the first speech.

With the sun in the first quarter of the sky, and the truck loaded with Brent's glass sheets and a whole host of other items for both settlements, they were off on their return journey, after first being pushed out onto the flat plain above the settlement, so the wind could do its job of propelling them along.

'I'm sure that damn hole has got bigger since we passed it the other day,' Brent commented, as they approached the giant funnel, 'and there are only a few metres left before it takes the track with it.' Macie remained silent while he tried to contemplate the consequences of it happening while they passed the dreaded thing, heaving an audible sigh of relief as it dropped behind the speeding truck. Brent chuckled.

With the wind behind them, and only a simple boom change over when the track changed direction, the truck, despite its heavy load, raced along like a thing possessed.

Macie was looking increasingly worried as the usual drumming of the wheels acquired a distinct squeak every now and again, Brent knew what was happening, and dropped the sail. The truck slowly came to a halt, and the brake was applied, then Brent got out to grease the axles.

'Come on, get out and stretch your legs,' Brent called out, 'it'll be a little while before you can do it again.'

Macie got out of the truck nervously, holding onto it with one hand, he was beginning to feel a fear he had never experienced before. Brent saw what was happening and decided to take a hand.

'Come on Macie,' he called cheerfully, 'nothing's going to happen. The sail's down, the brake's on, the truck can't move, so let go of the damn thing.'

Reluctantly, Macie let go of the truck, ready to grab it instantly if it should so much as creak, and then he took a couple of paces away from it, still not happy, but pleased with himself for having done so.

'That's better,' said Brent, putting away the grease pot, 'lets go just a little further, it'll give you the feel of the barren lands like you'll never experience by just walking out from the settlement.'

'What about the dust thing that nearly took your truck?'

'From what I can make of it, they only hang around rock piles, and there are no rocks around here, so we should be all right.'

'Should be? You don't sound very certain.' Macie replied, holding back.

'Do you think I'd leave the truck if it was dangerous?'

'Probably,' Macie retorted, 'you're an unpredictable old sod sometimes, and I think this is one of them.'

'Come on,' Brent said coaxingly, putting his arm around his friends shoulder, 'let's just take a few paces to see what it's like, you can go back whenever you want to.'

They strolled over to a slight rise in the ground, Macie visibly relaxing as they went, Brent talking all the while.

'There you are,' said Brent gently, 'it's not as bad as you thought, is it? You can certainly get the feel of what it would be like to cross this lot on foot, that's why I don't think the meeting of our settlements came about by chance wanderings, you could wander about here for ever without ever coming across a settlement, or anything else for that matter.'

They turned to go back to the truck, and Macie's legs gave way, Brent catching him just before he finally collapsed.

The truck and the track were nowhere in sight.

Brent slapped his friend's face hard, and was just about to deliver another blow when Macie uttered a groan and opened two terrified eyes.

'Where...where..?' he began, to be cut short by a somewhat impatient Brent who was doing his best to hold him upright.

'You silly sod, the truck's just below that mound, you can't see it from here, unless you can suddenly see through solid sand and gravel, and I doubt that very much.'

They reached the top of the mound in stony silence, the missing truck slowly revealing itself as they climbed higher.

'Sorry about that,' Macie began, 'I just couldn't help it.'

'Sorry I had to whack you, but we can't have you fainting all over the place.' Brent replied cheerfully.

They both clambered back into the truck, slipped the brake off, hoisted the sail and with a few creaks and an occasional squeak which soon disappeared, were on their way again.

All went smoothly for the next few kilometres, both men chatting amicably about things in general while the barren lands flew by. And then the ravine loomed up.

Macie went white again, with both arms outstretched and hands gripping the sides of the truck, his mouth opened, but no sound came out of his paralysed vocal cords.

'Look, just sit down, keep your head down if it's too uncomfortable to look at, and we'll be over in a trice. I'll even go over a little more slowly if that will help.'

'Yes please.' Macie croaked, miserably.

Brent dropped the sail long before he would normally have done, to enable the truck to slow down a little before they reached the bridge, but in doing so he made a miscalculation.

There was a slight bump as the truck left the normal track system and went onto the special extra thick bridge rails. The drumming sound of the wheels changed pitch and began to slow down long before they were halfway over, and Brent silently swore under his breath realizing what would happen next.

The truck ground to a halt halfway over the nebulous structure of the bridge, allowing the all pervading silence of the place to crash onto their ears like a physical blow.

Macie looked up to see the frail looking structure ahead swaying in the wind, or from his point of view, the land and the end of the bridge were sliding back and forth in a sickening manner. According to his rational mind, land wasn't supposed to move, but his senses told him it was.

He was awakened from this paralysed moment in time to see Brent stand up to free the trapped sail, and then hoist it up the mast. The wind caught it, and it billowed out with a soft explosion of sound, and the truck jerked forward as the creaking rigging took up the strain.

Slowly the truck gathered speed, Brent playing the sail like a musician coaxing the best possible sound from a reluctant instrument. The edge of the ravine rushed closer and then they were on solid land again. Macie gave a soft whimper, Brent gave a sigh of relief, and jerked the sail up to its full height. The truck surged forward up the gentle slope and over the top, the ravine quickly fading from view.

'That was rather unpleasant,' Brent said brightly, to break the spell, 'next time we'll do it at full speed, it's much better than dangling like a quin fruit in the middle of all that space.'

'Less of the we. You won't catch me doing that again in a hurry,' Macie finally blurted out, 'I'd rather run naked under the giant trees smothered in quin juice.'

After a bite to eat, and a cool drink, Brent having wrapped their water flask in wet cloth, they both felt better, and the conversation took off where it had stopped before the ravine.

Several times Brent had to slow the racing truck down just before one of the turns for fear it would jump the rails, but apart from that, the rest of the journey was uneventful.

Unless of course you include the pair of cold red eyes which watched the two tasty little morsels as they trundled by in their little box, but as they hadn't noticed anything, all was blissfully well.

They were both thankful to have reached the metal workers settlement in one piece, arriving far earlier than expected.

Eager hands unloaded the glass and fired earthenware pots which had been exchanged for the tools they had sent earlier, Brent being very careful to protect his flat sheets of glass lest they be broken in the general rush.

When the truck was nearly empty, the old man came over to see if he had been lucky in obtaining his glass blobs.

Brent saw him coming and gave a cheery wave, handing over the samples of glass as though they were the most precious things on earth.

'I have something special laid on for you two, would you like to join me?'

'Wouldn't dream of going anywhere else,' Brent replied, 'we'll just tidy up here, load up the stuff we have to take back tomorrow and we'll be with you.' The old man smiled.

'Pity we can't stay a little longer,' Macie said, 'I'd like to see a bit more of the tool makers at work.'

'Thinking of changing your settlement then? We'll be back again soon, and we have to stay overnight each time as it's not possible to get back in daylight on the same day.'

Their chores done, the two strolled down between the workshops of the metal workers, glancing into most of them and getting a cheery wave in return. The truck sailor was usually the most popular person in any settlement as he was the link man for distant relations, a carrier of goods and a bringer of news, plus any favours he could do on the way.

A discreet knock on the old man's door, and they were in another world. He had lit all his crystal lamps, and that amounted to quite a few, the main room was ablaze with sparkling pinpoints of fire, far outshining the setting sun seen through the open window.

'You know, news travels faster now than it used to,' the old man began, waving them to their seats around the table.

'Just heard about the party they threw for you to celebrate your new idea making flat glass. Very good it is too.'

'But can you guess what I'm going to use it for?'

'Why, to replace these wooden shutters, of course,' the old man replied with a chuckle, 'can't think why no one thought of it before.'

'It needed someone like you to come along who wanted flat glass enough to figure out a way of making it.'

They all raised a cup of fortified fruit juice to that, and the evening began.

'Where do you get all this marvellous food from?' Macie asked, 'surely you don't make it yourself.'

'No, no,' the old man replied, grinning, 'I know a couple of elderly females who have very little to do, except out do each other in their culinary gifts to me. It's not all bad being old, but a little frustrating when you want to get going on something physical.'

They both looked at each other, wondering if the old man had meant what they thought he meant, and whether to pass a comment, but what if he hadn't? So they didn't.

'I had a word with the metalworkers, and they are very pleased and excited about the silvery metal container you brought them. Obviously it is a leftover from the days of the ancients, and I would think there would be more of the same around the area you found it in. Had you thought of looking again? There may be some working artefacts lying around, and that would be a great find indeed.'

'Hadn't given it much thought,' replied Brent, pleased the subject had been changed, 'as far as our Elders are concerned, it's strictly out of bounds, and we got a telling off for our troubles.'

'I would not have thought that would have put you off such an interesting venture,' the old man came back with, a definite twinkle in his eye, 'I seem to remember similar happenings when I was a lad, but look at my collection.'

They had, and with considerable envy. In Brent, it had sparked off a deep interest in those who had gone before, and a fair amount of defiance towards those in authority.

'I don't think the Elders have any actual power,' said Macie, 'they seem to rule by consent. We just say yes or sorry, depending on what's happened, and life goes on.'

'A bit dull for you?' the old man queried.

'Yes, it is really,' Brent added, after a short pause, 'I hadn't really thought about it much, but you're right, we need something exciting to add a bit of spice to life.'

Many things were talked about that night, some technical, some not, but when they retired to their sleeping quarters Brent was all fired up, Macie's head was swimming, and the old man had trouble recalling a better spent evening.

As the sun chased away the mists of night from the long gully which once connected the settlement to the forest, the truck was hitched up to the extra one they had brought, and the water flasks filled for the return to Brent's settlement.

Once clear of the buildings, the sail cracked against the mast a couple of times before filling out and the truck surged forward. The old man had come out once again to wave them off, like a father saying goodbye to his only son.

'You know, that old man has taken quite a shine to you,' Macie commented, as they settled down in the truck, 'perhaps he sees something in you which reminds him of his own youth.' Brent just gave a non committal grunt; he had other things on his mind, and was already making plans.

They slowed down for the loose section of track, the rails bouncing up and down alarmingly as the twin load went over them, and then it was on to the next hazard, the large funnel pit.

A snack of meal cakes at midmorning and a drink which had been laced with fruit juice cleared their throats of dust, and Brent was almost wishing something would happen, if only to break up the boredom of the journey.

He was surprised, as he had never known boredom on his travels before, and now he had a companion, and he was still looking for something else.

As they approached the funnel pit, they could see another large section next to the track had been eaten away and Brent let the sail out a little to reduce speed.

'Don't like this,' he commented, as they went into the curve around the edge of the ever encroaching pit, 'they'll have to move the rails out a bit now, I'll not run this track again until they do.' Macie could detect a slight belligerence in his friend's voice, which had not been there on the outward journey. Brent had changed, and was becoming a man to be reckoned with, he surmised.

They looked down into the pit, the sloping sides dropping off into a central black hole from which there would be no escape.

'Where the hell does all the stuff which falls in go to?' Brent asked thin air, and just then another section of the crumbling edge of the funnel broke free. Gathering speed quickly it rumbled down the slope, scooping up more material as it went until it shot into space and disappeared for ever, without a sound.

With the funnel behind them once more, the truck picked up speed on the straighter section of track, Macie released his white knuckles from the sides, and with a whoosh let the breath out he had been holding.

'I don't know that I understand the old man's explanation of these holes,' Brent came out with some minutes later, 'that bit about something falling from outer space, and knocking out of existence the ground it falls on.

'I can understand it making a hole, but why does the hole keep getting bigger?' He didn't really expect an answer.

Macie's failure to answer or comment on his friend's question was not only because he was unable to, but because his attention was now on the fast approaching jumble of rocks where Brent had heard the scream. His nerves had been jangled up enough of late, and he did not want to arrive home a gibbering wreck.

They sped past the strange black rocks which seemed to suck in the light, without mishap, but both were listening intently just in case.

They were just relaxing again, when up ahead the track disappeared behind a bank of mist.

'Oh no.' Brent said, more in anger than fear. 'Here we go again. I think the best thing is to get up as much speed as possible, and belt right through the damn thing. It's only dust or mist.' Macie instinctively squatted down in the truck with only the top of his head showing, saying nothing.

The mast creaked as Brent pulled the sail in even tighter, and the trucks responded by bounding forward like living creatures released from some invisible restraint. Everything shook and rattled as they careered towards the fog bank which was growing bigger by the second.

Just before the trucks plunged into the mist, it split in two, rolling aside in twin rotating columns, but still quite close to the vibrating track.

They shot through, and looked back nervously as the two misty columns expanded out into much bigger hazy masses, and then faded away into nothing. The track was clear again.

'Did you notice how cold it felt?' Brent asked, his teeth chattering as they slowed down to their normal speed, 'it was like being hit by chilled water.'

'Yes, and I feel weak.' They both slumped down in the truck, exhausted from fear, and something else indefinable.

'Looks like we'll have to take an armed guard with us in future.' Macie said, after a while. 'Although I feel doubtful they could do anything against a cloud of mist or dust.'

'I don't think that's the answer,' Brent replied, 'we need to know exactly what it is before we can get any control over it. The old man didn't seem surprised when I mentioned it last night, perhaps he may know a little more than he said. I'll see what I can find out next time I go there.'

'You mean you'll go again before you know what it is?' asked a surprised Macie, 'I would have thought that last experience would have made you a little more cautious.'

'No one else seems to know about it, or at least, they've never mentioned it, so the only way we'll find out more is to face it, and see what happens.' Macie noted with dread the use of 'we' again.

The trucks went through the split in the dividing range between the two sections of the barren lands, and then rattled down the long slope towards home. Two very weary and shaken men climbed the ladders to Macie's home, staggered in through the door and flopped down without saying a word.

Eslie took one look at them, and returned to the cooking area bringing back a large steaming jug and two big cups.

'Get some of that down you, and then you can tell me exactly what happened.'

The broth, fortified with something only known to Eslie, revived them quite quickly, and after tucking in to some of her cooking, they related what had happened to them.

She took it in her stride, neither chiding or commiserating, just listening intently, until they had finished.

'Sounds as if there's something out there quite beyond our understanding,' she said at last, looking very concerned.

'I think you should try to find out a bit more about whatever it is before you go charging off again. Perhaps if several of you went out together, fully armed, it might frighten it away, or perhaps you could devise some new weapon which would have an effect on it.'

'I don't think spears or arrows would be much of a threat,' Brent stated, 'but I do have one thing in mind.'

The other two looked up with renewed interest, Macie leaning forward in anticipation.

'I brought back a bag of flame rocks, just to mess around with,' Brent continued eagerly, he could never resist an interested audience, 'I got to thinking about that stuff. They heat it up, and it releases burning air, leaving behind a porous grey mass which the metal workers use to heat their metal with as it is much hotter than the burning air. So I thought if we could reduce the flame rocks to a very fine powder or dust, so fine it would remain suspended in the air, it should burn if we put a light to it, and be very much hotter than the burning air itself.'

'I asked the pot makers to make me a grinding pot and a rounded bar to grind with, and they said it would be sent when the trucks came for the replacement rails. So, if they get through, I can begin experimenting.' He sat back, a satisfied look on his face as if the problem had been solved.

'How would that frighten the dust cloud thing?' asked Macie, not quite understanding what would happen, Eslie just nodded her head.

'Well, the dust thing isn't solid like us, so it can't be strong in the sense we are. That much heat should blow it apart.'

Unable to prove anything to the contrary, they both nodded their approval to the scheme, looking as doubtful about it as politeness would allow.

Eager to change the subject so as not to show his ignorance on the matter of flame rocks, Macie mentioned the matter of finding more metal in the forest, as suggested by the old man.

'As we have a few days before my grinding pot arrives,' Brent began, thoughtfully, 'we could have a go, but I don't think we should go in from the usual place, as it would be too obvious, and there's no point in upsetting the Elders more than necessary.'

'How else can we enter the forest?' Macie asked, completely baffled.

'A little deception is needed,' said Brent, warming to the idea as he went along. 'Four of us could borrow one of the fishing boats and follow the edge of the lake until we are out of sight of the settlement, and then go ashore.'

'But no one goes out that far,' a worried Macie said, 'because of the water monsters, and that would only add to our problems.' he added hopefully.

'I'm not so sure they exist,' Brent retorted, 'I think they are just a story to keep the fishermen close by the settlement, the Elders don't like anyone exploring or doing anything to upset their stable little world.'

Eslie agreed, surprisingly, and it was left to Brent to organize the expedition, asking two of the men who had stayed behind from the silver cylinder experiment, as they looked as if they were made of sterner stuff than the others.

Sleep came easily that night, but he did dream of dust clouds which had acquired hideous faces and which were quite impervious to his flaming powder device, and that frequently failed to ignite in his dream.

Brent awoke next morning a little grumpy, but determined to make his mark on the day, come what may.

The first two men he asked, agreed eagerly, and rushed off to organize the use of the fishing boat, while Macie set about the food supplies, water not being a problem with the lake being within easy reach. Each was to be armed with spears and bows and arrows, surreptitiously taken down to the boat and hidden beneath a spare sail.

Just before midmorning they were ready, pushing off from the shore like four boisterous young men out for a bit of fun, their intent concealed from anyone who happened to be watching. They used the oars until they were free of the windbreak formed by the high cliffs, and then the sail was hoisted, the little boat surging forward like a thing possessed.

Some way out on the lake, they dropped the sail, and threw out the fishing lines, 'Just in case anyone is watching', an over cautious Brent insisted, and then they were off again.

The forest followed the edge of the lake for as far as could be seen on the western side of the water, the eastern edge consisting of the ubiquitous barren lands with their sinister outcrops of rock. No one knew how far the lake stretched southwards, nor did they seem to care, their main concern being the harvesting of the abundant fish which inhabited the shallows around the lake's edge.

Tales of the water monsters kept the fishermen close to shore where it was thought they would be unable to swim, not that anyone had ever seen one in living memory.

All but Brent grew a little nervous as they sailed on into uncharted waters, ever watchful for anything breaking the surface of the tranquil lake.

Once around a promontory, and out of sight of the settlement, Brent brought the boat close to the shore, but there was nowhere to land, as sheer rock walls rising up many metres separating them from the forest above.

'Don't worry, there's bound to be somewhere we can land soon,' Brent called out from the front of the boat, 'I'll keep a lookout.'

Some while later, they were still confronted by steep rock walls, blocking their access to the forest. One of the men, for something to do, had trailed a fishing line behind the boat and now had a catch, indicated by his excited cry.

'Haul it in then,' Brent said, a little impatiently, 'at least it'll look as if our intentions had been to fish.'

The line was pulled back into the boat bit by bit, but suddenly the resistance increased considerably, something on the other end was not so keen to join them.

There were now two of them on the line, and they were still having a bit of a struggle.

'Don't like the look of that,' Macie commented, as the men continued to heave on the line, 'I don't think a normal fish would put up that much of a struggle.'

'Well, if it's a big one, we can share it out with the Elders, that'll please 'em, and back up our story.' Brent muttered.

Five metres from the back of the boat the water suddenly swirled and foamed. A large dark grey snout broke the surface; two enraged beady eyes surveyed the line pullers malevolently, while a quite large fish was struggling hopelessly impaled on one of the larger creature's massive fangs.

'Cut the bloody line,' Macie squeaked in a high falsetto, 'it'll have the lot of us if it gets into the boat.'

Brent hurried to the rear of the now violently rocking boat, a knife in his hand, and slashed at the strong fishing cord.

It took several swipes of the flashing blade before the line went slack, and the huge head slid back out of sight.

Then someone noticed a huge dark shadowy shape cruising alongside the boat, and the boat rocked alarmingly.

During the next few minutes, the boat received several heavy blows from the creature, either trying to spill them out to add to its menu, or to dislodge the still struggling fish impaled on its fang.

Two men grabbed the oars and pulled with all their might, while Brent tightened the sail in to increase their speed, but still the dark shape below kept pace with them, butting the boat every now and then. Macie fitted an arrow to his bow and braced himself against the side of the boat, waiting for the dark shape to show itself.

'An arrow won't be much use against something that big,' Brent called out, fearful they would enrage the creature still further, 'our only chance is to get to the shore and out of the damn boat.'

At that moment the creature decided to take a look to see if the battering had produced any results, and Macie's arrow flew true into one of its eyes. Only half the sturdy shaft protruded, the rest was buried deeply in the creatures head.

Whether it had penetrated the creature's brain and killed it, or just blinded it on one side so hampering its navigation they were not sure, but they took the opportunity to head for the shoreline at full speed, not that they could actually get ashore as the rock barrier was still there.

With the boat bumping up against the sheer rock wall, they realized they were no better off than when out on the lake, it just felt better being closer to land.

There's no sign of it now,' Brent said, more in hope than certainty, 'so we may as well continue along the edge of the shoreline.'

They stayed a few metres off shore to catch the wind, drifting along gently so as not to disturb the water too much and thereby advertise their presence.

A pause for food was taken and the water flask passed around, making a pleasant break from the monotony of the slap slap of the wavelets against the boat's bow as it slowly edged along the side of the lake.

They were just about to resign themselves to the fact that they would never get ashore, when one of the men standing on lookout in the bows of the boat called out excitedly,

'Something up ahead, can't see what it is, but it juts out into the water.'

'Looks like a large flat rock,' Macie commented as they drew nearer, 'we may be able to get off at last.'

Slowly they approached the long grey slab until the bows of the boat grounded on the submerged section of the fallen bridge, the shattered support pillars lying many metres below them, and out of sight.

'It looks like stone,' said Brent, gratefully stepping out of the boat and onto something solid, 'but I've never seen stone quite like this, it runs up into the forest in one continuous sloping length. Pull the boat up out of the water, I think we've found our entry into the forest.'

With the boat safely two metres clear of the water, they picked up their food bags, water flasks, and weapons, and warily walked up the ramp and into the fringe of the forest.

'Most of these trees are the same as the ones near us,' Brent noted, looking around him, 'so we should be all right for food. Anyway, top up your food bags just to be sure, we don't know what it'll be like further in.'

They followed the wide slab of concrete for several hundred metres, a dense tangle of growth on either side of them.

'Good thing we found this, I wouldn't fancy chopping my way through that lot.' one of the men stated, peering into the matted mass of creepers and vines.

As they tramped on, they failed to notice several pairs of eyes following them, the owners of some savouring the thought of the tasty crunchy little morsels who had entered their kingdom.

The light filtering down from above had taken on a green tinge as they pressed on through the tunnel of plants vying for space in which to grow, but nothing touched the concrete.

'Wonder why nothing grows on this stone?' one of the men asked, 'there's not even a trace of moss.'

'I don't think it's stone as we know it,' Brent replied, 'most likely made by the ancients. Perhaps it contains something like the barren lands, which stops things growing.'

They walked on a few hundred metres more and were then out into the cathedral like spaces between the forest giants.

The concrete causeway continued on ahead, but it was now covered in leaf litter which was more comfortable to walk on, but could contain hidden dangers.

The little troupe paused for a moment to gaze up at the mighty trees, a little unnerved by the total silence and the absence of anything moving.

A thin agonized screech filtered down from far above, reminding them that this was no benevolent haven to saunter about in, but a tooth and claw world where the slowest usually became a meal for the faster, and no quarter was given to anything.

'Keep a sharp lookout for any movement,' Brent said in hushed tones, 'we'll only get one chance to take evasive action, and we'll have to be quick about that.'

As their eyes got used to the gloom of the forest floor, more details began to show. Some of the giants had massive vines dangling down from the dizzy heights above, their bases firmly rooted in the rich leaf mould below.

Macie went over to one of the nearby vines, and before anyone could stop him, slashed the half metre thick stem with his long knife. He jumped back just in time as a thick green oily liquid spurted out of the wound, and fell to the forest floor. Within seconds a myriad of small creatures, some crawling, some jumping and some taking to gossamer wings, fled the area. Something in the juice of the vine was noxious, poisonous, or possibly corrosive.

'I wouldn't advise any unnecessary actions like that if I were you,' Brent suggested, 'let's just keep to exploring, and be fully aware that this place is geared up to consume anything that moves, and I've got a feeling that size doesn't come into it.'

They contritely formed up into a little group, two by two, thereby affording the smallest target and maximum defence should anything catch them unawares.

A variety of small creatures scuttled away from under the leaf litter as the advancing quartet tramped along, leaving them to contemplate what else there might be under there that had failed to make an escape, or had no need to.

'I don't remember so much life under the big trees near the settlement.' Macie said, stepping aside as a particularly slow worm like thing wriggled off to one side, snapping its giant pincer-like mouth parts either as a warning or in the hope of catching something to eat. 'And they're a lot bigger.'

'Looks like we have something up ahead,' Brent said quietly, a few minutes later, 'and I don't think it's a natural rock formation.'

As they drew nearer to the dark mass, they could see that whatever it had been, it was now in a sorry state, the top portion being rough and jagged, as if ripped off by some enormous force.

Only a few metres of the structure still remained above the surface of the forest floor, but the symmetry and clear cut corners suggested something constructed rather than an accident of nature. Three corners stood proud of the ground, the third only just breaking the surface of the damp leaves, while the entire centre of the construction was an empty square of some sixty metres along each side. No vegetation grew within its bounds, but a copious layer of leaves hid whatever else might be there.

'Are you going into it?' asked one of the men, well back from the rest in case he was invited to do the honours, 'I think it might be a good idea if you were secured by a rope, if you don't mind my saying.' he added respectfully.

'Yes, that's a good idea,' Brent replied, stopping dead in his tracks, 'who knows what's in the middle, it looks like leaves, but they may be covering up a hole, or worse still, something hungry.'

With a rope attached to his waist, he cautiously climbed over the lowest section of the remaining wall and set foot on the flat mass of leaves which filled the centre of the square.

'So far, so good,' he called out, with more confidence than he actually felt, 'I'll walk right across to the other side.'

He failed to do this because the rope was of insufficient length, so he untied it and carried on walking, probing the ground with a spear, just to make sure it was solid.

Having reached the other side of the square enclosure, Brent turned, waved his hand and called out that all was well, and to come on over. The others followed, but not quite with Brent's degree of confidence.

A sharp ripping noise followed by snaps and squeals high above in the canopy caused them all to look up in fear.

A massive branch from one of the forest giants had rotted, probably due to damage from a lightning strike, and fallen away, tearing out lesser branches on its way down and disturbing the wildlife in the process.

With an earth shaking crash, several tonnes of rotted timber hit the forest floor, accompanied by a flurry of stripped leaves and an odd assortment of creatures from the different levels of habitation above.

Within seconds all was quiet again. The creatures dislodged from their lofty perches had all scampered to the nearest tree trunk and begun the long climb back to their chosen level, while those who were unable to climb quickly enough were either consumed by other creatures emerging from the leaf litter, or burrowed into it to escape detection until times were more favourable.

'Just our luck to have something like that happen, it could have landed on our heads.' Macie said wryly.

'I think it happens more frequently than you realize,' Brent answered, 'I reckon that mass of wood is already well on its way to being used by the forest for its own ends, we'll have a look at it when we leave.'

No one looked too happy at the thought of a close inspection of the mountainous pile of fallen timber, and what it might contain, but said nothing.

'Look, over there,' one of the men said, pointing, 'it looks like the shiny metal thing we found earlier.'

They trooped over, prodding the ground to make sure they were not taken by surprise by a leaf covered hole.

'It looks like a flat sheet of the silvery metal, stuck on the wall, that's a useful find.' commented Macie, realizing just how many tokens of credit it would earn for the settlement from the metal workers.

Brent gave the sheet of metal a thump with his clenched fist, and a deep sonorous boom came back at them.

'I don't think it's stuck on the wall,' he said, pensively, 'it looks more like a door of some sort, but I can't see any hinges or a latch, so perhaps they used something else.'

'It's bigger than our doors,' someone commented, 'that's if it is a door.'

'Perhaps they were bigger than us,' Macie suggested, 'this whole structure is bigger than anything we've ever built.'

The door intrigued Brent, and he was determined to find some means of opening it, if only to prove it was a door.

They scraped the dead leaves away from the bottom of the big silver sheet, disturbing several small creatures which scampered away hurriedly, not liking even the dim light which filtered down from the canopy above. A close inspection of the stainless steel sheet revealed a slight square depression near one edge, with a small hole and two protruding bumps set within it.

All attention was now focused on the release mechanism, although none had the faintest idea of how to operate it.

One of the bumps moved when Brent pushed it, receding to lie flush with the surface of the door, but the other stubbornly refused to respond to any amount of pushing, banging with a spear end or Brent's muttered curses.

Someone suggested poking something into the hole, but they had little about them which would fit, much to their frustration.

Macie suggested whittling a piece of wood down so that it would enter the hole, but could not find anything suitable in the vicinity.

'There should be some twigs from that branch fall,' one of the men suggested, 'I'll go and look.'

Returning with a hard stick, he handed it to Macie, who began whittling it down to size.'

'There's a lot of noise going on by that pile of fallen wood,' he said, as he watched Macie's skilled fingers trimming the stick into a thin delicate probe, 'crunching and grinding sounds.' he added, as his body gave an involuntary shudder.

'That's nature at work, using waste material to create new.' Macie said, as he pushed his stick into the hole.

It went in so far, then hit an obstruction and would go no further. In sheer frustration, Brent pushed one of the bumps next to the hole, and the stick went in a few centimetres more. Encouraged by this unexpected reaction, he pushed the other bump, and a loud click was followed by the door opening few millimetres, accompanied by a loud hiss.

No one had noticed that what appeared to be a single sheet of metal was, in fact, a frame encompassing the actual door itself.

They had all jumped back a respectable distance, but as nothing else happened, Macie slipped his fingers around the edge of the door and pulled. Slowly the door opened enough for them to peer inside.

'Don't like that smell.' one of them said, wrinkling up his nose to emphasizes the unpleasantness of the odour.

'Just stale air,' Brent said, knowledgeably, 'it's been shut for a very long time I would think.'

'What are those marks?' asked Macie, pointing to the faded words 'Emergency Exit' as the door was swung fully open.

'Don't know,' Brent replied, 'but I've seen similar markings on other things belonging to the ancients, so it must be an instruction or warning of some kind, I would think.'

'Dare we go in?' one of the others asked, hastily shuffling to the back of the group, 'once the smell's gone.'

Brent had already entered the opening, peering around the corner of the doorway to see what lay beyond.

'There's a flat bit, and then steps go down into the darkness below, can't see much else,' his voice sounded hollow and strange, 'we'll have to use lights if we want to go down.'

'I've got my fire sticks,' one of the others said, 'we could make a fire brand.'

Finding a bundle of dried sticks meant going over to the remains of the fallen branch, and no one was keen to do that after the stick gatherers comments about the odd noises.

In the end, Brent went over, grumbling about wet nursing a bunch of girls, but fortunately the others had their heads in the doorway and failed to notice his derisory remarks.

'It's certainly very active over there,' Brent commented, returning with a large bundle of dry sticks, 'bind these into two bunches and we'll have a look down there.'

With the light from the smoky flames lighting their way, and grotesque shadows leaping behind them on the walls, the four slowly crept down the spiralling steps until they reached a flat section of corridor, and there they stopped.

'We'll have to use oil lamps to go much further, if we get stuck down here in the darkness, we'll never find our way out again,' Brent said reluctantly, 'so let's go back up while we can still see.' The other torch had to be lit as the first one had burnt down to the holding stick.

They were nearly at the top when the second torch burnt out and fell apart, sending a shower of sparks and smouldering twigs down the steps they had just climbed. The pale grey green light of the forest framed the open doorway above, and they all hurried out, relieved to be in open air.

Three:
The Confrontation

'I'll bet there's some stuff down there we could use,' Macie said, as they filed out into the remains of the old building, 'that's if we can haul it back to the settlement.'

It was decided to return home, as without adequate means of lighting their way, there was little else they could do.

'Let's have a look at that pile of stuff which fell from above.' Brent suggested, the others agreeing somewhat reluctantly, not wanting to appear squeamish about it.

Most of the mighty branch had been well eaten into long before it fell. Either a final nibbling or the passing of something too heavy for it to bear, had sent it crashing to the forest floor where it lay in shattered lumps.

Macie idly kicked one section which promptly split apart, revealing a multitude of different creatures from things the size of a large sand grain to a pallid worm like creature with a black head and a sticky tongue, with which it greedily mopped up the smaller insects.

An excited cry from one of the others, who had screwed up enough courage to wander off a little, brought the others running. Several large honeycombs lay scattered about, broken from their hiding place inside the branch by the fall.

They were surprised that nothing seemed too interested in the honey, only the brown flying insects which tried to guard the huge combs. These were being grabbed in the pincer like jaws of dark brown shiny six legged creatures, whenever the defenders tried to land on their combs, and whose voracious appetite for the flying defenders seemed insatiable.

The forest wasted very little. Microscopic filaments of fungi attacked any dead wood, extracting nutrients and softening the fibres for tiny grubs and worms to eat, the tunnels they created attracting larger predators.

These slightly larger creatures consisted of a range of multi-legged worm-like insects with hard outer skins, a selection of slim brown and black beetles whose outer jaws enlarged the holes made by the smaller insects and chased them down their tunnels, and an ingenious little creature which exuded a compound the smaller ones found irresistible, their appetites sealing their fate.

These in turn fell prey to a squat, pimple skinned horror which followed the sound of the others as they scurried about their hunting, and grabbed them as they came to the surface, sometimes smashing through the thin bark to catch them if they should get close enough.

Just about everything was eaten by something a little larger, until the largest moved up a layer in the canopy, and was consumed by something even bigger and more vicious, which had been patiently waiting for its arrival.

These creatures only represented a small portion of what could attack a piece of dead wood, the upper layers of the canopy having their own diverse collections of hunters and hunted, while the leaf litter and the ground below it housed a subterranean army of creatures which survived best by being hidden, except for those who could hunt in the dark, and there were many of those.

When the defenders of the honeycombs had been eaten, and before anything else decided it liked honey, the four men each gathered up the largest portion that they could carry of this welcome gift, and began the journey back to the boat. The honey was a real treat, as it was almost impossible for them to collect it from so high up, and the rare honeycombs to be found in the fringes of the forest were a very poor imitation of these giants, and had defenders who stung viciously at the slightest provocation.

Arriving back at the lake's edge, Brent suggested they wrapped the honeycombs in large leaves, as by the time they had reached the settlement, some of the honey might have leaked from the combs and attract insects, especially the ones who built small combs at the forest edge.

Thin vines were used to tie the leaves in place, and a final deterrent to any interested insects was to spear two stink fruits on a long cane-like growth, and this was lashed to the rear end of the boat so that they would not have to endure its fetid smell, but it would mask the sweet smell of the honey as they sailed along.

'What do we tell the Elders?' asked Macie, as they made ready to leave, 'they'll want an explanation.'

'We don't tell them anything, and if they ask, just say we got the honey in the normal way. When we get back, we'll break the combs up into smaller pieces, and store it. Give some away if you like, but don't give details of how we acquired it.' All nodded their agreement to the order.

The journey back took a little longer, as they had to tack back and forth against a head wind, and they kept as close to the shoreline as possible, remembering the creature they had encountered when on deeper water.

No one tried fishing on the way back, just in case.

With the boat returned to the fishermen, and a piece of honeycomb given to show their thanks, the group split up and went their separate ways, agreeing to meet in five days time to arrange another foray into the forest.

Later that day, the timber trucks arrived from the glass workers settlement, and while the timber rails for the track relaying were being loaded, one of the men delivered Brent's grinding bowl and pestle.

'What are you going to use it for?' he asked.

Brent explained his idea about the flame rocks without going into great detail, or what he intended to do with the resultant powder. He carefully steered the conversation around to the journey the truckers had made, and then asked if they had noticed anything unusual.

'Not really, apart from the track being a bit loose in one place, and a bank of mist on the track. It cleared away as we approached,' the man said, 'never seen anything like that before, at least not out on the plains.' he added. Brent said nothing, not wanting to raise unnecessary fears. Perhaps it was harmless after all.

The new oil lamps the settlement used had glass funnels supplied by the glass workers and the flow of air going up inside tended to pull the flame higher than if it had been unshielded, giving a much better light. Brent traded around his friends and acquired three to add to his own, and then fitted larger gourd oil holders to them, and handles.

The grinding up of the flame rocks proved more difficult than he had anticipated, but after several hours of hard work he had acquired a small container full of very fine powder, and then called around to Macie's home to see if he was interested in the experiment.

The two of them took the powder, a bellows and a hollowed out log to the back of the store sheds, well out of the reach of prying eyes.

Using hollow vine stems, Brent had coupled the bellows to the pot containing the powder such that the rushing air would pick up some of the black dust and puff it out in a cloud of fine particles and into the hollow log.

'Light the taper,' Brent said, working away at the bellows, 'and put it to the end of the log when I tell you, but stand well to one side.'

A grey mist of powder seeped out of the log, and Brent gave the word to light it.

Both were surprised at the result. A gush of red smoky flame leapt from the log with a whoosh, the log jumped back half a metre and a large crack appeared along its length.

Once over the initial shock, they quickly gathered up their equipment and hid it behind a pile of old timber as a large black cloud of smoke rose above the store sheds, and drifted away in the ever constant wind.

'Hope no one sees the smoke,' Brent panted as they ran to the other end of the line of buildings, 'we'll have a hell of a job explaining that away.'

Later that day, they retrieved the log and puffer unit, to see exactly what had happened.

'We could bind the log with strong vines,' Macie suggested, 'that should stop it splitting.'

'It might work, but I'm thinking of a metal tube. We may be able to get some metal from the building in the forest, and the metal workers will make anything if we give them enough metal in exchange.'

'What about the Elders?' Macie asked, 'we can't keep it from them for ever, they're bound to find out.'

'Sod them. This is our experiment,' Brent replied hotly, 'and if it gets rid of the mist thing, I don't see how they can object. Anyway, what can they do? They can only ask us to stop, they can't do much physically.'

'I know,' Macie said, uneasily, 'but we're supposed to accept their rulings on things, it's always been that way.'

'If they made useful decisions, I might agree, but they don't. They only stop things, they don't help us to develop things to improve the settlement. Look at the trouble we had with the oil lamps,' Brent was getting into his stride.

'Left to them, we'd still have the old ones, with every puff of wind blowing them out every time you move too quickly, and they're less smoky. I think the Elders only hold us back these days. They may have been a good idea once, but we need some young blood with good ideas to take over.'

'Is that what you're aiming for? To take over?' Macie asked aghast, 'you can only do that when you're an old man.'

'That's the damn trouble,' Brent replied, 'when you're old, you're too staid, and usually don't like change, so what's the point of it? Anyway, I don't have any aspirations to be an Elder, yet.'

Leaving the split log where it was, Brent took the puffer back to his hut, thinking he would try it with a metal pipe.

No one seemed to have noticed the puff of black smoke, or made any comment about the sudden appearance of the large quantity of honey, so both men felt a bit more relaxed, and looked forward to their next expedition.

A team was sent out to re-ballast the track where it was loose, and re-route the section which was threatened by the ever increasing funnel pit. Completion of the work was then relayed back to Brent, as he was the main truck sailor in the settlement.

Three days later the rail trucks returned, requesting more rails as the funnel pit had expanded, taking a huge section of the plain down to the depths below, and for safety's sake, they wanted to give it a wide berth. There was only just enough of the prepared rails in stock, and a lumber team was sent out immediately to cut new timber, so it could be shaped while it was still green. The rail link between settlements was the most important thing they had, and always took precedence over everything else.

This delayed Brent's next planned visit to the forest and the ruined building, but they set out the following day equipped with the modified oil lamps on another 'fishing trip'.

There were no further incidents with the water monster but the ruined bridge section was not so easily located. Macie thought they had gone past it, and they were about to retrace their steps when the lookout in the bows saw it.

Leaving the boat on the concrete, just clear of the water, they headed off into the forest. Passing the area where the fallen branch had landed with such terrific force a few days before, they were surprised to see no sign of it, except for a slight depression where the leaf litter had been compressed from the impact, and that would soon recover to leave no trace of the awesome event.

Brent pulled the door to the subterranean section of the building open, but this time there was no rush of foul smelling air, just the stale dank smell one would expect from a building which had been abandoned for so long.

'Right, let's get the lamps lit.' Brent said impatiently.

'We'll have to leave here well before evening in order to find the settlement again.'

Each carried one of the new modified lamps by its handle, the lights throwing leaping shadows on the walls as they descended the spiral steps, their voices echoing eerily as they talked just to make some comforting sound in the strange surroundings.

The corridor, when they reached it, went in two directions, Brent favoured the one to the right of their entry point for no other reason than he felt he should assert his leadership in case it came into question at a later date, when quick decisions might need to be implemented.

With their footsteps echoing loudly, they set off along the corridor, checking the walls for any sign of a door or other means of entry to what they thought may lie hidden within the ancient's construction.

'Here's one,' Macie called out, 'but it's got a funny looking latch on it, shall I give it a try?'

'Let's have a look at it first.' the ever cautious Brent said, bending down to see what his friend had found.

'Looks like a lever type of thing,' he said, pressing down with considerable force, 'must be locked like the other one up above.' he added, putting his full weight behind the next thrust, but there was no movement.

'Is there a hole in it like the other one?' asked one of the others, pushing in closer. Brent stood back a little to shine his lamp directly on the handle.

'There's a knobbly bit on the end, I'll push that.' The handle clicked and went down.

They opened the door into pitch blackness, and Brent thrust his lamp into the opening and looked around.

Light sparkled and glistened off several objects deep within the room, but the details were far too indistinct to see what they were. Cautiously they entered, and going up to one of the sparkling objects, gasped in surprise.

'It's like the metal workers display of things they have made,' Macie said, 'only they're not metal, are they?'

'Don't think so,' Brent replied, thrusting his face up against the glass of the display cabinet, 'looks like pots of some kind.'

They moved in a tight-knit bunch around the huge sales hall, their feet crunching on broken glass from the occasional cabinet which had not stood up to the shock generated when the top of the building had been ripped off.

It took over an hour for them to systematically go from one cabinet to the next, until all had been seen. Not that they understood what all the items were for, but many were close enough to their own creations for them to recognize the uses to which they could be put.

Piles of china plates, some of which were broken, caused the most excitement so far, as their plates were so thick and crude in comparison.

'We should have brought some baskets to load these things into,' Macie said as they moved back towards the doorway, 'we'll not be able to carry very much as it is.'

'Not unless they have baskets down here,' Brent said, pointing to a stairway leading down to what looked like another floor, 'lets see where that leads to.'

What had possibly once been carpet, turned to dust as they tramped down the stairs, rising in misty swirls around their feet until they reached the floor below.

'Wow, look at that,' exclaimed Macie, as they surveyed an array of stainless steel cookware, 'we'll be the envy of the other settlements if we can get that lot home.' Pot and pans of every size and description lay in piles, where the vibrations of long ago had shaken down the carefully balanced displays.

A bay to one side of the showroom held electrical goods for food processing, but most of the plastic had distorted, cracked, or just crumbled away, giving little clue as to what the items were originally for, not that they would have understood anyway.

Another alcove held gardening tools, those handles which had been made of wood or plastic having long ago turned to dust, but the business ends still remained bright and shiny, illustrating their purpose beyond doubt.

They went down one more floor, but there was little of use there as all the clothes had rotted, leaving the bare stands like so many skeletons, and they hurriedly left.

'Let's take off our shirts and make bags from them,' one of the men said, 'we won't miss them on the way back, and we'll be able to carry quite a lot of this stuff.'

A collection of knives, scissors, a few small hand held gardening tools, cooking pots which stacked inside each other and some of the more robust glass and china were bundled up and transported up to the surface, amid much puffing and grunting. The main exit door was closed, and after a short break to refresh themselves, they were on their way to the boat.

'We'll have to tell the Elders now,' Macie said, between gasping breaths under the heaviest load, 'they'll never believe we've made this lot.'

'I know,' Brent replied, in a resigned tone, 'although once the others see what we have to offer, they'll be on our side, so that should make a difference if it comes to taking sides.'

Everything was loaded into the boat and they set sail for home, hardly believing their luck at what they had found.

Dusk had begun to creep over the landscape by the time they reached the small bay set below their dwellings, and two anxious fishermen were waiting for the return of their boat. They stared in fascination when they saw what the four had brought back, asking who they had been trading with. Brent was as evasive as possible without being too discourteous, as he wanted to set the scene, as it were, before too many people knew about their find.

With the bounty safely shut in a store room, Brent was invited to Macie's home for a meal and to give some back-up to the telling of their adventure to Eslie.

After the meal, the story was related, and a few small objects Macie had managed to secrete about his person were given to Eslie, after which, they now had one firm backer to their future exploits. Brent suggested that Macie went to see the Elders first thing in the morning to arrange a meeting, as he had already antagonized them to some extent, and he wanted the meeting to at least begin on a good note.

None of them slept too well that night, the excitement of what had happened, plus the contemplation of the possible changes to their lives precluded a sound sleep, even the infrequent snatches they did manage were filled with bizarre dreams which left them exhausted next morning.

A good breakfast from Eslie's cooking alcove helped a little, and by the time they had consumed a jug of her special brew of hot fruit juice and the mystery ingredient which she kept to herself, they were ready for anything the Elders could throw at them.

The gathering took place in the general meeting house, the Elders on a raised platform at one end with the others scattered about according to their whims.

The four adventurers trooped in at what they thought was the most opportune moment, just as the Elders were getting a little edgy as nothing had happened.

'We understand that you have a statement to make concerning the future of our settlement,' one of the Elders began, 'please make your statement.'

Brent stood up, half turned towards the rest of the audience, as he wanted them to feel part of the coming decisions rather than just listeners, as was the usual case.

'We four have made a very important discovery which could be of great benefit to the rest of the settlement, making our lives easier and more enjoyable.'

There was total silence, as if no one had been present. Brent cleared his throat and looked around nervously,

'We have found an old dwelling place of the ancients, and it is full of the things they used to make. They are wonderful things, much better than we can make, and could be of great service to us.'   One of the Elders looked directly at Brent,

'How do you know these things belonged to the ancients? And where did you find them?'

There was no going back now, the die had been cast.

'We went on a fishing trip down the lake and saw part of their building sticking out of the water. It was a huge stone slab, just like rock, but rock does not happen like that in nature, so we went to look at it. We found a door which lead us below ground to rooms much bigger than this, and they were full of things, some of which we didn't understand, but most we recognized as being similar to ours, but better. We have brought a few things back for you to see.'

Brent looked towards the door and raised his hand, and two men carefully carried in a flat board with their bounty laid out neatly upon it.

There were a series of large and small china plates, cups, a jug, two ornate glass vases, shears and scissors, knives of various sizes and a collection of cutlery. The silence deepened, as the Elders looked at one another, and then a hushed muttering from the rest of the assembly gradually grew in volume as they realized the importance of the find.

The four waited with bated breath for the verdict from the Elders, feeling that the noise from the general assembly indicated that they, at least, were already on their side.

'This should have been discussed with us first to ensure your safety and that of the settlement.' one of the Elders said hesitatingly, feeling that someone had to say something.

'We would have done so,' Brent responded respectfully,

'Had there been an Elder present. We didn't know exactly what we had found until we found it, and then it was too late. We have brought these things back for you to see and judge if they are harmless, and of use to the settlement.'

Brent's careful choice of words and reverential manner left the

Elders little room to manoeuvre. Somehow they had to take control of the matter, but it was obvious that the main assembly was interested in the goods on offer, and more than likely would side with Brent and his friends if they tried to deny the settlement the benefits of such a find.

'These things,' Brent continued quickly, 'would be useful for trading, as there are more of them than we would need, and this would be of benefit to all the settlements.'

The Elders were left with little option, the items on display seemed harmless enough, and were certainly of better quality than anything available at the present. Somehow they had lost control of the situation, and as usual in such circumstances, they employed procrastination to gain a little time and to re-marshal their forces.

One of the Elders slowly stood up to address the assembly,

'This matter needs careful consideration, it could upset the balance of trade between the settlements and unleash the power of the ancients, who, it is believed, brought destruction upon themselves long ago with the things they had made. We will advise you of our finding later.' At some unseen signal, they all rose up and marched out in single file, trying to look dignified and failing miserably.

As the last Elder disappeared through the doorway, the crowd rushed forward, eager to see at close hand the wonderful things from long ago.

Brent and the other three spread out along the board, explaining what some of the more obtuse items were for, based mainly on guesswork. But in so doing, it cemented their relationship with the crowd as men who knew what they were about.

'When more of these goods are available, and they will be soon, they will be shared out among you.' Brent said, sealing the fate of the Elders should they try to stop the pillage of the ancient's shopping arcade.

'Shall we go again tomorrow?' asked Macie, eagerly.

'Yes, at first light, and we want more lamps, see what you can get based on the promise of things we'll bring back.'

Three more of the group who had shown interest in Brent's earlier experiment were invited to join them, and did so willingly. The fishermen gladly agreed to the additional use of another larger boat, while Brent and Macie spent the rest of the day modifying the donated lamps, fitting larger gourd oil containers.

The new eating utensils were tried out that night when Brent was invited to eat with Macie and his family again.

'These metal spoons are great,' Macie said between mouthfuls, 'do you think there will be enough down there for all of us?

'I expect so,' Brent replied, swallowing quickly, 'what we saw was a display of their goods, like those at the metal workers. I would think they must have store rooms full of the stuff, otherwise what's the point of showing it off in the first place, if you can't supply the demand. Most of those things were in glass cases, you wouldn't want to keep opening them and replacing the stock every time someone wanted something.'

Another sleepless night followed for those concerned.

Next morning, the two boats set off at the crack of dawn, the waters of the lake looking cold and grey, and there was still a distinct chill in the air from the night before.

Macie and the three newcomers took the larger boat while Brent and the other two who had been on the earlier expedition led the way in the smaller craft, just far enough from the shore to catch the wind, the box of lamps jingling as they encountered the odd larger wave.

They were well on their way down the lake before the sun broke the horizon, turning the lake into a shimmering sea of silver with its welcome warming rays.

A lookout had been posted to watch for the water monster, but there was no sign of it, so they assumed Macie's arrow must have proved more deadly than was first supposed.

The fallen concrete bridge was spotted, the boats pulled well clear of the water, and after picking up their weaponry and the box of modified lamps, they set off through the forest. There was now no sign of the fallen branch or the depression where it had once been, nothing remained the same in the forest for very long.

The lamps were lit, and the door was opened with a few sceptical looks from the new additions to the team, and they began the journey down, leaving lamps at strategic places so they could bring their haul up without having to carry a lamp at the same time.

Brent organized piles of what he thought would be most suitable to take back to the settlement, making sure there was a good selection of knives and other cutting tools along with the china tableware and a few choice pieces of glass.

He scoured the displays for small things unfamiliar to their world, hoping to later learn something from the ancient's way of life and their manufacturing skills.

When all the bags had been filled and transported to the surface, Brent suggested they explore a little further, making a mental map of what each room held and its possible use to the settlement.

At one point, exploring a side passage, they came to the maintenance department, with various metal working tools lining the walls, and huge amounts of metal sheets and tubes in racks. A large pile of dust could be seen in one corner, which they assumed to be what was left of timber or some other perishable material, which had succumbed to the passage of time.

They finally reached the lowest level, where a pair of huge glass doors were the only exit point visible.

'I wonder what's in there?' Brent said, as he held his lamp up against the glass, 'it can't be another way out as we're deep underground.' Most of the light from the lamp was reflected back from the thick glass door, and after a long and thorough search, they found no means of opening it.

Macie suggested that he go back to the room with the tools on the wall, to see if there was anything there which could be used to prise the door open. Brent agreed, insisting that he take someone with him.

Armed with a tool used for opening packing cases, they tried to prise the tightly fitted doors open, but only managed to chip some glass from the edges. Brent called a halt to the assault as he felt bad about damaging such a huge piece of glass. And then someone noticed a series of bars running along the top of the doors, and wondered if they were holding the glass in place.

With Macie standing on the shoulders of two others, he drove the jemmy between two of the bars and pulled down hard, lost his balance and began to fall.

The extra weight on the lever forced the bars apart, causing one of them to spring free from its junction with a loud crack, while Macie's fall was broken by the quick action of the others as he tumbled grounds wards, arms flailing.

He seemed none the worse for his acrobatics, giving the others a good laugh and releasing the tension which had been building up due to the unusual circumstances they were all under.

After dusting himself down, he gave the door a perfunctory push, more as a gesture than anything else, and it opened.

With the door now open just enough for them all to file through, the mystery behind the glass doors was revealed.

A thirty metre long platform stretched out before them with a curved roof overhead. Brent walked to the edge, looked down in the feeble light of the oil lamp, and gasped.

Below him, twin rails ran off into the darkness of a tunnel at each end of the platform, with a third rail raised on white insulators between the main pair.

'Come and look at this,' he said in a high squeaky voice,

'The ancients had a track system too.'

The others crowded round, the light from their combined lamps lighting up the rail system quite clearly. For a moment they just stood there, too surprised to speak.

'But there's no wind down here,' Macie said, 'so how did they make the trucks go along?'

'They must have had some means of moving them,' Brent replied, impatiently, 'or they wouldn't have built the damn thing in the first place.'

He stood there thoughtfully for a moment, and then said,

'I think this is a means of bringing people from somewhere else to visit the store. I wonder why they did it under the ground instead of on top, like us.'

'I'll bet the Elders won't believe this,' Macie said with relish, 'especially as we have a rail system too. It sort of joins us to them, in a way, having the same ideas.' The others grunted their accord, still too shocked for words.

They walked up and down the platform, trying to make out what the tattered remains of the pictures on the walls with their strange words meant, but time had destroyed all but the toughest of them, and they were none the wiser.

'Better get up top again,' Brent said at last, 'we've got a lot of stuff to get down to the boats, and I've no idea how long we've been down here.'

On the way, they called in at the maintenance room, and found some lengths of metal tubing which Brent insisted they bring up. The tubes were of different sizes and diameters, and mostly quite thin as they were for air ducting, but a few were of thicker material, and he had his eye on these for the burning powder he had made.

Slowly they made their way back to the surface, collecting the extra lamps they had left to mark the way, and extinguishing them as they went.

The pile of loaded carry bags needed several journeys to and fro from the forest, and they had a struggle to launch the boats back into the water with their extra loads.

This time the forest had been benign to them, and nothing had shown its teeth, but a few had watched the little people running around, and wondered what they tasted like.

With the boats now in the water, they were a little nervous about getting in themselves as their bounty weighed more than they expected, and there being little freeboard left.

'Just take it easy,' Brent called out, 'no sudden movements, just spread your load out as evenly as possible and we should be all right.'

On the way back they had to go slowly so as not to ship water and sink, as the gunwales were only just above water level. To help pass the time constructively, they discussed every possible scenario they could think of which might occur when they landed their goods and the Elders made their pronouncement thereupon.

'I think,' said Brent, summing up all that had been said, 'When some of this stuff has been shared out among the people, the Elders will have a hard time of it trying to put a lid on our operations. They'll have the whole of the settlement to contend with, and I don't think they'll take that on.'

Everyone felt easier having seen the logic of Brent's statement, and were in a much calmer and more cheerful mood when they finally reached the settlement. The goods were offloaded and carried up to the store shed, Brent having put on one side those items he thought fit to offer in exchange for the lamps which had been donated earlier.

The next morning, a small allocation of tableware was given to those who had visited the store shed to see what they had brought back. Once word got out that gifts were in the offing, the rest of the settlement joined the queue, and just about everyone had something to take home, except the Elders, who kept themselves a little apart from the others.

The first part of Brent's plan was in place, it now only needed the Elders to put in an appearance to complete the action, but for some reason they chose to stay away.

Macie later found Brent hammering away in the store shed.

'Your dust burning device?

'Yes,' Brent replied, pounding away at the end of the metal tube with a hammer, 'I'm trying to peen this end over to lock in a piece of wood which will form the end plate.'

He finished his hammering, picked up the puffer, and stood back to admire his handiwork, grinning broadly.

'Let's take it out and try it.' They both took hold of the tube and made their way out behind the building to a position facing away from the rest of the settlement.

Brent placed the tube up against a rock so that it would not take off with the back lash, handed Macie the lit taper on the end of a long stick, and began working the puffer.

'OK, light up.' and Macie swept the taper past the pale grey cloud which was drifting out of the end of the tube.

Neither of them expected what happened next. There was a loud whump, the tube bucked like a frightened deer and a three metre flame shot out of the end.

It was not quite an explosion, but the concussion wave from the expanding gas rattled a few things near by. This time there was little smoke to give them away, but they still hurriedly picked up the tube, burning their hands on the hot metal, and hid it in the shed.

'You know,' said Macie thoughtfully, as they strolled back to the ladders, 'if you count the number of puffs you give that thing, you might get the same size flame each time.'

'That's a damn good idea,' Brent replied, 'I'd not thought of that. How about a bigger tube?' Macie looked horrified.

That night they celebrated, filling their bellies to the full and imbibing far too much of Eslie's potent fruit juice.

It was with a thick head that Brent received the summons to visit the Elders, and he hurried off, calling in on the way to tell Macie where he was going.

He had resumed some measure of composure by the time he reached the chief Elder's abode, and only hoped he could remember all the subtle arguments he had rehearsed to handle any resistance from them.

He knocked politely on the door; a deep resonant voice invited him to enter. Two of the senior Elders sat behind a table on which three glasses stood, but no pouring jug.

'Please be seated,' one of them said, 'and relax. We do not intend to stop your adventures into the ancient's old buildings, as you have cleverly got the rest of the settlement on your side. It's surprising what a few little trinkets will do, isn't it?' He tried to smile, but his eyes didn't.

'Our main concern is that we do not upset the balance of trade between the settlements, as this is what keeps us all together. A limited amount of trade, consisting of harmless items will be permitted, but we must approve of them first. You will, at all times, keep us informed of what you intend to trade, and with whom, and our decision will be final. Do you agree to this?' Brent felt his hackles rising.

'Well, I....'

'A simple yes or no is all that's required.' the Elder said, trying to look stern.

'Now just a damn minute,' Brent almost shouted the words, making both men jump, 'I didn't come here to be dictated to, but to discuss the best way forward for all of us. We have a great opportunity here to better ourselves, to learn from the ancients how to make things we can't do at the moment.' He paused to get his breath. 'Look, would you allow these scissors to be traded with the metal workers?' taking them from his pocket and handing them across the table. The Elders looked at the scissors, and tried them, cutting an imaginary something in mid-air.

'No, we would not.' said one of them, 'they are far too advanced, and would make the metal workers feel inferior.'

'That is just your short sighted point of view,' Brent replied, 'just the sort of thing that stops progress.'

'I think the metal workers would be delighted to receive such a gift, they could then see the best kind of metal to use. This design is better than anything they have ever made.'

Both Elders looked very uncomfortable, as if they had realized their argument had been flawed to start with, and there was no way around it without losing face, and they were not about to do that. Sensing that he now had the upper hand at last, Brent now took full advantage of the situation,

'Now it is your turn to listen to my terms.' he said, leaning forward, and closing the space between them.

'It wouldn't take very much for the whole settlement to ignore all you Elders, and elect a new lot of younger men who are in touch with the needs of the people. I do not see why you have to be old to be an Elder, in fact I think it is a disadvantage, as you are far too stuck in your view points and ways. If my group have any more interference or threats from you, steps will be taken to remove you from the power you think you possess. Do I make myself clear?'

Both Elders looked thunder struck, and at a loss for words, until eventually one of them gathered himself together, and in a faltering voice did his best to regain a little ground.

'How dare you speak to us like that. It is the greatest impertinence I have ever heard.' he said shaking.

'I just have, and will again if I have to.' Brent retorted, getting into his stride. 'I mean no disrespect, I have only spoken to you in the same manner in which you addressed me, and if you can't handle that, you shouldn't be in the position of Elder anyway. I now conclude this meeting, you will be hearing from us in the near future.' he added, unable to resist the opportunity to be as dramatic as possible and loving every minute of it.

Before the shaken Elders could marshal their thoughts and try to regain control of a hopeless situation, Brent arose from his seat, spun on his heal and left the room, trembling slightly from the vicious exchange of words a few weeks ago he would have thought impossible.

Time would tell as to who had actually won that confrontational exchange, he thought, and sought out his friend to update him on what had taken place.

'No stopping you when you get going, is there' Macie said when he had listened to the encounter, 'but I think you're right. From what I've heard this morning, most of us are of a like mind, and the opportunity to gain a few of the ancient's possessions will convince the rest. What do we do now? Can we go back to the underground store?'

'We can, but not just yet. I've got to go to the metal workers again tomorrow according to the travel listing, and I want to mount the flame tube on the front of the truck before facing that cloud thing again. Can you give me a hand with it?'

The afternoon was spent attaching a wooden framework to the front of the truck and mounting the metal tube. Not being too happy about the way to achieve ignition of the coal dust, Macie came up with the idea of using one of the flint fire makers.

With the tube firmly fixed to the frame, and the flint fire maker attached to the front of the tube, it only remained to form some sort of linkage back into the truck for the device to be completed. They stuck a crude paper cover, with a small hole at the bottom, over the front end of the tube to contain the coal dust cloud, in case the wind blew the mixture out before they could ignite it, and then Brent wanted to test the apparatus, just to be on the safe side.

They trundled the truck out of the shed and a short way along the track, so that it was out of sight of the rest of the settlement.

'I'll only use a small charge,' Brent said, reassuringly, 'Just to make sure the ignition system works.' But Macie stood well back, knowing full well what his friend was like when he had the bit between his teeth. A few short puffs on the puffer and Brent pulled the rod connecting to the flint spark maker. There was a soft woof, a tongue of flame shot out of the tube, and a small cloud of dark smoke spiralled up into the late afternoon sky.

'Looks good to me,' Brent said, a satisfied smile on his face, 'that dust cloud thing is going to be in for a shock, if we ever see it again.' Somehow he knew they would.

'I'll take a few of our newly acquired oddments for the old man's collection,' Brent said, as they left the store building, 'he's been very hospitable to us.'

Later that evening, before it got too dark, Brent returned to the store shed and loaded a box of metal objects he thought the metal workers would appreciate, covering the box with coils of rope and twine which were the main load of goods to be delivered. Doing it this way, it would obviate any possible arguments if an Elder should decide to interfere.

He slept well that night, feeling that much had been achieved, especially as he felt they could raid the ancient's store of goods quite safely, as long as they were sensible and took the normal precautions one did in the forest.

The usual early morning start got under way without a hitch, the truck being pushed out onto the flat section of track just clear of the buildings so that they could take advantage of the wind which rushed across the flatlands.

Brent and Macie climbed in, and they were under way.

The chill of early morning began to wear off as the sun climbed higher in the sky, promising another blistering day.

Although Brent was deeply disturbed by the threat of the swirling dust cloud on the approaching section of track, he was keen to try the flame thrower, but still wondered if it was the right sort of weapon to deal with the thing.

The concept that a cloud of dust or mist could have a life of its own, reshape itself, and move about out on the barren lands was something well beyond his comprehension.

To reform its shape, and move about against the constant wind implied some sort of intelligence in his book, but how could something so tenuous as a puff of dust contain life? It was the lack of knowledge and understanding which fuelled his fear, and it would remain with him until the enigma was solved.

'I think we're coming up to the spot where the thing usually shows itself,' Macie called out helpfully over the drumming of the wheels, 'I'll bet it doesn't appear now we're ready for it.' Macie was no way ready for it, but didn't like to show it.

They both scoured the landscape for any sign of dust or mist trying to coalesce into a visible mass, and were well past the point where it usually appeared before giving up their vigil.

'Just thought of something,' said Macie brightly, 'I think it only shows up on the return journey. Have you ever seen it on the way out to the metal workers settlement?'

'Come to think of it, I haven't.' Brent replied thoughtfully.

'That was good thinking on your part.'

'And what happens just before you see it? You pass that pile of black rocks. I'll bet that's got something to do with it, perhaps it lives there,' Macie added cheerfully.

Brent gave his usual grunt of acknowledgement which he used when preferring not to use words, and turned his attention to trimming the already perfectly set the sail.

The sun climbed inexorably higher, beating down on the two travellers as they sat in their wheeled box rumbling over the baked landscape, taking it in turns to enjoy the shade afforded by the billowing sail.

'Looks like the repair team have been busy,' said a relieved Brent, as they approached the big funnel pit, 'swinging the track out this far should make it last quite a time.'

They rattled past the yawning chasm, not bothering to reduce speed as they now had several metres of solid ground between them and the edge of the funnel.

By midday they were coasting down the last slope towards the store sheds of the metal workers, having made very good time, which neither of them could understand as they had done nothing unusual during the journey.

After the ropes and fabrics had been traded and dispensed to those who desired them, the metal workers were invited to a display of the ancient's artefacts, and this caused more than just a little interest.

The Elders were called, and they too were dumfounded for a few moments, and then, realizing the benefit of acquiring such goods, tried to set up a deal with Brent directly, which was totally out of character for them, this being done by those of lower status.

He explained that one each of the different metallic items would be a gift to the settlement, while duplicates and the pots and plates were up for trade.

Keeping tally of the swiftly mounting credits kept Macie busy for a while, and then it was all over, just the empty truck and two very tired men leaning against it.

The foreman of the metal workers had stayed behind after the others had dispersed, and now approached them.

'The silver cylinder you brought last time has proved most useful, we are still using the burning air it contains and I wondered if it could be refilled, or another one found?'

'We've not seen any more,' Brent replied, 'and I've no idea where to get the burning air from, or how to get into the cylinder.' And then he remembered the flame thrower on the front of the truck and the hot flame it produced.

'Could show you one thing we've developed,' he said, 'it may be of use if you can control the burning.'

He showed the Foreman the device on the front of the truck, explaining how it worked and offered a demonstration.

The truck was pushed to the end of the line, well away from the sheds, and Brent got to work with the puffer.

When he thought he had half filled the tube with dust, he pulled the flint lighter rod, and the tube obligingly belched forth a great gout of flame, nearly singeing the Foreman who was standing a little too close for his safety.

'It's not quite the same kind of flame,' the shaken Foreman said, 'ours is pale blue, and produces no smoke. Come and see what we have done.'

The cylinder was in use when they went into the workshop, a worker playing the flame on a piece of metal which was glowing red hot, and then dipping it into a tub of water.

'That makes the metal very hard.' the Foreman explained.

'And we have added a short metal tube to the end of the burning pipe so that it pulls in extra air as it burns, and that makes the flame much hotter.'

'The glass workers use a burning air which they get from the flame rocks,' Brent said, trying to be helpful, 'you could try that, if you can get it into the cylinder.'

They discussed the properties of flame rocks, burning air and the possibility of getting it into the cylinder until they ran out of bright ideas, and then went their separate ways, the Foreman fired up with new concepts and the other two looking for the old man who had entertained them so well on their last visit.

As they rounded a corner, they saw him coming towards them, a hand raised in greeting, a broad smile on his face.

'Funny, you know,' said Brent quietly, 'he always seems to know where I'll be, and at the right time. Odd that.'

Before Macie could come up with a reasonable comment which made any sense, they had met, touching palms like old friends and exchanging greetings.

They automatically assumed they would be invited to stay for the rest of the day, and so it proved to be, the old man shedding the years as he chatted away with his younger companions, and plying them with copious amounts of his special fruit based beverage.

When Brent presented his box of gifts, the old man was overwhelmed, and for a few moments, unable to speak. He carefully picked up each piece, turning it this way and that, examining every tiny detail.

'These are wonderful things,' he said at length, reluctantly returning the last one to the box, 'you have found in a few days more artefacts than I have in a lifetime of searching, you are very fortunate indeed.'

'They are for you to keep,' Brent said gently, sensing the old man had not realized they were for him.

The old man looked up in disbelief, tears wetting his eyes, and then he embraced an embarrassed Brent.

'These are the finest gifts I have ever received,' he said at last, 'and I will treasure them greatly.'

After they had regained some degree of composure, the old man wanted to know the full details of where the gifts had come from, and what else might be there. He showed no sign of surprise when they told him about the underground track system of the ancients, even suggesting that they follow the tracks to see if they led to another store, something they had not thought about.

Brent had a few items in his pocket which he had held back, now he brought them out to see what the old man could make of them.

'This,' the old man said, turning it over in his hand, 'is something which you would carry on your wrist, I can tell this because of the diameter of the expanding bracelet. What the dial is for I do not know, but it must measure something, I would think. The little knob at the side could be some form of winding device I suppose,' The knob jumped out a little as he tried turning, and it made the two pointers go around, one faster than the other.

'The little signs around the edge must have a value of some kind, as the pointers point to them, but what it means is anyone's guess.'

After some fiddling and holding it to his ear, which puzzled his visitors, he announced that when the big pointer made a complete revolution it caused the small pointer to index up from one sign to the next.

'I do not think it is for finding your direction with, like the sticking stones, so maybe it was used for recording some quantity, and you turned the knob to indicate the value.'

He handed the luxury wrist watch back to Brent, who told him to keep it in case he could later work out what it was.

'What are these sticking stones you mentioned?' asked Macie, 'I've never heard of them, what do they do?'

The old man reached behind him to the shelf of trophies and handed a small cluster of grey black stones to each of them, explaining that the stones had some strange property which made them attract themselves to some metals and to each other, and demonstrated this by holding two stones a short distance apart and letting one of them go. The released stone immediately snapped up to the other one he was holding, and stuck to it.

'I do not recall why exactly, but one day I stroked a hard metal needle against one of these, and the needle took on the same properties. Some time later I was playing about with the needle, laying the it on a floating leaf in a bowl of water to see how far away the stone would have to be in order to attract it, and it was quite some way. I later noticed that the needle always took up the same position if left alone, no matter where I took it.'

The old man looked to see if his friends were following his explanation, and by the intent look on their faces, concluded they were, so far.

'From this, I reasoned that if you took a bowl of water and a floating needle with you, wherever you went, the needle would always point in the same direction, and this could be used to navigate your way around in places where there was no other reference to go by.'

'That's very clever of you,' said Brent, greatly impressed by the old man's reasoning powers, 'that could be a very useful device if you were travelling over the barren lands on foot, do you think that's how the settlements got together in the first place?'

'No, I do not think so, I showed it to the Elders and although they showed polite interest, the idea was never taken up by anyone to my knowledge.'

'That's a pity.' Macie said, remembering the attitude their Elders displayed when approached with anything new, or a query about something.

Brent dug deeply into his pocket to bring out another trophy from the ancient's shopping centre and gave it to the old man after he had put his lode stones away.

'Can't make head or tail of this,' he said, 'we've tried to make it do something, but although it looks as if it has two tiny cutting blades on one end, they don't move, and they're too small to be useful anyway.'

The old man gracefully took the proffered item and grinned,

'The reason nothing moves is because it is not meant to, unless you release this top lever first.' He twisted the lever and swung it around through one hundred and eighty degrees, and clicked it back down. The tiny jaws had now opened, and moved up and down as he pressed the lever.

'Put your finger nail in there,' he said, 'just the tip, and hold your hand steady.' There was a click as the old man closed the lever and a small chip of Brent's finger nail flew across the room. The two younger men looked astonished.

'It is a device for trimming your finger nails, and time has made the lever mechanism a little stiff to operate, that is why you could not work it. I have seen one of these before, but it was not in such good condition, and would not cut anything as the sharp edges had corroded away.'

Several other things the ancients had left in their shop were examined, the old man enjoying himself like a young child with a new toy, explaining some, baffled by others, and making a few of them function as they were intended.

It was very late in the evening when they finally said goodnight, the old man seeming to be reluctant to let them go, but they had an arduous day ahead, the journey back.

It was midmorning before they set off for home, as one of the Elders had requested a meeting with them to discuss future possible finds from the ancient's ruins.

'If during any future explorations you should come across any large sheets of metal, we could organize a collection party to bring them back here, so saving you the trouble of hauling them out and transporting them,' the softly spoken Elder suggested, 'and of course you would be credited for finding the material in the first place. The idea behind this suggestion is not to deprive you of the trading possibilities, but to enable you to concentrate on exploration, which you seem to be very good at.'

'That sounds fine by me,' Brent replied, realizing the efficiency of such a proposal, 'but surely there are remains around here your people could explore, the ancients must have been spread all over the place in order to have evolved into such an advanced race.'

'That may be so, but we have found none. Whatever reduced the barren lands to their present state has probably destroyed any trace of an earlier civilization, certainly as far as the surface is concerned, so we have no idea where to look. A few oddments have been found occasionally, but they are either corroded beyond use, or we do not know what they are for.'

Brent agreed to the idea, with the reservation that it would only apply to large pieces of metal, which he would designate for collection.

'May I ask you a question?' Brent asked, observing the correct protocol when requesting anything from an Elder.

'Certainly, I would be only too pleased.'

'I understand your people once came from the great forest, a long time ago, can you tell me more about that?'

'Ah, you have been talking to your new friend,' the Elder said, with a chuckle in his voice, 'he is very knowledgeable, I must agree, but some of his theories are just that, theories.

'There is very little known really, except that once this settlement was on the edge of a forest, but we were driven out by some new creatures who had come into our area. We had to leave the forest because of this, but even so, they raided us from time to time, so the forest was cut back except for the really big trees which we were unable to fell, and when the cut wood had dried out enough it was burnt.'

'With the wind blowing in the same direction all the time, the fire took hold and got out of control, releasing enough heat to set fire to the long strip which joined us to the main forest. The deep gully is all that remains of the forested strip, and we salvage what's left of the dead roots of the giant trees for fuel. It put an end to the attacks, but left us isolated here, and that is all I know.'

'What do you know of your attackers? Brent asked respectfully, feeling there was a little more to be learnt.

'You must bear in mind that this happened a very long time ago, and I cannot vouch for the accuracy of what has been passed down through many generations. According to what I have heard from my predecessors, they were much like us, except that they were covered in dark reddish brown hair, had big fangs and dropped on us in large groups from high up in the trees, which they were able to climb with ease.'

'Most disgusting of all, anyone they caught was torn apart and eaten on the spot. We had no option but to leave the area, and followed the line of trees to this present place.'

They thanked the Elder profusely for his time and trouble and headed for the truck, and home.

Time flew as they discussed what the Elder had told them.

'Do you think long ago some of us turned into the hairy killers, or were they a leftover from the time of the ancients?' Macie asked thoughtfully, 'we are often finding new creatures in the forest, so perhaps changes like that are all part of a natural happening.'

'Don't know,' Brent replied, 'but I'm glad there are none of 'em around now. Not much point in asking our Elders, I don't suppose they even bother to keep the stories going.'

'I doubt they'd even speak to you now anyway.' Macie commented wryly.

They passed the vast funnel pit without mishap, this time it lay dormant, but still threatening, its enormous dark central hole beckoning any would be passer-by to investigate at their peril.

As they approached the dark finger rock, as they now referred to it, Brent checked his flame thrower, making sure the puffer was fully charged, and wondering what would happen if it failed to ignite. The thought of a misfire made him shudder, but he kept his feelings to himself.

The truck sped past the ominous rock formation with its skywards pointing digit, and on to the area where the dust cloud was expected. They were not disappointed.

'There it is,' squeaked Macie, his voice several octaves higher than he intended, 'what'll we do?'

'Go right up to it, and give it some heat,' Brent replied aggressively, 'give the little sod something to think about.'

As they drew nearer, Brent lowered the sail so that they were just coasting along, slowly losing speed until they were almost up to the misty cloud. The mist then began to rotate and thicken, taking on a more solid and threatening form than they had ever seen before.

Brent furiously worked the handle of the puffer, counting the strokes, and then the front of the truck touched the swirling menacing cloud.

They both felt a blast of chilled air as the cloud thickened, blocking out the light from behind it, and then Brent pulled the spark maker's rod.

A deep whump was followed by a gush of flame enveloping the front of the truck, and punching a hole through the rotating cloud. Sparks of light flashed throughout the swirling mist, like a miniature thunderstorm, the air crackled crisply and they both felt the hair on their heads suddenly acquire a life of its own as it stood on end.

A thin loud keening sound rent the air, and they both instinctively clapped their hands over their ears to shut out the awful shriek of torment as the cloud expanded to three times its original size and was then dispersed on the constantly blowing wind. The chill was gone, and the welcome radiance of the sun once more bathed them in its comforting rays.

By now the truck was stationary, and slowly its occupants gathered themselves together and looked around. There was no sign of the cloud, and everything seemed normal again except for some singe marks on the sail which had flopped forward when the truck stopped, and momentarily been bathed in the expanding fire ball.

A string of expletives preceded Brent's first comment,

'Don't think we'll see that thing again any time soon.' he said.

'If ever,' Macie added, slumped down in the back of the truck, 'do you think we killed it, or just frightened it away?'

'Don't think it really matters much,' said Brent callously.

'I don't think it'll risk another meeting with us, unless it's totally stupid or mad, or both.' he added for good measure.

With the truck underway once more, they both relaxed, although a close observer would have noticed the odd slight tremble as the final tensions ebbed away. The rest of the journey went smoothly enough, racing down the final stretch towards the settlement and into the storage area.

Eslie had a meal waiting for them when they arrived, Brent commenting that he now felt a full member of the family and would shortly be bringing his bed along. The children were thrilled to bits at the announcement, until their father explained that it was only an adult joke, but on second thoughts he was uncertain if adult had been the right word.

After the meal, and when the children had been put to bed, Eslie wanted to hear the full details of their adventure, listening intently as she always did. She made no comment when they had finished, except to agree it had been very exciting with just a touch of danger thrown in.

She did show some concern when she realized they intended returning to the underground store as soon as possible, suggesting that a few more be added to the group to increase the safety factor.

The moon had climbed high into the night sky when Brent finally staggered up his ladder, a little too inebriated to fully appreciate the beauty of the silver light reflecting off the water below, subtly bathing everything in its gentle glow.

Next morning, Macie found him cutting his flat glass sheets to size; ready to fit into the window frame he had constructed earlier.

'How will you hold the glass in place?' Macie asked, not being particularly gifted in the building crafts.

'These little beads of wood. The glass sheets drop into the frame and the beads lock it in place. And before you ask, these little pegs hold the beads firmly in the frame.'

'Oh.' Macie responded, glad he was not required to explain the system of clear window building to a third party.

Of the Elders there was no sign. Either they had gone on holiday en masse, which was a concept the settlement had never encompassed, or far more likely, they were holed up somewhere chewing over the problem of the troublesome Brent and his merry band of heretical dissenters.

He was glad they had left him alone, as having got rid of his pent up emotions about their general attitude to things, he was now feeling a little more co-operative, but not much.

With the window in place, hinged from the top so that it could be propped open to let cooling air in when needed, they both stood back to admire Brent's handiwork.

Before long, they were joined by others who had seen something going on, and had now come to see what all the fuss was about. By midday, Brent had collected several orders for windows, and was wondering where he was going to get all the glass from, until Macie pointed out that the underground store had glass aplenty, if they could release it from the frames which had held it secure for so long.

It was agreed that three more men should be invited to join the team, making ten in all, this being a number which could be controlled easily, and enough to give some backup if anyone should find themselves in trouble.

The fishermen were approached for the loan of yet another large boat to which they eagerly agreed, having seen the rewards the others received from the last outing.

Brent set about making a smaller portable version of his flame thrower to take with them, intending that nothing should stop their entering the forest to acquire its hidden bounty, also the memory of the brown hairy creatures they had been told about had not gone away.

The third expedition, when it set off early next morning was in jubilant mood, their ribald comments and jokes echoing across the still waters of the lake, eliciting a response from the creatures of the forest's edge. Once the sails had been set, the little armada was soon out of sight of the settlement and heading out into deeper waters.

All had been warned that they may have to stay the night in the safety of the building should they not have enough daylight left to make a safe return.

Brent had told the newcomers about the water monster and its supposed demise, and that a strict watch must be kept at all times as it was more than likely there were others.

The concrete slab came into view, and the boats were hauled well out of the water. Armed with extra lamps, copious amounts of nut oil and the new flame thrower, Brent felt invincible as he led his troupe into the gloom of the forest. All were skilled bowmen, and four of them held bows at the ready while the others staggered along with the carrying bags and the other equipment.

The newcomers were shown the doorway and the steps down to the dark depths below, their reactions being noted by Brent, who then judged there was no reason to believe they could not be relied upon should things take a turn for the worse.

With lamps lit, and being placed at key points on the way down as before, they soon arrived at the main hall, Brent giving the new members a chance to take in the wonder of it all before allocating specific duties.

The main store was found, and this amazed even Brent with its complex system of rooms and interlocking corridors.

Again, lamps placed at the right places acted as guides through the labyrinth and back up to the main hall.

Once Brent and Macie had selected the goods for transferring to the surface, the original two additions to their first venture were invited to go down to the underground track system with them, as the others would be fully employed transferring the bounty upstairs for some time to come.

They left instructions that the others should wait in the main show room for their return, and if a whole day went by without them returning, they should go back to the settlement.

On the way down, Brent tried unsuccessfully to remove a sheet of glass from its frame, breaking it in the process.

'We'll go to the tool section next time,' he said in frustration, 'and get the correct tools.'

'How will you know which are the correct ones?' asked Macie in all innocence. He just got a poorly disguised dirty look for his troubles.

One of the great glass doors leading to the platform stood ajar, with a steady cool draft blowing through it.

'You know what this means,' said Brent, after they all had felt it, 'there must be an opening to the outside world somewhere, as fresh air is coming in.'

They clambered down onto the track level, wondering which way to go, there being no particular incentive to choose either. In the end, it was decided to follow the tracks on the left-hand side of the platform, as it seemed the gentle air flow was coming from that direction.

Once their eyes had got used to the blackness of the tunnel compared to the reflective properties of the rooms above, the lamps gave adequate light for their purpose. A sudden curve in the tunnel awoke them from their almost dream like tramping, and Brent quite irrationally thought there might be something interesting up ahead.

A few more metres and they came to a turn off in the track way, leading into a much wider tunnel and a complete train. They stood in awe for some moments before finding a way of opening the doors and exploring the interior.

'How do they make it go along?' someone asked. A thorough search of the carriages failed to give a clue as to its means of locomotion, no one thinking to look underneath.

Macie had wandered off, his lamp bobbing about up a side track, when his excited call brought them all running.

'Look what I've found,' he said proudly, pointing to the hand propelled maintenance truck, 'I'll bet those handles make it go along.' he said with unfounded certainty.

'Let's give it a try then.' said Brent, climbing up onto the truck's flat top. He put his weight down hard on one of the horizontal handles, and the truck slowly moved forward.

'All we need to do is get it onto the main track, and we have a means of transport.' Macie said, stating the obvious.

Once they had figured out how to manually work the points system, the maintenance truck was on the main track, they were on it, all the lamps were up front to maximize the light, while two of them were pumping the handles vigorously. The others were straining their eyes looking into the darkness of the tunnel to give warning if there was an obstacle ahead, while the truck rumbled and squeaked its way along.

'If there's another store on this track, it's one hell of a long way away,' commented Macie breathlessly, taking his turn on the handle, 'I for one would prefer to shop at the first store.'

'Shut up and pump.' someone said in the darkness, they never did find out who said it, but it gave them a laugh, so breaking the tension which had built up.

Four:
Attack from the past

THEY CHANGED SHIFTS on the crank handle several times, and after a few twists and turns of the track Brent was thinking of abandoning the attempt to find where it led when a glimmer of light showed up ahead.

'Let's slow down a bit,' he said, 'we don't know what's ahead, and there shouldn't be any lights down here anyway.'

The light grew brighter as they approached, making their oil lamps ineffective, and then the truck hit something and shuddered to a stop, nearly spilling its occupants.

They clambered down from the truck, nearly blinded by the brilliance of the light and shuffled around for a few moments until they got used to the glare.

'The track's got a lot of debris on it,' someone called out,

'Perhaps the roof's collapsed.' They all looked up, but the roof was undamaged, the smooth vault of its curves intact.

'I think that's daylight,' Brent said after a while, 'let's go see, but tread carefully, there's a lot of rubble.'

He led the way, the light getting brighter until they had to shade their eyes from the dazzling white blaze.

A cool draft of air greeted them as they came out into the open on a ledge high above a shimmering lake.

'If that's not the damnedest thing,' exclaimed Brent in disbelief as they looked down, 'we're up above our settlement. But that can't be, we'd have seen this hole in the cliff face, surely.'

Going to the very edge, he looked down on top of the dwellings perched all along the curving cliff, their ladders looking like spiders webs, connecting the various levels.

'I can't understand it either,' Macie added, shaking his head, 'why would the track end here? There's no boarding platform, and how could you get up here anyway?'

'I think I can see what might have happened,' Brent said after a pause, 'the track must have continued on to somewhere else, and the missing section of the cliff has fallen away into the lake, taking the track with it.'

By now they had all crowded out onto the ledge, looking around in amazement at a totally new view of their homes.

'Look over there,' said Macie, pointing, 'there's another hole in the far end of the cliff, I'll bet the track tunnel curved around and went in there.'

The sun had passed the midday mark, and Brent decided they should return to the underground store as there was no way they could get down the cliff at the moment, and there was nothing further for them to do on the ledge, except gaze out at the magnificent view set out below them.

'I think I can see why we didn't spot this hole before, the ledge protects it from our view when on the ground, and the other hole would just look like a piece of black rock being so far away.' Brent said, as they returned to the truck.

They removed the rubble from the track which had stopped the truck, climbed back on and began the return journey, Brent saying he saw no reason not to go at full speed as they had encountered no obstacles on the outward journey.

They were all a bit hot and sweaty as they flew past the siding where they had acquired the manually operated transport, and sped on to the main station platform, the truck skidding to a stop opposite the entrance doors.

It transpired when they met up with the loading group, that they had taken the goods up to the surface and on to the boats, and were now patiently awaiting the arrival of the truck party. Brent was not too pleased that the others had taken the goods out without his say so, but it showed initiative, and as no harm had befallen them, he said nothing.

They left the underground store and headed for the boats, having closed the door to keep out any creatures of the forest who might wander in and lay in wait for their return.

Brent looked up at the sun, trying to judge if they had enough time left to reach the settlement before dark, or if they should return to the store and stay the night there. Macie was all for leaving now, using the lights from the settlement as beacons to guide them the last part of the journey.

Brent saw the logic of the proposal and agreed, saying they would have to stay well away from the shore once it got dusk, as the settlement lights could otherwise be obscured.

It took the whole team to launch the two bigger boats as they were so heavily laden and extra care would be needed to keep the boats stable in the water once the men embarked.

Because of the constant tacking against the head wind, they knew the journey back would take much longer, and began to worry as the light faded after the sinking sun dropped below the horizon in a splash of vivid red, and the forested area on their left took on menacing black shapes.

As the night closed in on them, flashes of light suddenly appeared below the boats, darting to and fro in a frenzy of activity. This display of luminescent fish was not lost on the travellers, and Brent had to call out several times to remind them to change course and keep together.

Once the novelty of the flashing fish had worn off, real panic set in as they were surrounded by a total velvet darkness which had crept up on them unawares.

Thinking ahead, Macie had suggested each boat light a lamp to act as a marker, and fortunately this had been done. Three lonely lights now bobbed about in the inky blackness of the lake, with only the constant head wind to act as a rough guide as to where the settlement was.

'Lights ahead,' a voice called out, and they all stared hopefully into the darkness, until the lone voice was joined excitedly by others as they too saw faint lights twinkling in the distance.

The glittering fish suddenly left the area around the boats in one huge coordinated movement, as if at some unheard command, and the waters were jet black again.

'Don't like that,' Brent commented, looking over the side of his boat, 'something must have frightened them away, and that only leaves us.' Just then the boat shuddered and began to rock from side to side, something was butting the craft furiously, trying to spill its occupants into the water.

'Quick,' Macie called out from the darkness, 'tip the oil from a lamp onto a shirt tied to an oar, and light it. Then hold it out as far from the boat as you can.' Brent fumbled about in the pitch dark among the loaded bags, swearing, and trying to find the lamp box. Having found one, he tipped the oil out onto the shirt handed to him by his companion who, had already tied it to an oar. Dangling the oily cloth over the lamp in the bows of the boat, it caught fire, and he then held it out over the water, wondering why. The horrendous thumping of the boat stopped, and seconds later a huge dark shape broke surface alongside, its cavernous jaws fully open. The flaming shirt and the end of the oar disappeared in one lightning fast snapping action, nearly pulling the remains of the shaft from Brent's grasp.

Within seconds the waters were calm again, the three lights continued to bob up and down, and everyone was shaking.

The lights of the settlement beckoned, and as they drew nearer, the high cliffs shielded them from the wind so they used the oars for the last few hundred metres, Brent sculling from the back of his boat with a single remaining oar.

A small crowd was waiting for them as they pulled up to the jetty, Eslie in the forefront, waving a lantern, and then eager hands were helping the weary travellers up onto the boards, and tying up the boats.

'We were getting worried.' said Eslie, trying to stop her lower lip from trembling. 'We came down to the shore just in case you came back today, and then we saw the lights and knew you had not stayed the night, what happened?'

'Tell you all about it later,' Macie said quietly, 'don't want to make a fuss about it in front of the others.'

A lone Elder stood at the back of the little crowd, listening intently to what was being said and gathering any information he could.

After the exchange of greeting, they all split up and went their own ways, Brent being invited to join his newly adopted family for yet another meal.

Feeling better for having eaten, they related the whole story to Eslie, who listened intently as usual and surprised them both by suggesting that the newly found track could be used to transport goods from the store to the cliff top, and then down to ground level on a platform and winch.

They finally retired to bed, the three of them having worked out a system which would efficiently strip the ancient's store of its treasures by making a new truck to put on the front of the manually operated unit, and a lift system of ropes and pulleys to lower the goods down to the settlement.

By mid morning, they had a willing band of volunteers to help with the construction of the new truck and a system of ladders to reach the tunnel opening up above the dwellings on the cliff face. The enthusiasm for the project had to be calmed down a little while a sequence of events was worked out which would be most efficient.

The ladders would be made first, pinning them to the cliff face with Ironwood pegs driven into fissures in the rock, and then the tunnel would be cleared of the debris which had collected in the entrance over the years. Careful measurements would be taken of the maintenance truck's wheels, duplicating them in Ironwood. The new truck to carry their bounty would then be hauled up the cliff face in pieces and assembled in the tunnel mouth.

A platform which could be winched up and down the cliff, would be suspended from a framework at the tunnel entrance, and Macie suggested that they power it with a wind mill mounted on the cliff top.

All the while, each part of the operation was being watched over by one or more Elders. Although they kept well back from the activities, nothing was missed. Brent had expected some interference, but there was none, just the odd stony look when he caught their eye.

The problem of the water monster still niggled Brent, but as Macie pointed out, there was no problem really. The fishermen kept to the shallow waters where the creature never went, and they would soon have the rail link directly to the ancient's store, so there would be no need to travel the deeper waters of the lake anyway.

With most of the artisans of the settlement usefully employed on these new projects, the place had taken on a buzz of activity not seen for a long time, and although the Elders watched from a discreet distance, they still held back from any form of interference.

Brent had taken on the role of leader, organizing the work and checking to make sure that everything was done correctly. It was to him that the members of the settlement now came with their queries and suggestions.

Two days later, and the ladder network up the cliff face had been completed, the debris cleared from the tunnel entrance and the parts for the new truck hauled up.

They were still working on the winching platform when Brent, Macie, and two others from the original team set off by boat for the underground store. They would bring the maintenance truck up to the cliff opening, hitch up the new truck, and then return with a few others to begin the plunder of the ancient's super store.

This time they were ready for the water monster, with an oil soaked bundle of rags tied to a pole, and an alert lookout.

The concrete slab was reached without incident, much to Brent's secret disappointment, and they set off for the store, Brent carrying his portable flame thrower while the others were laden down with as many lamps as they could carry.

The entrance was opened and then closed from the inside for the last time, their new route being directly from the settlement via the rail link.

The maintenance truck was where they had left it, and clambering onboard, they took it in turns to pump their way through the long tunnel to the settlement.

'There's something odd about this track,' Macie said as he took his turn on the handles, 'we go into the store just above the level of the lake, and then go down some way to this track, but the track comes out well above the level of the lake, so how come we're not going up hill?'

Brent thought for a moment, as this anomaly had not occurred to him before, having taken it all for granted.

'We may well be going up hill,' he said at long last, 'but look at the length of track between the store and our settlement, any gradient, and I'm sure there is one, would be hardly noticeable over such distance.'

Eventually, the light at the end of the tunnel began to show as a pale glimmer in the distance, growing brighter as they pumped the handles up and down. As they neared the opening, the lamps were extinguished and the truck began to slow down as it approached its new addition.

A pile of boxes lined the walls of the tunnel, ready for loading onto the new truck if the towing trial was successful, which it was. Although many wanted to begin the operation of pillaging the ancient's store right away, Brent suggested they begin next day at first light, as the truck would have to be unloaded and the goods sent down the cliff in the dark, as it was now after midday.

The trucks were secured with wooden wedges, and the long climb down the ladders began, several of them having their heads trodden upon by those above, eager to get down and relate the latest developments to all and sundry.

As the two friends were about to enter Macie's dwelling for much needed refreshments, two of the Elders approached.

'We would like to speak with you,' one of them said, looking around furtively, 'in your home perhaps?'

Ghent ushered them in, introducing them to Eslie who was more than a little surprised at the visit.

When they were all seated, and the customary jug of fruit juice placed in the middle of the table, one Elder began,

'We do not voice the opinions of the whole group, but after careful consideration, we feel we must draw your attention to the possible harmful effects your venture may have on us all.' He looked around the table, trying to judge how strongly he could voice their concerns without alienating, and so losing the co-operation of those he wished to influence.

'Please continue,' Brent said, his voice flat and toneless.

'At the moment, our three settlements are in a stable condition, each of us producing or supplying goods the others do not have, and so we have a nice balance of trade between us. We think if there is a sudden flood of goods which do not have to be made by any of us, it could put many out of useful occupation, and thereby lead to a feeling of not being needed and possible restlessness. We think something like this must have happened to the ancients, for why else would there be such total destruction of their dwellings and the wondrous things they had made?'

If this were true, Brent could see his world of adventure and improvement for the settlement showing cracks.

'We can't be sure that's what happened to the ancients, there may have been some other cause. I mean, take the funnel vents, they say that is caused by something which fell from the sky, so maybe something else hit the ancient's world and destroyed it.' He knew his argument was weak.

'We accept that we do not know what happened for certain, but I am sure you can see the possible risk.' The Elder's voice had now taken on a firmer tone, but his face still smiled.

'We are not against what you want to do for the settlement, and there are several others who would back you in your venture, but there must be some control in the flow of goods so that the workers remain gainfully employed and feel useful, and part of their groups.' Brent could see that he could not argue against such a statement, for it made sense. He would have to give ground as gracefully as possible.

'I hear what you say, and I understand the points you have raised, but these things have been discovered now, there's no going back and pretending they don't exist. Sooner or later someone else will find them, and then what?'

Eslie poured another round of drinks, thus easing the building tension, and giving each side time to think.

'All we are asking is that there is a controlled flow of these goods,' the Elder continued, after moistening his dry mouth with a gulp of juice, 'this settlement could profit greatly at the expense of the other two, but for how long before they got aggressive and tried to take by force that which they did not have? Also, what could they provide to barter with? We would have everything we need from the ancient's store, and it would be of a superior quality to anything they could provide, we would not need their goods.' The Elder sat back in his chair, his face calm and serene, he had made an unassailable point, and he knew it.

Brent looked crestfallen, and was unable to hide it. He had felt so certain he was doing the right thing for all, but now realized he had not thought it out fully.

'All right, how do you propose to control the flow of goods?' he asked, trying to maintain a level voice.

'You will do that, by releasing only just enough of each item to stimulate improved manufacture of those things we already have. A few new items which the various artisans can duplicate would improve things all round, but not in such quantities as to make manufacture unnecessary.

'With suitable control of what is released, everyone can benefit. We do not wish to interfere with your aims, only to offer guidance and help where we can.'

At this point, the result of the meeting was a foregone conclusion, and they all knew it. Somehow, it had cleared the air, and Brent felt relieved that he no longer had to face the Elders head on, and they in turn, seeing the dangers of the situation, had obtained the co-operation they needed to maintain the status quo.

Eslie had diplomatically left the table, returning with a plate of hot spiced flat cakes. These, together with another round of her special fruit drink, relaxed all concerned.

'We are all for improvement of the settlement,' the other Elder said, forgetting his manners and reaching for another flat cake, 'and as my colleague has said, with some degree of control it can be achieved. Only a few of the other Elders are against change, and I think that is because they feel unable to control it. Your earlier accusation that we do nothing and offer little help is unfortunately near the truth. It was not always like that, but of late I think some of us have lost our way, and what you said had long been needed.'

Brent looked at Macie, who nodded discreetly, perhaps all was not lost, they could still do their exploration work.

'Will the other Elders agree to this?' Brent asked, just to make sure he had understood everything correctly.

'Of that, there is no doubt. Enough of us see the need for change, and will back your group all the way, all that is needed is a little discretion and sensitivity on the matter.'

The two Elders arose, thanked Eslie profusely for her hospitality, and left, one unsuccessfully trying to hide the flat cake he had surreptitiously sneaked off the table while getting up.

'Well I'll be...' and Macie stopped, seeing Eslie's half smile and the dip of her head.

Everyone slept a little better that night, except possibly a few of the Elders who had no idea of what had taken place, and would have had no sleep at all if they had known.

Next morning the new truck was loaded with empty boxes, a crew of eight took their places, and the crank handle of the maintenance truck squeaked and rattled to the energetic pumping of eager arms.

Arriving at the station platform, Brent took a lamp and walked to the far end where the tunnel disappeared into the darkness. Removing the glass shield from his lamp, he held it over the edge of the platform, and then called Macie.

'Look, the flame is drawn to one side, I'll bet we could go down this tunnel to another store or something, the rails must lead to another place the ancients used, just like our tracks do.' They both watched the tiny flame bobbing about with a life of its own as a gentle draft of air flowed through the tunnel. Macie just nodded his head, he was getting used to the fact that when something unusual was pointed out, it usually meant they were going to explore it to its limits.

The goods for taking back to the settlement were earmarked for stacking in the reception hall, and while the others loaded the carrying boxes, Brent and Macie carried on exploring the complex.

The maintenance room was raided for hand tools, leaving behind those which were motor driven as they were beyond their comprehension, and even if they had understood what they were for, there was no electric power.

The stock rooms seemed never ending, but not all of them held things which would be of use to the settlement. A room full of books had disintegrated into piles of dust, as had the clothing store, but there were a few exceptions.

One room contained clothes made from some kind of plastic thread which had defied the passage of time, and they were still in pristine condition. A selection of these was transferred to the main hall, causing much amusement to the others, mainly due to their bright colours.

With the boxes full of things they thought useful to the settlement, they were taken out to the truck and the journey back was begun.

The lamps threw distorted animated shadows on the wall of the tunnel as those on the crank handles worked away, beads of sweat soon forming on their brows due to the extra load they were pushing.

After a while, Macie asked if they could stop off at the siding, as there was something he wanted to do. Brent was about to query what it was, but thought better of it, he would soon know anyway.

They left the trucks on the main line, and walked towards the row of carriages parked in the maintenance section. Macie immediately climbed into one of the carriages and pointed to a plate above the door.

'See, it's a map of the tracks, I remembered it from last time, but didn't know what it was.' The enamelled plate showed the underground layout as a series of coloured lines with the termini as circles joining the different sections.

'Pity we don't know which stop this one is,' said Brent,

'We could then work out where the others might be.'

In the dim light, none of them had spotted the platform name plate above the huge glass doors.

As they were about to jump down from the carriage, they froze, a rustling sound was coming from below them, accompanied by wheezing and grunts.

Cautiously Brent peered over the edge of the exit door to see one of their number squirming out from under the carriage, pushing his lamp before him.

'You'd better have a look at this, it might be the thing which makes their truck go.' he said, straightening up.

'There's a big lump thing with gear wheels like our windmills, linking it to the truck's main wheels, and there are blocks of metal on the rails joined up to the lump. I didn't touch anything, just had a good look.' he added.

It was too much for Brent, he grabbed the lamp and squirmed under the carriage to see for himself.

'You're right.' he said triumphantly, wriggling back out.

'There must be something in the rails which the truck picks up and uses to propel itself along, but I can't think what, the rails are just metal.'

'Do you think the Elders would know?' someone suggested helpfully, only to get a scornful look from Brent which was totally lost in the poor light.

'They didn't know this whole thing existed until we told them.' he added, for good measure.

Because of the loaded truck, it was hard work getting back to the settlement, and they were all soaked in sweat by the time they arrived. One useful suggestion which came out of the darkness as they pumped along was to extend the pumping handles, so that two or more could work on each end. This would then need an extension of the platform each end of the truck for the extra personnel to stand on, as someone else pointed out. Brent thought it was a good idea, and thanked the contributors, none too sure who they were.

Getting the first load down to ground level had its problems, but they soon got the hang of it. After hauling the heavy platform up several times, Macie's idea of a windmill powered winch gathered a few more supporters, much to his delight.

With their bounty safely tucked away in the main store shed, Brent and his friend began working out just what they would release to the other settlements, such that the items would inspire improvements to existing goods, or perhaps encourage the development of new ones. Having made their list, Macie took it to the Elder who had visited them the previous evening, just to show willing.

The Elder greeted Macie like an old friend, which threw him a little, as this was not the norm when meeting one of such exalted position. Macie then showed him the list.

'This looks like a very good choice.' the Elder responded.

'I am very much relieved that our talk last night has had such a constructive effect, I am sure you can see why we were so concerned.' Macie had, and said so.

'You do not really have to show us your lists in the future, unless you want to. We are quite satisfied that you will act in a responsible manner now that the possible problems have been explained and the remedies agreed upon.' With that the Elder took one small discreet step backwards, which was a signal the meeting was over, and Macie returned with the good news that their list had been accepted. The usual non committal grunt from Brent was all he got for this trouble.

'Tomorrow,' Brent said casually, a few moments later,

'I have to go to the glass workers, want to come along?'

'Yes, that would be fi....,' and Macie stopped, remembering the spindly bridge they would have to cross.

'Oh, come on. It's quite safe. Do you think I'd go over it if it wasn't?'

'More than likely.' Macie responded miserably, realizing there was no way out now.

'I've got to go anyway, so while I'm there I'll get the glass makers to make me a special glass cover for a new type of lamp I have in mind.'

Macie realized that a new something usually meant a venture into something they had not done before, and that intrigued him. 'What do you have in mind?'

'We shall need a stronger light to safely explore the other tunnel at the store platform, so I'll need some new bits.'

'I thought several wicks in a row, with a shiny curved metal plate behind them to reflect the light forward and a glass cover to stop the wind blowing them out. Have to make one and try it on the truck.' he added.

It had been agreed that the quantity of goods they had retrieved from the ancient's store would remain a secret as far as the other two settlements were concerned, thus enabling a controlled flow of the new artefacts which would not then disrupt normal manufacturing, and so keep the trading between them in balance.

They set off next morning in the single truck, loaded to the brim, and only just leaving enough room for the two of them to sit down at the back. As they approached the section of track where they had encountered the cloud thing, they both tensed up, looking around nervously for any sign of mist or dust, but there was only the usual sand, gravel and rocky outcrops for as far as the eye could see.

Passing the funnel pit, the customary chunk of material broke free from the side and slid down to the depths below, enlarging the giant sore on the landscape still further.

'That's another mystery I'd like to look into,' said Brent as they passed, 'there must be an explanation for it.' Macie silently decided that was one event he would certainly give a miss, no matter what.

As soon as they arrived at the metalworker's settlement, Macie organized the unloading of their merchandise and distribution of the artefacts from the ancient's store, while Brent sorted out a particular artisan for his metal reflector.

The old man appeared just as business finished for the day, inviting them to spend the evening with him, as they had hoped he would. It was a relationship where everyone gained something, which made it all the more enjoyable.

Over the usual refreshments, they brought their host up to date with their latest findings at the ancient's underground store, and Brent's theory about the tracks, born out by the rail layout map in the carriage.

'I am not surprised at your findings, or your ideas about the rail system,' the old man said, 'they must have had some means of travelling about efficiently, and a rail link would be ideal for the transportation of bulk items. I think you will find quite a complex system, if it has not been destroyed by whatever ended their reign.'

'What do you think it was that destroyed them?' asked Macie, 'it would seem that everything on the surface has been reduced to what we now know as the barren lands, so it must have been something very powerful indeed.'

The old man looked thoughtful for a moment, as if deciding whether to tell all he knew, or just enough to satisfy his visitor's curiosity.

'No one knows for certain. Some of the Elders have a theory that something came down upon us from the skies, but they will not discuss it with anyone. I think it might have been a great conflict between the huge settlements they must have had, and no doubt they had very powerful weapons with which to fight each other'.

'What could they have had that would reduce huge buildings to rubble and wipe out all life?' Brent asked, sensing there was more to tell.

'We have had bows and arrows and spears for a long time, and now you have come along with your flame thrower.

'That could be made much bigger, and therefore more destructive, so even more powerful weapons are quite possible. I do not think they wiped out all life, just most of it, and it is quite possible we come from the few who survived.'

'I only hope with these new things you have brought us, we do not advance to such a state again. Next time we may not survive at all.' the old man concluded sadly.

'I think it far more likely the funnel pits will devour everything long before that,' Brent commented, 'they are growing bigger every time we pass them, and one day they'll join up and there'll be nothing left.'

As usual on such occasions, they talked on well into the night, so the two travellers were a little bleary eyed next morning when they set off for the glassworker's settlement.

Macie cowered down as much as he could as the truck accelerated down the slope leading to the flimsy looking ravine bridge, Brent having already lowered the sail.

The thrumming of the wheels drowned out Macie's rasping breath as he hyperventilated, and then they were over on solid ground, the sail up again, and rattling their way on to the settlement.

A quick word with one of the glassworkers, plus an ancient glass trinket Brent had given him elicited a promise of the lamp globe for the following day.

The overnight stay was obligatory, as by the time all the deals had been done there would not be enough daylight left to make the journey back with any degree of certainty.

After acquiring a load of flame rocks, some more glass sheets for his ever growing requests for 'see through' windows, and pots for both settlements, there was little else to do except enjoy the hospitality of one of the workers, and that was generous enough to thicken their heads again for next morning.

They set off, a little the worse for wear, just as the sun cleaved the horizon splashing the sky with red and yellow streaks, and the promise of another very hot day.

Macie had dozed off in the bottom of the truck, and Brent, not wishing to wake him until they had crossed the rift bridge, flitted about like a ballet dancer, flicking the sail boom back and forth as they changed direction at each end of the many curves in the track which led back to the metal workers.

He was keeping an eye out for the stumpy remains of what he though may be another of the ancient's buildings, when Macie awoke with a yell. His face was white, and he shook.

'What the hell's the matter with you?' Brent asked.

'I thought I'd had it. Must have been dreaming. The truck stopped in the middle of the bridge, and then the damn thing started to fall apart. We got out to walk, and I fell off.'

'Couldn't have made more noise if you had.' A dispassionate Brent replied, momentarily frightened by the yell.

'Anyway, we're past it, so you're safe, for now.'

'What do you mean, for now?'

'We're nearly up to the old building I was telling you about. Going to have a look at it, as it might be on the route of their underground track system.' Macie made no reply.

A short while later the sail was lowered, blocks brought along for the purpose were jammed under the front wheels after the brake was made fast, and they set off across the barren plain for the distant outline of what was once a great building of the ancients. Macie kept looking back at the truck 'just to make sure it was still there,' he told himself.

The ruin, when they eventually reached it, was little more than the corner of a building poking up out of the surrounding gravel bed. There was no sign of a door, or any other opening that they could see, so Brent began to scrape away the gravel in the corner with a flat piece of stone, determined to find something for his efforts.

When the pit was about one-third of a metre deep, he hit solid concrete, and then lengthened the hole to form a shallow trench until it reached the adjacent wall.

'If this is like the other building, this is the roof of the room below.' he said, banging his stone on the concrete.

'There must be a way in.' Several other pits were scraped out, but no entrance was found, much to Brent's frustration.

Macie was getting a bit edgy, with frequent glances in the direction of the truck, not that he could see it as it lay hidden behind the brow of a gravel bed.

'I'll try just one more pit,' Brent said, sensing his friend's discomfort, 'and then we'll go.' The next hole had no concrete base at nearly one metre, but he could go no further as the sides kept caving in.

'Looks like we've found a deep hole in the roof, but we'll need proper digging tools to shift the gravel efficiently. 'We'll come back one day and dig it out.'

'You'll need more than digging tools,' Macie said, 'if there's a room down there it'll be full to the top, and any other rooms below that will be too.'

'Suppose you're right,' Brent replied, reluctantly dropping his scraping stone, 'but I'll find some way of getting in.'

They tramped back up the slope, Brent looking back longingly at the stubby remains. This time he knew he was beaten, but there would be other times, and other ruins.

Back in the truck with the sail up, the drumming of the wheels soon grew into a deep rumble as they headed for the metalworkers settlement at full speed, not realizing the length of time they had spent at the old ruin.

And then the unimaginable happened, the wind dropped to a soft sigh in the rigging, and then ceased altogether. The truck slowed down and then creaked to a stop.

The sail hung like a limp rag against the mast, and the total silence almost hurt their ears as they looked at each other in disbelief. The wind had always been a constant thing, blowing steadily from the North, day and night, for as long as anyone could remember, and now it had stopped.

'What's happened?' asked Macie, realizing they were now stranded out in what amounted to endless kilometres of barren desert, 'and how do we get home?'

'We don't, unless the wind returns,' Brent answered, his voice unusually hushed, 'although we could follow the track, it's too far to walk in this heat, and we'd be dried out husks before we got half way.'

With the absence of wind, heat shimmers began to form as the scorched ground warmed the air above it, causing it to rise in eddies and swirls, so distorting the view of the surrounding area as though it were seen through turbulent water. Without the cooling effect of the wind, the heat from the naked sun beat down unbearably on the two as they sat in the truck, wondering what to do next.

'Let's pull the sail around and tie the boom down, it'll give us a bit of shade while we think this one out,' Macie suggested, 'there must be something we can do.' If there was, they were unable to find it. Their very existence relied on   reaching the settlement before their water gave out, and they only had enough for the speedy travel afforded by the wind blown truck, with just a little to spare, and the truck was now as still as the surrounding wastelands.

The enormous bubble of heated air began to rise vertically from the parched land, creating its own weather system. A layer of haze began to build above the barren lands, taking the edge off the heat from the blazing sun and adding an unearthly glow to the desert below.

'What's happening now?' asked a frightened Macie, as the hair on his head began to rise of its own accord, 'I can feel my skin moving.'

'So can I,' Brent replied, looking puzzled. The air above them had now taken on a dirty grey colour, and the light was fading fast.

'I seem to remember something like this when I was working on the rope winding machine years ago,' he continued, after a few moments reflection, 'it's something to do with things moving in a dry atmosphere, we used to spray water on the strands to stop it, otherwise you got a sharp prickling sensation, and a tiny spark would jump from you to anything you touched.'

'But there's nothing moving out here.' Macie replied.

'Yes there is, the air. It's going straight up instead of across the land, so that might be causing it.'

Before he could expand further on his theory, the air around them crackled and hissed, and then a vivid streak of lightning struck the ground close to the track, instantly followed by an ear splitting bang which stunned their senses.

Flash after flash rent the sky, digging into the barren sand and fusing it into clumps of knobbly glass. The air had taken on a pungent smell due to the massive electrical discharges which raged all around them, the light from which far out did the now feeble sun, hiding behind the overhead blanket of deep haze.

'Quick, get under the truck,' Brent yelled, yanking the brake to the fully on position, 'it may protect us from a direct hit.' They lay there, huddled under the only protection available while the electric storm vent its fury on the surrounding terrain, whipping up its own miniature gusts of wind tainted with fine sand and the smell of burnt air.

They were not sure how long they had lain there, their senses battered by the hideous cacophony of sound as the forces of nature tried in vain to reach a new balance. Eventually the lightning strikes became less frequent, until there were only the faint distant rumble as the final bolts of energy discharged themselves into a riven landscape.

When they crawled out from under the protection of the truck, they noticed a cool and gentle breeze had sprung up, taking away the dust which had accumulated on their clothes as they shook themselves and tried to get some feeling back into cramped limbs. Brent walked around the truck, inspecting every part to see if it had been damaged.

'Seems all right,' he said, slapping the side of the wheeled box, 'we'll have to watch out for damaged track though, if we come off at speed it could be fatal.'

They climbed into the truck, checked over the goods, and took a long drink before running up the sail. The breeze was getting stronger all the time, but nothing like the constant blast they were used to. Slowly the truck began to move, squeaks and groans which would normally have been inaudible, now became apparent in the almost silent desert.

'Can't say that was a lot of fun.' Brent commented, as the breeze grew stronger and the truck picked up speed.

'You certainly make light of it.' retorted Macie, still shaken by what had happened.

'No point in doing otherwise,' he replied cheerfully, 'we're still alive, and heading for the settlement. Had a bit of a fright though.' he added, to mollify the distraught Macie.

Before long the wind was almost back to its normal constant blast, hurrying the truck and its two occupants along the many twists and folds of the track way as it snaked its way towards the settlement.

The sun was low on the horizon as they entered the metalworker's settlement, a small group of people seemed to be waiting for them, waving and shouting greetings as the truck rumbled down the last section of track.

'What gives with the reception?' asked Brent, stepping down from the dust caked truck.

'We could see the disturbance over the barren lands, and wondered if you were in the middle of it,' one of the Elders said, holding out his hand for a palm touch, 'it looked ferocious from here. We are very pleased you survived it.'

'Only just,' Macie added, 'it was a close thing, believe you me.' The truck was wheeled into the store, the goods for the settlement removed and those for woodworkers loaded for the return trip next day.

After a general recounting of what had happened out in the barren lands, and a deal of welcoming back slapping, the old man singled them out and invited them for a meal.

'We could see the storm building up from here,' the old man said, as he dished out the food, 'and wondered if you would be caught in the middle of it. It is a very rare thing, in fact I have only seen two of them in all my years, and I was on the edge of one of them for a while.'

'What happened?' asked Macie, a spoonful of food poised half way to his mouth, his attention fully on the old man.

'Having heard about a similar storm many years before, I sheltered in a pile of rocks, which I think saved my life.

'I had been out in the barren lands, looking for artefacts left from the time of the ancients, when I noticed the air getting, thick, is the only way I can describe it. I watched fascinated as a haze built up, high in the sky, and the wind dropped almost to nothing.' He paused for a moment, amused at the two pairs of eyes locked onto his.

'And then?' they both chorused at once.

'I felt my hair stand on end, and the air around me crackled, like walking on dried leaves. The first flash was some distance away. As the discharge hit the ground, it threw up a little spurt of sand which seemed to sparkle with a light of its own. It was all very beautiful, but very dangerous, and I eased myself back into the crevice I had found.

'Shortly afterwards, the sky lit up in a blinding flash and the rock just outside my shelter was struck. I could not see for some time, but eventually my sight returned, and I was able to see the main storm was some distance away, and that was the most amazing thing I have ever seen. If I had been out in that, I would not be here now.

'Later I went to see what effect the lightning had wrought on the terrain, and found it had been ripped apart, great lumps of sand had been fused into dark green glass-like masses, still far too hot to touch, and the normally smooth surface of the ground looked as if it had been trampled by forest monsters.' He paused to get his breath back, and give the others a chance to take a mouthful of food.

'What causes these storms?' Brent asked, partly in general interest, but mainly so he could avoid such horrors in future.

'Like many things, it is not known for certain. I think it is created when two things rub against each other in very dry conditions, like hot air and the ground. It seems to build up some sort of energy, which when it reaches a certain level, discharges itself in a huge flash of heat and light.

'I feel sure the ancients knew it well, and managed to master its powerful forces for their own ends.'

'What makes you think that?' Brent asked, still looking for a method of moving his truck without using a sail.

'By some of the things I have found.' the old man replied.

The old man filled their drinking cups again, he now felt sure he had found someone younger and more able who would carry on his quest for knowledge, and hopefully bring the results back to him.

'Remember the sticking stones?' Both nodded their heads as their mouths had also been refilled during the pause.

'Look at this?' the old man reached behind him and took a small amber coloured lump from his shelf of trophies, rubbing it on his sleeve. As he moved it across the table, several tiny crumbs leapt to its shiny surface and stuck there.

'I found this when digging about in the deep gully which leads back to the forest. I think it is a fossilized resin from one of the great trees which used to grow there. Now keep very still.' the old man furiously rubbed the lump on his sleeve again, and then brought it up close to Brent's hair.

'I can feel that. It's like just before the storm broke.' he said in astonishment, backing quickly away. The old man smiled, and then got up from the table to go to a cupboard.

'This is something very special,' he said, placing it reverently on the table before them, 'notice the shaft at one end, and these two little wires I have attached to these studs.'

'Watch the space between the wires very carefully.' He adjusted the wires delicately, bending them gently so that they were almost touching, and then he deftly spun the shaft between his fingers. A tiny blue spark leapt between the wires in a continuous stream, fading away as the shaft slowed and then stopped.

'I think the sticking stones, the amber coloured resin, and this device all use the same sort of energy, as did the storm you were caught in. I feel sure that if you could harness that energy and feed it into these two wires, the shaft would spin around, and then you would have a power source.'

It was all too quick for Macie, but Brent got the message and made the connection almost at once.

'That explains something we saw in the underground store, or more precisely, under the big truck in the track siding. There was a big lump thing under the truck, and it had connections to metal blocks which rested on the rails, and gears linked it to the wheels. Do you think they somehow got energy from a storm onto the rails and drove the truck with it?'

'I do not think the energy came from a storm,' the old man replied, 'there are too few of them to make it worthwhile, and it is too strong. But I think they did make this energy somehow, and used it for all sorts of things.' He sat back, a contented smile on his face, his disciple was a lot brighter than he had expected, or even hoped for.

They took it in turns to spin the shaft, marvelling at the tiny flashes of light, and then Brent took the amber lump, rubbed it hard on his sleeve and applied it to the two wires.

The old man later told them the look of disappointment on Brent's face was something he would remember to the end of his days.

The rest of the evening was spent looking at every possible way to create the magic force needed to spin the small electric motor the old man had found and kept for so long.

Next day Brent collected his highly polished lamp reflector and a metal oil container he had designed, and then the pair set off for their home settlement.

The wind had returned to its former self, a constant rush of hot air, whisking away any dust and only leaving behind the heavier grains of sand. Brent often wondered where all the dust and finer particles finished up, 'must be a damn great pile of it somewhere,' he mused.

For the first time, the giant funnel pit was motionless and quiet as they passed it, but the threat of what it could do was still uppermost in their minds as the truck rattled by.

They passed the menacing black rocks, and then kept a sharp lookout for any signs of the mysterious cloud which had caused so much trouble in the past.

'I guess your flame thrower did the trick,' Macie commented, as they rumbled past the last place they had seen it, 'do you think you killed it? That's if such a thing can be killed.' Brent looked deep in thought for a few moments.

'Can't tell. It had the feel of something alive, and it made a sort of noise when the flame hit it, but I don't see how a cloud of dust or mist can be alive, at least not in the sense we know of.' He scratched his head, as if in doing so would release an answer to the mystery.

'Funny how that thing chose you to have a go at, it just got out of the way of the others when they came through.'

'That's a good point.' Brent replied, thoughtfully.

They arrived back in the settlement without mishap, and as there was plenty of daylight left, they got on with Brent's special lamp. The metal container was made such that four wicks could be mounted, each with its own trimming wheel to adjust the flame. The glass globe fitted perfectly, shrouding the flames from the wind, and the reflector sent out a much stronger beam than they had expected.

As dusk fell, they went out on the walkways to try the lamp out in real conditions, causing quite a lot of interest from others they met on the way.

'Looks like you've got another nice little line to barter with,' Macie said enviously, 'you'll have to set up a workshop, what with the lamp and the see through windows.'

'I've got something else in mind too.' he said, grinning.

It was during their evening meal, which had now become a permanent feature of Brent's life, that Macie raised a concern which had been troubling him for some time.

'All these things we have been finding of the ancient's, and the new ones we're making,' he began hesitantly, 'do you think there's any harm in it for the settlement? I mean, we've been going on quite well for a very long time now, I just wondered if all these changes are a good thing.'

'Oh come on,' Brent replied cheerfully, 'you're beginning to sound like the Elders. How do you think the ancients achieved so much? Certainly not by just sitting still and doing the same old thing day after day.'

'But look what happened to them.' Macie retorted.

'We don't know what happened to them, for certain,' he retorted, getting a little impatient with his friend's over cautious attitude, 'that's why I want to explore everything in their world to see what really happened, and then, if it was their doing, we'll know what to avoid.' Macie gave in, he knew when he was losing the argument, and perhaps he was being just a little too cautious anyway.

Eslie came to the rescue, sensing the building tension.

'What's this new idea you told Macie you had?'

'Oh, that.' said Brent, the smile coming back on his face.

'It's quite simple really. What do you think would happen if we strengthened the flame thrower tube and made it longer, put a wad of material about half way down, and put in some stones and another wad to hold them in place?'

'Not a lot.' said Macie, wondering what was coming next.

'And then you light the flame rock dust.' Brent added impatiently, 'I thought you would have understood that.'

'I think I know.' said Eslie quickly, realizing how touchy Brent had been of late and wanting to defuse the situation.

'From your description of what happened when you met the dust cloud thing, I would think the stones would come flying out of the tube with considerable force, and do a lot of damage to anyone standing in the way.'

'Exactly,' said Brent, 'that's what I reasoned out. It would be a powerful weapon against anything we might come across in the forest. We would then be free to go anywhere we choose, and who knows what we may find.' He sat back, having made his point, and glad that someone had understood the possibilities.

After that, things calmed down a little, and the rest of the evening passed amicably enough, especially when the fruit juice was brought out.

The next day saw a little workshop set up to make the new windows. Brent showed three wood workers how to cut and then fix the glass sheets into the wooden frames, then he left them to get on with what they did best.

He was just about to climb the ladders and try his new lamp in the tunnel above, when two fishermen came rushing up, greatly excited.

'Not the old monster again?' asked Brent, a little annoyed his intentions had been thwarted yet again.

'No, no, it's another boat,' one of them gasped out, between gulps of air, 'and it was much bigger than ours, many times bigger.'

'Did it have a sail?' asked Brent, his interest aroused, 'and people onboard?'

'It had a sail, a huge one, in fact two, but we were not close enough to see if there were people on it.'

'Do you think they saw you?' he asked, concerned that their settlement might be contacted by an unknown group of people who's intentions were not known.

'Don't think so, they didn't change tack and come towards us, just sailed across the lake and disappeared around a headland. They were some distance away, almost on the horizon. We came straight back, thought you'd want to know about it.'

'You did well. Thanks. I'll tell the Elders about it, and see what they want to do.' The two fishermen looked at each other in surprise, and then left, the breath still rattling in their throats.

Wondering if it was really worth his trouble, Brent sought out the Elder who had been most friendly towards them, and explained what had happened.

'There is little we can do, except keep watch in case they return. I would assume they would be friendly.' he added.

'Don't know, I've an uneasy feeling about 'em, can't explain it,' Brent replied. 'I'll set up a watch system.'

He talked it over with Macie who agreed the watch system would be a good idea, especially if the old man at the metal workers could make them a magnifier so they could see the boat before it could see them.

'What do we do if they are unfriendly?' Macie asked, looking worried, 'they may be more advanced than us.'

'We could make the new type of flame thrower to fire stones, that should give 'em something to think about.' Brent replied, glad of an excuse to increase his weaponry.

'Sounds to me we're going the way of the ancients.' Macie was not happy, 'but I suppose you're right.'

Over the next few days they visited the underground store, found a length of heavy gauge tubing, and took it over to the metal workers to have the end sealed over. The old man looked sad when he heard about the possible threat to the settlement, and agreed to make them a magnifier at once.

A constant watch was kept from the tunnel exit high up on the cliff, and when the magnifier arrived a few days later, there was no shortage of volunteers for the position of lookout. The new flame thrower was mounted on a small hand truck so that it could be moved about as required, and the test firing brought the whole settlement running.

Brent had set it up on a solid ledge of rock halfway up the cliff, pointing out across the lake. The stones were loaded, halfway along the tube and held in place with wadding, and then the puffer was brought into play. The ultra fine dust was blown into the gun via a small tube which had been forged onto the end of the main barrel, and when all was ready, Brent yelled out a warning to the small group of onlookers, and pushed the flaming taper into the filling hole.

A jet of flame shot out of the filler tube, and the whole assembly jumped back to hit the cliff wall with a thump as a great gush of flame and smoke leapt from the open end of the tube. The explosion made their ears ring as they watched a stream of stones shoot out over the lake to land in the water some three hundred metres away, sending up a great cloud of spray. The sound of the explosion echoed back and forth for some seconds, bringing the rest of the inhabitants out in a rush to see what had happened.

'Well, that seems to work,' said a very satisfied Brent with a grin on his face, 'don't think anyone's going to come back for a second dose of that.' They all nodded their assent, some more enthusiastically than others.

They later had to explain to some of the Elders what they had done, and why, most of them reluctantly agreeing that perhaps it was a good idea to have some means of defence in case the mystery ship returned one day, and their intentions were less than noble.

Macie later came up with the idea of packaging the stones in a cloth bag such that it would fit the bore of the tube, and would thus save time when they had to reload, should the occasion ever arise. Two young volunteers set about making a large quantity of super fine flame rock powder, while the new weapon was modified to enable it to be angled up or down, thus altering the point of impact of its missiles.

When all had been completed, Brent felt they were ready for anything, but some of the others were not so sure, being unable to get their heads around the idea that anyone would want to harm them.

The tight control over the release of the ancient's artefacts seemed to be working well, both other settlements improving their goods considerably due to the extra materials and inspiration provided by those things left by the ancients.

A considerable amount of metal was recovered from the underground store as the storage racks were dismantled, and the use of nuts and bolts discovered. Broken glass was boxed up and sent off to the glass workers, who found it far superior to that which they were able to make, keeping most of it for casting lenses and other optical objects.

Trucks were now running in pairs to cope with the expanding trade, one pair leaving Brent's depot for the metalworkers, while at the same time another pair would leave the metalworkers for the glassworkers. This needed careful scheduling, but so far there had been no mishaps of any great importance.

Brent was keen to get on with exploring the tunnel at the store, quite convinced that another store would be found with even more interesting things to pillage, but his time was being taken up organizing the feverish activity which had gripped the settlement.

They built extensions to the front and back of the hand driven truck, and extended the handles so that four men could work them at the same time, two on each end. The new lamp made a great deal of difference, lighting the tunnel up for some considerable distance ahead and allowing them to travel much faster in relative safety.

The first time they tried it out they were able to bring back a huge amount of metal from the store without much extra effort, and the increased light output from the new lamp made the journey more tolerable.

Macie had found a strip of metal which rang with a clear note when struck, and it was hung it at the lookout post, so that an audible warning could be given of approaching danger, as Brent was still convinced the ship would be back.

The image magnifier was causing a great sensation. Someone had trained it onto the top of the distant forest, and for the first time seen some of the strange creatures which inhabited the forbidden zone. People were queuing up for just a quick glance, but once having got control of the instrument, were more than a little reluctant to give it up. Several scuffles had broken out, and it took a good dressing down from a red faced Macie before reasonable order was restored.

Of the Elders, very little had been seen, especially the ones who were against trading the ancient's artefacts. The two who had visited Brent and Macie made the occasional call, mainly enquiring how things were going and offering general support.

The queues for the telescope shrank once everyone had seen the forest monsters a few times, and the lookouts got on with their job of looking for the big ship, but that too got a bit lax after a few days and no sign of it.

It was the early hours of the morning, and still very dark, when Brent was awakened from his sleep by a persistent knocking on his door. The flint igniter soon had his lamp alight, and he staggered to the door, still half asleep and not in the best of moods. Four men with bobbing lamps greeted him, two in great distress. Brent recognised one of them from the Metalworker's settlement.

'What's going on?' he enquired grumpily, throwing the door open, 'it's still the middle of the damned night.'

'Sorry Brent, but we don't know what to do,' one of the strangers blurted out, 'this huge metal thing is smashing up the settlement and collecting any metal bits it can find.'

'If this is some kind of a joke, someone is going to get a thick ear,' Brent said crossly, 'I've got a busy day ahead.'

'It's no joke,' one of the others broke in, 'these two have travelled over the track way through the night, and that's something no one else has ever done, I think it's serious.'

'All right, what happened.' he said a little more graciously, waving the two strangers to the only available seats.

'Yesterday afternoon, this huge metal thing came up the gully where we collect our wood, and started smashing our huts down. It seemed to be looking for anything metal, and when it found some, it picked it up and put it in a big box on its back. It really did.' he added, when he saw the look on Brent's face.

'Was there anyone on this thing, I mean driving it, like us on our trucks?' Brent asked, now sure the man was telling the truth, although possibly in a somewhat garbled fashion.

'No, we couldn't see anyone, but there was a pipe sticking out the back of it, and it was puffing smoke.' The man was visibly shaking at the recall of the horrific incident, and Brent felt sorry for him. 'All right, let's take it from the beginning again, in case you've missed anything.'

Apparently the wood gathers had come hightailing it into the settlement, yelling their heads off about a large monster which was chasing them. The Elders went to the edge of the settlement where the barren lands began, and sure enough a large oblong object was slowly trundling up the gully, puffing out clouds of smoke and heading for them.

One of the less bright Elders stood in its way with his arm up, asking it to stop, and it promptly flattened him. The others having a little more sense had stepped aside, and were wondering what to do next. They tried putting obstacles in its way, but these were ignored as if they hadn't been there at all, and there seemed nothing they could do to stop the huge machine's progress into the settlement.

It soon became apparent that the device was looking for anything made of metal, which it then picked up with a pair of arms mounted on its front end, and deposited it in a large box on its back.

As soon as they realized what was happening, everyone rushed into their huts and workshops and dragged out anything metallic, spreading it out as far apart as possible around the settlement. As the machine was quite slow moving, they hoped this would slow down the destruction a little, until they could think of something more positive.

Nothing they could do seemed to make any difference to the machine's intent to acquire every bit of metal available, and so the two had risked their lives in crossing the barren lands by sail truck in the dark to get help.

'Why come to me?' asked Brent, wondering why their Elders had not acted more positively.

'Because Kelt, the old man you visit, said you would probably know what to do,' the man answered miserably,

'No one else has any ideas.'

'What was happening when you left?' asked Brent, now fully awake, 'what was the thing doing?'

'We tied rope to a couple of large pieces of metal and dragged them in front of the thing. When it went after the metal, we then dragged the metal away just before the arms grabbed it. It only goes for metal which is still, that's why we used two pieces of metal, moving one and then the other.

When we left, our people had lit all their lamps and formed a large circle around the settlement to act as guides in the darkness so that the metal pullers could go from lamp to lamp safely. It only goes at a good walking pace, but it is very tiring trying to keep ahead of the thing, so we do it in shifts.'

'You seem to have worked that out very well,' said Brent,

'So why do you need me?'

'We can't stop the thing, and we can't keep going around in circles for ever. Also we want our metal back.' The man looked pleadingly at Brent, while his companion added 'please.'

'All right, I'll come over, but I can't be sure I can do anything to stop it.' Brent picked up one of the new lamps, his water flask, and the thickest jacket he could find, it would be cold out on the barren lands this early.

He did think of waking Macie to join them, but thought better of it, there was possible danger in travelling at night and what might happen at the other end was anyone's guess, and besides, Macie was a family man.

They clambered down the ladders, their lamps bobbing about like fireflies on a warm evening, but there was nothing warm about the night air and the task ahead.

With the new lamp firmly strapped to the front of Brent's truck, they set off for the metalworker's settlement.

Brent sailed the lead truck, his two companions squatting down as low as possible to avoid the swinging sail boom, and with their heads just over the edge of the vehicle keeping a lookout for anything on the track. The two visitors followed a short distance behind, terrified of being left behind Brent's racing truck, but even more afraid of ramming it if they got too close.

As they neared the settlement, dawn was just about to break, the first glimmers of light from a hidden sun streaking the horizon in brilliant reds and yellows. The sheer beauty of the scene masked the dangers of the funnel pits and the scorching heat to come when the sun reached its full height.

As they went down the slope to the store sheds, they could see a ring of lights guiding the metal bait pullers in their never ending enticement of the huge metal gathering machine. Although it moved slowly, its inexorable intent was frightening, crushing anything in its way as it sought to collect anything metallic.

The bait pullers had done a good job, steering it away from most of the buildings and workshops, but occasionally it diverted from their intended path, and another workshop disappeared in a cloud of smashed mud bricks and timbers as the machine blundered through, its insatiable appetite driving it mindlessly on.

They left the trucks, Brent taking his lamp with him as he hurried up to the clanking machine.

'Don't go too near it, it'll grab you.' someone called out.

'No it won't,' Brent shouted back, 'its only interested in metal, we don't exist as far as it's concerned.'

Close up in the breaking dawn light, the metal gatherer, almost as big as one of the workshops, towered over Brent as he tried to look at the driving mechanism.

The box like structure was propelled by two endless bands of linked metal plates, one on each side. Part of the shielding had been torn away on one side, where it had probably hit a rock, thus exposing the driving wheels which pulled the drive bands endlessly round.

A smell of hot oil accompanied the clanking and throbbing of an internal combustion engine, adding an extra element of fear for those brave enough to get near the scavenger.

Brent picked up a large stone and trotted along side the monster, lobbing it through the gap afforded by the rent shielding. There was a crunching grinding sound for a few seconds, but the machine didn't hesitate in its pursuit of the metal bait dragged just a few metres in front of it.

By now, several Elders and the old man had joined Brent as he warily walked alongside the machine, trying to think of some means of stopping it.

'By the smell of the smoke it's pouring out, I'd say it was powered by burning oil of some kind,' said Brent to no one in particular, 'and that poses another problem. There's no point in it gathering metal and then running out of oil and stopping. I think it will return to wherever it came from while it still has enough oil left, so that means we'll have to stop it before it heads back down the gully.'

'If we could dig a deep trench, perhaps we could entice it to fall in.' someone suggested.

'It would have to be a mighty big trench,' Brent replied,

'and it would probably be able to pull itself out with those drive bands. If we could jam enough metal in through that hole, that might make it go around in a circle.'

'What happens when it wants to go back to where it came from?' one of the Elders asked, not having thought the problem through enough.

'It can't with one of its drive bands stopped,' Brent replied impatiently, 'just think about it.'

The metal scavenger[1] veered off to one side, demolishing yet another workshop in its hunt, and then they had it back on the intended path around the outskirts of the settlement.

Brent called for a quantity of metal bars about a metre long, and four brave volunteers carried these walking along beside him, waiting

---

1 See *The Single Twin* (chapter 4, 'Of Wheels and Oil') by the same author for more on the robot wars.

for instructions.

'What we'll do is this. I'll push the first bars into that gap in the shielding, and when I've finished the next man must rush up and push his bars in. We'll need to do this quickly or the machine will be able to crunch them up, and it won't work. One of you hold the lamp steady so we can see the hole.' The look of horror on their faces told it all.

They formed up in a little line, Brent at their head and the lamp holder off to one side, shining the beam onto the rent in the side of the machine. Brent lunged forward, and threw in the first bars. The next man hesitated as the screech of metal on metal split the early morning air, and then rushed forward to do his bit. As the last man hurled his bars into the gap, the vast machine shuddered and spun around, the drive tracks on one side jammed by the twisted mass of bars they had managed to get in. The engine roared in protest, black plumes of smoke pouring from its exhaust stack, but it could only spin around in its own length.

'Quick, more bars,' Brent yelled out, 'it may go in reverse.'

And it did a few seconds later, but they were ready with a new supply of bars, and suddenly the vast machine shuddered to a stop, its engine quietly ticking over while it tried to figure out what to do next.

Five:
The Visitors Return

'We'll have to stand by with more bars,' Brent said, wiping the sweat from his brow, 'it may try to shake that lot loose.'

The true dawn broke, lighting up a bizarre scene of a hulking machine puffing little clouds of pale blue smoke into the clear morning air, and surrounded by a very jumpy group of people with metal rods in their hands.

The scavenger, having tried unsuccessfully to shake out the impeding bars, tried a few more circles before giving up and sending out its distress signal to base.

Fortunately for the settlement, the base had been destroyed long ago, and the scavenger had laid dormant in its shelter until some freak of nature had galvanized it into action.

By midday, the main engine had slowed down to a gently whump, whump, whump which echoed around the settlement, reminding all that the machine was not dead, only sleeping while it waited for the rescue unit to come.

'If the machine is burning oil,' Brent reasoned, 'it must be pulling air in. If we can find the hole it gets its air from and put a bung in, it should stop.' Everyone agreed, even those who had not the faintest idea of how it worked.

Brent asked for a bundle of old rags which he tied onto a pole, set fire to it, and then blew out the flames. Walking around the slumbering giant, he pushed the smoking mass into every crook and cranny, watching for the smoke to be drawn in, but to no avail. Someone brightly suggested the hole might be on top, and with the large audience he had acquired, there was little alternative other than to clamber up with his smoking rags, and check it out.

Apart from the huge cage like collecting box and the grabbing arms, the top of the machine was almost featureless, and then he found it.

A hole some twenty centimetres across had a metal grill over it, and the smoke from his burning rags was being sucked down into the internal workings through the grill.

'Pass up a metal bar,' he called out, 'and get someone with a block of wood about so big,' he spread his hands out, 'and a sharp cutting blade.'

Egged on by the entire population of the settlement, a very nervous man with a blade and wooden block, climbed up beside Brent who by now had the grill off, and was dropping bits of his smoke tracer down the hole.

'Carve one end of the block to fit that hole,' Brent instructed, 'but don't drop it in until I tell you.' He then called for some food and a drink, as if this were the normal thing to do when perched atop some alien machine which was gently throbbing with latent power beneath his feet.

Brent almost drained the large water flask, and then tipped the remains down the hole. The mighty engine continued to turn over slowly, but a few puffs of white water vapour came out of the exhaust tube which elicited a round of applause from the admiring onlookers.

A while later, and the bung was finished. Brent held it over the hole, as the carver had gracefully declined the offer of doing the honours, nodded to the assembled crowd, and dropped it in.

The engine slowed down, coughed twice, shuddered, nearly throwing them off, and stopped with a sigh.

'It's dead.' someone called out in the ensuing silence.

'It's not an animal,' Brent retorted hotly, 'it's only a machine, it's not alive.'

'Certainly isn't now.' someone else called out, and a nervous laugh echoed around the area. The monster had been laid to rest, for now at least.

Brent and his assistant climbed down amid a round of cheers and applause, the Elders lining up to touch palms, as did most of the others in their turn.

Some of the brighter metal workers were concerned that the machine might start up again if they interfered with it, especially as they wanted to recover their own goods and then dismantle it for the metal it contained. Brent thought it unlikely as the machine could no longer breathe.

'Keep the bung in until you've figured out how it works, and take it apart carefully so that you can see what does what inside. We could all learn a lot from a thing like that. Just imagine a smaller version of what makes it go along put on a truck, you wouldn't have to bother about the wind, and you could go at any speed you liked.' Brent was already thinking about a wide wheeled version of the rail truck which could go over any terrain without the need for tracks.

The old man, Kelt, joined him as the crowd broke up.

'Come along to my place, if you have nothing else to do,' he suggested, 'we have a lot to talk about.'

Brent had not realized how tired he was, the lack of sleep, a journey across the barren lands in the dark, and then trying to outwit the salvage machine all took their toll and he sank gratefully into the offered chair. The usual juice and a plate of flat buns restored his energy levels, and he then felt more inclined to discuss the events of the day.

'I hope you didn't mind my suggesting you being called over,' the old man began, 'I'm afraid our lot would have taken several days to have solved the problem, and by then there would have been very little of the settlement left.'

'No, that's fine,' Brent replied, relaxing, 'in fact it's given me some new ideas to be working on, and one hell of a lot of unanswered questions.'

'Thought it might,' Kelt said, smiling, 'that's the main reason I mentioned your name really. I must say, I admire the two who came to fetch you, it must have been very frightening for them, travelling all that way in the dark.'

Brent just nodded, his mouth was still full.

The conversation carried on in general terms and pleasantries until Brent mentioned the salvage machine.

'Where do you think it came from?' he asked.

'I cannot be sure, but I think it came up the gully which leads to the forest. Someone said they had been collecting wood when it appeared out of nowhere, and chased them. I think it could somehow sense metal in the settlement, and headed for it, although how it does that is a mystery.

'It certainly made a bit of a mess of one of the Elders who thought he could stop it by holding up his hand.' the old man added with a chuckle, no supporter of fools.

'If it was made by the ancients, which is the only explanation I can think of, why do you think it has survived for so long in working condition, and more to the point, are there any more of them?'

'I do not think it was made by the ancients,' Kelt said thoughtfully, 'it looked too crude for their kind of workmanship, and besides, why would they be concerned about collecting odd bits of metal? They must have had huge quantities of it, judging by what they made. I think we may know a little more about it when we have taken it to pieces.

'As for another one, I doubt that somehow, I cannot explain it, but it has the feel of being the only one.'

'Just as well,' Brent said, relieved, 'can't say I'd look forward to a whole line of 'em coming out of the woods, one proved troublesome enough. What intrigues me is what moves it along, I think it runs on oil, but how?'

'Well, oil burns and produces heat, like your flame tube, and that, so I have been told, will propel stones some considerable distance. Perhaps the machine uses the force from the burning oil to push something which is coupled to the driving tracks. As for how it can sense metal, that is well beyond my knowledge, unless it is based on the principle of the sticking stones.'

'How would that work?' asked Brent, an idea already forming in his mind.

'You remember the floating needle and how it would move if a sticking stone was brought near it? Maybe the machine has something like that. If any metal is near enough it could cause a movement of the detector which would guide the machine to it. It is the only thing I can think of.'

'Well, if the ancients didn't make the machine,' said Brent, 'Who did?' And then he told Kelt about the big sail boat and the bad feeling he had about it.

'That's interesting,' the old man said thoughtfully, 'I did not think there were any more groups of people apart from the three we know, but then the forest is very big, as are the barren lands, and who knows how far they stretch. It is quite possible there are others, and who knows what they will be like. I think you are right to be forearmed and wary.'

They talked on well into the night, as usual, and next morning Brent went to see if the metalworkers had made any progress in dismantling the scavenger machine.

Several side panels had been removed, exposing the drive wheels which pushed the tracks around, and that gave a good clue as to how the machine worked.

'You remember the metal fixing things you gave us some time ago?' one of the men said to Brent, 'this whole machine is held together with them.'

He pointed to a pile of crudely made nuts and bolts which were being added to at a great rate as a team of workers stripped the huge machine down to its bare bones. The skeletal framework was made from substantial girders which supported the big collecting box and the drive unit below, which was of most interest to Brent.

He was impressed with the speed of the workers in manufacturing spanners and a series of levers and chisels with which to strip the huge machine, and then realized the bargaining price of metal was about to take a tumble.

The crudeness of the nuts and bolts and the general structure of the machine confirmed in Brent's mind that the ancients had not made it. It was structurally sound and functional, but lacked the curves and niceties the ancients would have incorporated, which left him still none the wiser as to who or what had constructed the monstrosity.

By midday, he decided he should return to his own settlement, and set off, working the sail to get every bit of energy from the wind, and looking forward to the day when it would be powered by an oil engine.

Macie, upon his return, was a little put out that he had not been invited along, but accepted Brent's reasons when they were explained.

All was quiet for a few days until the lookout sent warning of a white sail on the horizon. Brent hurried up to the lookout post, and through the magnifier could see a large ship coming up the lake towards them. He sent word down to warn the Elders and to get a few bowmen ready with plenty of arrows, who were to be well concealed from the approaching ship in case they were friendly. The flame thrower was ready for action, with a good stock of bagged up stones and a spare puffer. He was taking no chances.

The Elders assembled on the main jetty, their white robes blowing in the wind, and looking very grand. The bowmen were hidden behind the usual collection of boxes and barrels to be found around the fishermen's area, while a few had tucked themselves away a bit higher up behind the dwellings which clung to the cliff face.

One of the Elders had seen a bowman crouched behind his barrel, and ordered him to leave, but Brent could see the man shake his head defiantly and slip an arrow into the firing position to reinforce his decision to stay put.

As the boat drew nearer it paused as one of its sails was lowered, and then came slowly closer. By now Macie had joined Brent, along with a couple of others who were well trained in the use of the flame thrower and its stone missiles.

They were all well hidden from view behind a stone wall on the ledge overlooking the lake.

'We'll see what happens when they make contact with the Elders,'

Brent said quietly, knowing how voices travelled over water, 'if it looks like a fight, the bowmen will take care of anyone who tries to land, and we'll blast the ship.'

The sailing ship eased her way into the cove, turning herself broadside to the jetty and just out of bowman range. The watchers could now see down on the vessel, and it was obvious that there were many people on board who were taking great pains to remain out of sight from those on the shore who awaited them.

From the jetty it must have looked as if there were only six or so persons standing along the bulwarks, a couple of them waving in a friendly enough fashion. One of the Elders raised his hand in answer and then beckoned them in. Strange words floated across the water from the ship, but they were unintelligible to those on the land.

One of the Elders called back across the waters, welcoming their visitors, but there was no response from the ship.

'I don't like this,' Brent muttered, 'there's something odd about that lot, why are so many of 'em keeping out of sight?'

A command was suddenly shouted, and both sails went up, billowing out as they caught the wind. The ship turned and headed out to the centre of the lake, Brent training the magnifier on it as she got underway.

'Now that they think we can't see them, they've all come out on deck, and there's one hell of a lot of 'em. I think they were going to attack us, and something put them off at the last moment.'

'It can't have been us or the bowmen, we're all too well hidden.' Macie said, looking down on the jetty below and the small group of inhabitants who had collected to watch the arrival. 'Maybe they were just looking us over to see how many we were, and if we'd put up any resistance in the future. Can't think of anything else which makes sense.'

'You may well be right.' Brent answered thoughtfully.

'We'll tell the Elders and set extra watches, they may come back at night to surprise us.'

When they got down to ground level, one of the Elders was still remonstrating with the unfortunate bowman, who was standing his ground gallantly. Brent went up to the pair.

'What seems to be the problem?' he asked politely.

'Oh, it's you,' the Elder replied sarcastically, 'I wondered where you had hidden yourself.' Brent ignored the gibe.

'What is your dispute with my bowman?' he asked, a little more firmly, and backed it up with hard eye to eye contact.

'This insolent armed man refused to leave the area when I asked him to. We were here to meet our visitors, a man present with weapons would be most inappropriate.'

'This man is here because I told him to be. He is carrying a weapon as part of our defence force.' Brent replied hotly.

'Defence against what?' the Elder enquired smugly, 'six unarmed men and a boat, we could have handled that many if the need had arisen, which it did not. They probably saw the weapons arranged against them and fled in terror, we may never see them again.'

'I wouldn't count on that,' Brent said sternly, 'they'll be back, more's the pity, you mark my words. You were looking at the ship from just above water level, and only saw what they wanted you to see, six or so men waving. We were higher up, looking down on the ship and could see many more in hiding, all of them armed.' he added for good measure. 'Anyway, all our men were well hidden. All the boat people would be able to see were a few of our inhabitants standing around on the quay and you lot on the jetty in your long white robes, that's what probably put them off.' he added scornfully. He turned to the bowman,

'You did well, thank you.' The bowman nodded curtly and stood back one pace. The other Elders had walked off, except for the two who had visited Brent and his friend some days before, and they were standing a little way along the quay, obviously waiting for him.

'What did you make of that?' they asked.

'Trouble, I would think. They were looking us over before coming back in force, and if we want to survive, we'd better be ready for them.'

'We too felt there was something wrong, and so did some of the others. How can we help, and what do you need?'

'Thanks for the offer,' Brent replied, 'but I think we're prepared for a frontal attack, we have plenty of good bowmen, and the flame thrower on the ledge up there.'

'If they are hostile and try to land, the bowmen will pick them off from behind cover, and we can pepper the ship with stones from above. I know it's an awful thing to say, but I doubt if many will survive that. If they attack us, we have every right to defend ourselves.'

The two Elders nodded sadly, knowing many peaceful generations of life may now be shattered by a bloody battle for territory, and it was not of their making.

'We will tell the other Elders who are sympathetic to your ideas, I am sure they will back you wholeheartedly.'

They parted to go their separate ways. Brent too, was feeling sad that an otherwise peaceful existence was soon to be gone, and replaced with suspicion and the need to fight.

Several days went by with no sign of the threatening ship, even by the fishermen who were now going much further down the lake than ever before. It was almost as if the incident had never happened, except for the ever watchful lookouts, and they kept well out of sight.

Brent was pleasantly surprised one morning, when a truck from the metalworkers drew into the store sheds area.

'We thought we owed you something for stopping the scavenger machine, so we brought you this.' Brent looked over the top of the truck to see a complicated piece of machinery mounted on two beams.

'What is it?' he asked, guessing what it might be.

'The thing which works the collecting arms of the scavenger. There are two units like this, and one great big one which drives the tracks. We found where the oil went in and tried it on lamp oil, and it works fine. Would you like us to show you how to start it?' Brent had already dropped the end section of the truck down to pull it out.

Four of them lifted the engine down onto the ground while Brent stood watching, open mouthed and hardly able to believe his luck.

'The oil goes in here,' one of the men said, 'and you start it by pushing this lever over like this.' There was a sharp hiss and the drive shaft began to slowly turn. A couple of coughs, a puff of black smoke, and the engine burst into life, the chuff chuff sound of its exhaust echoing around the store sheds.

'Push this to make it go faster, and this one to stop it.' the man said, raising his voice to almost a shout. 'These levers were joined to other parts of the main machine which must have controlled it, but it is a complete thing in its own right.'

'I know you push that lever to start it, but what makes it go round?' Brent asked, deeply puzzled.

'We aren't too sure, but we think when the thing is running, it sends air into that cylinder where it is stored. When you push the start lever, the air rushes out and somehow turns the shaft, and it starts. Clever, isn't it?' the man said, beaming.

'I think you lot are clever to have worked it all out,' said Brent admiringly, 'and to have got it out of the machine in one piece. Thank you very much for your gift, you couldn't have given me anything better, this is wonderful.' He was quite overwhelmed by the gift, and, of course, the possibilities it offered.

The noise of the engine had drawn quite a large crowd, but few were brave enough to get really close to the noisy smoking monster, except Macie, who was grinning from ear to ear as he put an arm around Brent's shoulder.

'I'm very pleased for you, and I'll bet you can't wait to get going on that thing,' he said, 'and none of us will get any peace until you have it driving something along.'

When all the fuss had died down, the engine was dragged into one of the store sheds, while Brent held one of the metal workers in deep conversation for a while. Macie asked what was going on, but all he got was a 'you'll see' and had to be content with that.

Life returned to near normal, trading continued and the watch on the lake was diligently kept from crack of dawn to nightfall, Brent reasoning that the boat would be unable to navigate the lake during the hours of darkness.

A large metal spike with a pulley block attached was driven into the rock of the quay, but Brent would not say what it was for, except it was part of their defence against invasion.

The two men spent several days tinkering with the newly acquired oil engine, and then had to organize a nut gathering expedition to replace the lamp oil they had consumed.

Brent was torn between mounting the engine on a standard truck for use on the rail system, or building an overland version with very wide wheels so they could go wherever they liked.

The final decision was put on one side when another visit to the underground store fired up his interest in the unexplored tunnel at the other end of the platform.

After unloading their haul, they set about refilling the water flasks and acquired a stock of food together with plenty of lamp oil, and set off back down the track.

Passing the station platform, the team of ten, in two trucks, plunged into the darkness of the unexplored tunnel, eyes straining ahead for any signs of damage to the tunnel walls.

With four men on the elongated pump handles, the trucks sped along the rails with little effort, the featureless walls rushing by in a hypnotic blur, until they came across another siding.

They had gone past the points system before they could stop, and had to reverse the trucks, leaving them at the junction in the track while proceeding on foot to see what lay in the darkness of the siding.

It must have been used for storing several transport units at one time, although it was now empty. They found a doorway with a metal grill barring their entry, and one deft tweak with a metal rod gave them access to a flight of steps spiralling upwards. Two volunteers cheerfully climbed out of sight, their footsteps echoing back down the stairway, and then there was silence.

Those waiting were on the point of sending two others up to what had happened, when footsteps could be heard, getting louder by the moment.

'It goes up one hell of a way, and then it's blocked with a huge lump of stone. There's no way we could move it or get around it, so we came back.' The man looked disappointed at not being able to bring back better news.

They resumed their journey along the track, stopping for refreshments twice, and then the next station hove into sight.

The trucks slowed down, managing to stop at the far end of the platform and they all debarked, glad to stretch their legs after the cramped conditions of the second truck, the handle pumpers just glad to stop.

The same pair of glass doors faced them as they reached the middle of the platform, but this time they were not so easy to open despite close inspection and a little brute force.

'Looks as if we'll have to break one to get in.' Brent said disappointedly, and a metal bar was brought from the truck.

Repeated attacks failed to gain entry, only a producing few chips of glass flying across the platform amid frequent cursing from those wielding the heavy metal bar.

Someone suggested directing their energies towards the bottom corner where the two doors met, and that somehow released the locking mechanism, and they were in.

The store was much like the first one they had visited, the layout being the same and only a small difference in the stock on display. The store rooms were crammed full, Macie commenting that the sales people couldn't have been very good at their jobs, or the exchange rate asked was too high.

'That's a point,' Brent said, 'we've not seen any sign of goods offered in exchange for those they had to offer.'

'Perhaps they had a token system.' someone suggested,

'We do if our goods are worth more than those we trade with.'

They found what they thought was the maintenance department, and stood in awe at the huge amount of materials stacked on racks, and a line of machines along one wall.

'It's more like the metalworker's place than a store,' Macie said, 'I wonder what these machines do.' They all had a look, walking along the line of machines and offering many suggestions, a few of which were quite accurate, but they had no way of knowing that. A quick inspection of the main showrooms and they were back on the trucks and heading off down the tunnel, Brent having suggested they go a little further, and then return home.

After two shift changes on the pump handles, a glimmer of light showed up ahead, and they slowed the trucks down.

'Must be coming to another opening like the one on our cliff,' someone said, 'or maybe the tracks go in the open.'

The light grew stronger, and they slowed down accordingly so as not to be caught out by any surprises. As the trucks slowed to a halt, it became apparent that this was the end of the line, although it had not always been so.

The track ended, dangling a few metres over a vast chasm, light streaming down from above lighting up the continuing tunnel on the other side.

Brent swore copiously in frustration, his ambition to explore the ancient's network of tracks thwarted by the missing trackway over the yawning gulf which separated them from the rest of the system.

They left the trucks and carefully walked to the end of the broken line which curved down into the depths below.

'This looks like one of those damned funnel pits,' Brent said angrily, looking up at the open sky far above them.

'And it's cut right across the track. There's no way we can get across.' Macie heaved a sigh of relief, the thought of crossing the void on ropes making him feel dizzy.

The funnel pit had created a shaft some hundred metres across, and the rail lines had either been eaten away, or broken off under their own weight, just leaving a short length at each end hanging over the precipice.

Tying a rope around his waist and asking the others to hang onto the other end, he carefully crawled out along the stub end of the rails to peer down into the chasm.

'It seems to go down for ever,' he called back, 'can't see the bottom, just a black hole.' At that moment the pit decided to swallow another chunk of the surrounding ground above, and several hundred tonnes of rock and general debris heralded its approach with a grinding rumbling sound, and then rushed past him with a monstrous roar.

A piece of rock struck the end of the rails and nearly catapulted Brent off into space, but he managed to hang on while his attached rope tightened reassuringly.

'Nothing for it, we'll have to go back.' He sounded thoroughly dejected as he crawled back to solid ground.

They climbed aboard the trucks, putting the new lamp on what was now the lead truck, and began the journey back.

Stopping at the newly found store, they loaded up some of the tools from the maintenance department which had been left on the platform, and continued on to the settlement.

Brent had left instructions for some false barrels and boxes to be made, the idea being that they would have no backs to them and could be strewn about the quay in a random fashion, so affording cover for the archers to conceal themselves. Slots allowed those behind the shields to judge the most appropriate time to stand up and loose their arrows at an attacker, while being protected from incoming missiles.

The following day Brent put his concealed archers to the test. As the voices from the big ship had sounded as though it was another language, he reasoned they would be unable to understand theirs, and so used the difference to his advantage. The hiding places would be numbered, so that when an appointed person called out 'one', 'two', or 'three', the archer in that place would fire his arrow, the theory being that those on board the ship would not be able to anticipate the direction from which the next salvo came.

A couple of floating barrels were thrown into the harbour, and the archers put through their routine until Brent was satisfied that it could not be improved.

The two friendly Elders had been watching the proceedings, and said at first they were highly amused at the antics, but by the end of the operation had to concede that any attacker would be in for a very unpleasant time indeed, with little chance of reprisal.

Two days later the truck from the metalworkers arrived, and Brent hurried out to meet them along with Macie and two others who had attached themselves to the couple.

Brent eagerly looked inside the truck, and smiled. A strange looking metal device was carefully handed down to his waiting arms, and he staggered under the load.

'Is this what you had them make for you?' asked Macie, his brow furrowed as he tried to make out what it was.

Brent just grinned at him as they carried it between them to the quay, followed by the two friendly Elders.

'Come on, what is it?' Macie asked impatiently.

'I got the idea looking at a fishing hook,' Brent said at last, 'and that's just what it is, a giant fishing hook, only with three hooks all stuck together by their shafts.'

'But what the hell is it for? Surely you're not going after the water monster?'

'No, well not the one you are thinking of.' they laid it down on the stone quay, and Brent stood back a little to admire his new acquisition. The grappling iron was made from three giant fish hooks welded together, with a ring at the end of their shafts for a rope. Just below the ring, three hinged metal plates would form a full circle when extended, fitting in the barrel of the flame gun, and making a reasonable seal. One of the Elders stepped forward.

'We are just as intrigued as your friend. It looks a fearsome thing, so do please explain what it is for.'

'Right.' said Brent, having got as much out of the mystery as he possibly could. 'What happens if the big ship attacks us, looses the battle, and goes away again?' The others looked at each other, and Macie shrugged his shoulders.

'Oh, come on,' Brent retorted impatiently, 'think about it, what would you do?' There was a long pause, and then,

'Come back with more men, and try again?' asked one of the Elders, not too sure if this was the right answer, and not wanting to face the possibility of it happening anyway.

'Exactly!' said Brent. 'And if we don't want a repeat performance, they must not be allowed to go back to their home base. That's what this thing's for. We put it down the tube of the flame thrower with these spikes on the outside. These metal plates, when I've filed them to shape, will form a seal in the tube, and when it leaves the tube, they'll flop down and act like the guiding vanes of arrows.'

'But surely that's a very elaborate device just to catch one man.' an Elder said, wondering if he had said the right thing.

'It's not to catch a man, the archers do that.' Brent exclaimed sharply. 'This is to catch the boat and stop it leaving so we can get the rest of the crew. We'll fire it at the boat when it gets near enough, and the spikes will dig into the wood when we pull on the rope, and we've got 'em!'

'And what do we do with them afterwards?' asked one of the Elders, posing the most awkward question of all.

'We'll sort that out if it happens.' said Brent, suddenly realizing he had given little thought to the possibility of prisoners. A strong rope was passed through the pulley anchored to the bedrock of the quay and attached to the grappling iron, which was then pulled up to the ledge where the flame thrower was kept. The other end of the rope was coiled up and stacked beside the pulley, ready for the day when it would be needed.

Glass window production had gone ahead to the extent that every dwelling in the settlement now had 'see through' windows, and they were now supplying them to the other two settlements, although the glass makers insisted on wooden frames only.

It did not take long for the main store sheds to become crammed full with loot from the two underground stores of the ancients, and the construction of two new sheds began.

As two night crossings of the barren lands had now been made without mishap, the metal workers had taken Brent's new lamp design and extended it to eight wicks. This gave enough light to travel safely at night, and left Brent just a little bit peeved that he had not thought of the idea in the first place.

New ideas sprang from seeing the artefacts of the ancients, and everyone was kept busy making things or experimenting with new concepts, but not always successfully.

It was a good time for the three settlements, trade being carefully controlled so everyone got a fair share of the goods and ensuing benefits, the only problem being that the metal workers settlement was having difficulty in obtaining enough water for their needs. The wells had got progressively deeper as time went on, and now they were at the bottom of the water table, with very little flow to replenish that which they removed.

Transporting water from the lake proved too inefficient, although it could be done in an emergency for drinking purposes. Something had to be done, and so a meeting consisting of representatives of each settlement came together at the lakeside.

Brent and Macie were invited to join a few of the more progressive Elders of the settlement, and the meeting got underway on the quay side where they had assembled some screens to give a little shelter from the blazing sun.

The glassmakers stated that at the moment they had plenty of water from a deep underground lake, which had been discovered many generation ago when they had begun their mining operations, but the level of that was very slowly dropping, and so in time they too would be faced with a water shortage.

Rain was something unknown to the settlements, as each was constantly bathed in the blast of hot dry air from the North, only Brent's people having experienced an occasional shower when in the edge of the forest gathering food.

The forest generated its own weather being so vast, and with the aid of the magnifier, to everyone's amazement, the massive storms over the main forest had been seen for the first time and marvelled at.

The meeting drew to a close, with every possible idea discussed to its limits, even those which would normally have been considered of a ridiculous nature were given a fair hearing. The conclusion was that when the water finally ran out, the metalworkers would have to be split between the other two settlements, taking their skills with them.

The glassworkers were none too happy about the proposal, as they thought it would hasten the end of their water supply, and so just move the problem on to the lakeside settlement at some time in the future.

Macie pointed out that the habitable area they had at their disposal was not big enough to house both other settlements, and so they reached an impasse, with no further action decided upon.

Finally, Brent's friendly Elder quietly asked him if he could think of anything which might at least alleviate the situation, to which he replied that he had something in mind, but needed to check out a few things first, as it would alter the whole way of life for those concerned.

Word of the big ship which had sailed into their cove had now got around to the other settlements, some offering help, a few welcoming new contacts no matter what the price, but most wishing they had not heard the news in the first place.

All the delegates had to stay the night, except for a few brave souls from the metalworkers who had brought their own improved lamp, and set off for home in a great show of bravado. One of them thanked Brent for the basic idea of the new lamp, and as most others around the truck heard the acknowledgement, he felt a little mollified as it had been his invention in the first place.

Three days later the alarm sounded. Brent's well trained archers rushed to take up their positions behind the dummy barrels and boxes scattered around the quay, while the gun crew scrambled up the ladders to the firing ledge much faster than they ever had during training.

The cannon, for that was what it basically amounted to, was loaded with stone shot, and the puffer was primed ready to inject the explosive dust.

On the horizon, a pair of dirty white sails could be seen, growing larger as they watched. Brent looked down to check on his archers, and was dismayed to see a troupe of Elders marching along the far quay towards the jetty. When he thought they were within earshot, he called down to them.

'Don't stay on the quay or jetty, you'll be an easy target for them. Get behind something or you'll not stand a chance.'

'We will greet them in peace,' a thin voice floated up to him, and he recognized the Elder with whom he had had the altercation so long ago, 'we are not all warmongers or barbarians.'

'You won't be any damn thing if you don't get off that quay you silly sods; they aren't coming here for a party.'

The Elders marched on to the end of the jetty and arranged themselves into a semicircle, with the tallest in the middle and all standing as tall and dignified as the cramped space on the end of the jetty would allow.

Brent quickly looked over the assembled Elders and was relieved to see his two friends were not among them, the rest would have to take their chances when the boat arrived.

A 'caller' had been placed among the hidden archers, and during their practice runs, he even had Brent guessing who would pop up next with a primed bow, so he felt confident that their losses in that area should be minimized.

The ship came closer, and through the magnifier he could see the deck teeming with men armed with bows and a few in the stern with long spears. Hanging on the side of the ship was a flat bottomed boat capable of holding about twenty people, and he guessed they would try to make a landing while those on board kept up a hail of fire.

One sail dropped, and the ship slowed, and then the other sail fell to the deck knocking several archers flying, much to the amusement of the onlookers. Slowly the ship glided towards the jetty, turning broadside a mere hundred metres from the waiting Elders. Someone threw an anchor overboard from the stern, and the ship stopped.

'Welcome to our sett.......' one of the Elders called out in the loudest voice he could whilst still retaining some degree of dignity, and he, along with the others, fell to the boards amid a shower of well aimed arrows.

The archers hiding on the quay were eager to loose their arrows in return fire, but their training held them in restraint until the word was given.

'When are you going to fire?' whispered a worried Macie.

'Not yet, I want to see what they do with that flat boat thing on the side of the ship first.' A scurry of activity saw the flat boat lowered into the water and fill with spear men, then two men at the rear paddled furiously to drive the boat towards the jetty.

'Charge the tube,' Brent said quietly, and the soft sound of the puffer hard at work failed to drown out his own pounding heartbeat. He waited until the flat boat was halfway to the jetty, and then plunged the burning taper into the charging hole.

With a roar which hurt their ears, the cannon discharged its load of stones straight at the standing spear bearers, all of which fell to the bottom of the boat or went overboard in a series of large splashes.

'Archers.' yelled Brent.

'One.' echoed up from below, and the first wave of return fire streaked across the water to embed in the surprised standing targets along the bulwarks of the invading ship.

Brent sent another shower of stones into the flat boat to take care of the few who had survived the first discharge, and who had now staggered to their feet wondering what to do next. They ceased to wonder about anything as the stones arrived. 'Two.' came the call, nicely timed to catch those foolish enough to raise their heads above cover to see what had happened to the occupants of the flat boat.

Brent loaded his secret weapon into the open mouth of the cannon, the sharpened barbs of the grapple sparkling in the hard light of the sun. He then hit the elevation wedge, finishing with a few gentle taps to set it just right.

'Load her up,' he called, and then shouted 'Standby below.' over the edge of the platform, and an arrow hissed by, narrowly missing his ear. A muffled 'Ready to fire.' came from behind him, and the taper went home.

This time the explosion was a little sharper, and their ears rang with the concussion, while the grapple, trailing a thin plume of grey smoke, flew in a graceful curve over the water to land on the deck of the ship, just short of the bows.

A hail of arrows prevented those on board the ship from reaching the grappling iron and throwing it overboard, while Brent gave the order to haul in the rope.

A lone figure sprinted for the grappling iron rope, grabbed it, and ran back to the five others who were waiting behind a line of shielding boxes. The first jerk of the rope embedded the needle sharp tines of the grapple into the bow timbers of the ship, and unless the rope was cut, the ship was now captive.

Two archers had been detailed to fire at anyone who approached the grapple, and with six men pulling, the sailing ship very slowly began to swing around, her bows now edging towards the jetty and her anchor rope taught behind her. It was now just a matter of the remaining crew to accept surrender to complete the incident, but they still popped their heads up to fire at invisible targets on the quay, and were picked off one by one for their troubles.

When no more arrows came from the ship, Brent called a halt to the massacre, but all the archers had an arrow primed ready to loose at anything which moved.

'Throw down your weapons and stand on the main deck.' Brent yelled out, knowing they would not understand his words, but he felt he should at least make some effort to give any remaining crew the chance to surrender. Nothing moved, except the ship herself, gently swaying in the placid blood stained waters of the lake.

Dropping down to the quay, he ordered two fishing boats with archers aboard to approach the vessel and to shoot on sight anyone who looked aggressive. The boats drew up alongside, but there was no sign of life. The deck was red with blood and strewn with bodies, most of which were pierced by more than one arrow.

By now, Brent had joined those on board and helped in the search for survivors, but there were none to be found.

'I can't understand why they fought to the last man instead of surrendering when they realized they wouldn't win,' he said to one of the Elders, 'it seems such a waste of life.'

'Perhaps they have a different way of looking at life, and to surrender would be the ultimate shame. Who knows? But it is a pity there was no one left so that we could find out where they came from, and if there is likely to be another visit.'

Orders were given for the bodies to be collected up and roped together in long strings, so they could be towed out to deep water where the sea creatures would take care of the disposal problem. But first they had to be stripped of their clothing and searched for anything which would give a clue as to their way of life and abilities.

It was late afternoon when the little armada of fishing boats set out for deep water, towing their macabre strings of floating bodies, and a certain feeling of sadness that the day should have ended with so much carnage.

Brent was in the lead boat with four straining oarsmen, their brows beaded in perspiration as they pulled their gruesome load into ever deeper waters where they had first seen the water monster.

'This will do,' he called out, much to the relief of those doing the rowing, 'back up until you reach the end of the line, and then cut 'em free one by one.'

After the first few naked and blood stained bodies had drifted free, dark shapes could be seen cruising around beneath the boats, and then the feeding frenzy began. Soon the waters were thrashed into pink stained foam as competing creatures tore into the same body, ripping it to shreds.

'Hurry it up.' Brent yelled, concerned that they could soon become a target if larger creatures were drawn to the fray.

'It's time we were gone.' One of the smaller boats was nearly capsized as something large and hungry snatched at the last body as it was being cut free, and then they were rowing for cleaner waters, leaving behind a hideous scene as the larger denizens of the lake joined in the free meal.

They were all totally exhausted by the time they reached the jetty, both physically and mentally, never before having had to confront such a shocking ordeal. The boats were tied up and the crews wearily climbed onto the jetty, hanging about in little disorientated groups, wondering what to do next now that the pressure of the last few hours was gone.

'OK, listen up,' Brent called out, realizing that somehow a full stop had to be applied to the dreadful incident, 'you all did very well, couldn't have asked for a better effort.

'It's a terrible thing we've done, but a much more terrible thing would have happened if we had backed off what we did, the whole settlement would have been massacred. You can rest in your beds tonight knowing that you have saved your loved ones from a terrible fate. We'll set up a watch in a few days, but I don't think we'll be troubled again. Thanks once again, men, and sleep well.' Not that any of them would. His little speech seemed to end off the traumatic events of the day, and the groups slowly dispersed.

The two Elders who looked favourably on Brent and his ideas, joined him and Macie as they made their way up to Macie's dwelling, Eslie inviting them in for refreshments.

When they were all seated, Macie began the conversation.

'One thing I haven't worked out yet, is why you didn't blast the big ship with stones?' he asked, 'we had a good stock of them in bags, and plenty of flame powder.'

'Two reasons really. One, at that range they wouldn't have been so effective as they were on the flat boat, the arrows doing a much cleaner job, and two, I didn't want to damage the big ship. I have something in mind for her, once we've changed her appearance a little.'

'Was it your intention, right from the start,' asked one of the Elders, choosing his words carefully, 'to wipe out all members of the attacking force? I mean, to actually kill them all?' There followed a long uncomfortable silence.

'Yes it was,' Brent stated firmly, 'if we had let any of them escape they could have brought back others to attack us, now knowing where we were, and revenge would have been uppermost in their minds.' He paused for a moment, gathering his thoughts. 'If we took prisoners, what would we have done with them? Kept them locked up in one of our sheds? And for how long? If we had taken them out into the barren lands, and let them loose, it would have been even more cruel, they would have died a slow and horrid death with no hope of surviving. I think we did the right thing, in fact, the only thing, to protect our own survival.

'They chose to attack us,' he continued. 'And with no quarter if you remember the slain Elders, and that's what they got in return.'

He sat back, defying them to criticize his judgement. When Eslie appeared with the ubiquitous jug of fruit juice, it gave them all the chance to drop the subject.

'That spiked hook idea of yours was a surprise,' one of the Elders said cheerily, trying to lighten the conversation. 'You must have thought out every possible move they could have made. I'm glad you're on our side.' When the flat cakes ran out, the Elders excused themselves, saying they had to report back to the others, who had seen it all anyway.

Early next day, Brent began the exploration of the big ship, noting the different construction methods used and timbers he did not recognize. Below the deck were living quarters for about fifty men, a little cramped, but adequate for short journeys. A store of bows, arrows and metal tipped spears seemed to be their only armament, although several large jars of a yellow powdery substance made him wonder what they would have used it for, if they had had the chance.

Internally, the ship had a giant skeleton of massive timbers joined together with wooden pegs, the outer planking being held in place by the same method. Nowhere could he find the use of metal in the construction, and assumed they had little access to the precious material.

Brent searched in vain for any sign of a map or record of the ships travels, as this would give him an idea of where it came from, and if they had a record of his settlement from the previous encounter, but there was nothing of this nature.

In a forward locker he found a spare set of sails, and following a most unpleasant smell, found a large chest full of dried human scalps. Shuddering at the thought of what might have happened to his settlement if he had not been so decisive and ruthless in his actions, he made his way back on deck just before he parted company with his hastily eaten breakfast.

In order to wipe out any memories of the previous barbaric owners of the ship, and to put their own mark on it, they decided to paint the outer hull above the water line a deep blue, using a paint mixture made from nut oil and a finely ground local rock, while the sails would be dyed yellow, just in case they came across others who had had the misfortune to have met the previous owners and survived.

The scalps would be dumped down the nearest funnel pit.

Over the next few days everyone was kept fully occupied, the nut gatherers perhaps the most, as they had to find a huge quantity of nuts to make the oil for the paint. Bands of the dark blue mineral for the pigment had been discovered a long time ago, and its strange property of turning the oil into a tough waterproof film was well known, but little used.

Leaves from one of the forest trees provided the yellow dye for the sails, but their sheer bulk was proving a problem until someone suggested using one of the fishing boats with the seats removed as a vat.

Three new flame cannons were made, one large one for the bows of the ship, and a smaller one for each side, Brent claiming they were for fending off any large water creatures they might encounter.

Things settled down to the normal routine of manufacture and trading, the memory of the horrific massacre fading as everyone was usefully employed rushing around doing something for someone, and then word came from the metalworkers that their water supply was becoming undrinkable due to an unpleasant metallic taste.

Special trucks were made to transport drinking water from the lake to the settlement, but everyone knew that was only a stop gap measure, and some other source of water had to be found, and quickly.

As the main aquifer of the region had been drained over the generations, and was now contaminated by seepage from fissures in the bedrock, any new wells that were dug only produced the same tainted water.

The extra traffic hauling water between the lake and the metalworkers began to interfere with the normal flow of other trading trucks, and so they were now being sent off six at a time, strung out in a line.

With the metalworker's water problem stabilized, but not solved on a permanent basis, Brent was able to concentrate on finishing the sailing ship. The painting had been completed and the sails dyed, and they had taken her out for a trial run to get used to handling her.

The twin sail system and the method of rigging was something new to them, and Macie suggested that they rip out the whole thing and replace it with their own much simpler system. Brent was reluctant to do this, pointing out that it had worked well for the original owners and it was just a matter of getting used to it.

They passed the old collapsed concrete bridge where they had gone into the forest, and sailed on to where the lake broadened out so far that the left-hand bank was only a blur and difficult to distinguish from the water.

Several small rivers cascaded down over the high rock walls which separated the lake from the forest, and this caused considerable interest, as they had never seen flowing water in this way before.

'Either there's a massive great hill in the forest or the trees are much higher than those in our area,' commented Brent as they sailed on, 'I didn't think a growing thing could get so tall without falling over.' They had all forgotten the interlacing of the branches which gave the forest its colossal strength, allowing the tallest trees to reach four hundred metres and more, with a different climate to suit each level and the creatures who lived there. The forest was, in effect, one massive great tree, with countless thousands of trunks going down into the ground below to seek nutrients, and the interlacing branches actually growing into and supporting each enormous trunk as it towered above its neighbours to reach the blazing sunlight above.

At one point they had seen smoke arising from the forest, and a debate ensued as to whether it was from a natural forest fire, which was a very rare occurrence, or a settlement of people like themselves. Macie was all for going ashore to solve the mystery, but the sheer rock face at the lake's edge curtailed any possible expedition from landing with any degree of safety. This pleased Brent, who maintained that no one could actually live in the forest because of the dangerous creatures there, and so they sailed on, with many a backward glance until the smoke was lost from sight.

Several sightings of very large fish, and what they thought might have been a relation of the water monster were seen, but nothing approached the ship in a dangerous fashion, and they felt quite safe as they got used to handling the new addition to their fleet.

With plenty of food on board, there was little incentive to hurry back to the settlement, and Brent was still looking for a suitable landing place to explore a new region of the forest, insisting that there was a good chance of finding more remains of the ancient's dwellings and possibly solving the mystery of their demise, which had now become something of a preoccupation of his.

When night fell, they dropped anchor close to the lake's edge. Someone had caught some fish with a trailing line, and these were cooked over a wood burning stove the metalworkers had made to Brent's design, anticipating the day when they would capture the ship for their own ends.

A few oil lamps were lit, giving adequate light for their evening meal, but not so much as to spoil the dazzling display of stars, and later the moon, as it rose over the almost pitch blackness of the forest. As they settled down for the night, the nocturnal creatures of the forest awoke.

As the night wore on, the hideous chorus of screams and shrieks grew louder as empty bellies were filled by protesting food sources, and nobody got any sleep.

By midnight, everyone was up, walking around the deck and grumbling about the ear piercing performance of the forest creatures, until Brent in desperation charged the big cannon in the bows of the ship, and fired it.

When the echoes finally died away, the lake was strangely quiet, with just the lap of the water on the hull and the odd creak expected of any wooden ship as she lay at anchor.

One by one, the forest creatures began to feed again, but by then the exhausted crew were snoring their collective heads off, unintentionally adding to the sounds of the forest.

Daylight was preceded by a violent electrical storm over the forest, but well clear of the lake. From a boiling mass of black clouds which had gathered over the massive area of greenery, vicious streaks of lightening ripped into the tree tops, sending the inhabitants scurrying down several layers for shelter, where they were pounced upon by those who were not used to such treats.

All were on deck to witness the spectacle, despite the lack of sleep, and being terrified the storm might come their way.

Brent did his best to allay their fears, explaining that they were quite safe on the water, as there was nothing above it to cause the discharge. He was nearly right, but not quite.

As the sun came up, the storm had spent its fury, and died away with a few deep throated rumbles as it moved westward, leaving the air clean and sparkling, a good omen for the coming day, they thought.

After the first meal of the day they heaved the anchor up and pulled away from the close proximity of the shoreline to catch the full strength of the wind, and headed south.

So far there had been no sign of the settlement they thought the ship might have come from, despite a careful surveillance of the lakeside by a lone sailor equipped with a magnifier, who sat perched on a little platform high up on one of the masts.

About midmorning, the watcher up the mast yelled down that there was something unusual up ahead, and all eyes strained into the distance to see what it was. It was quite some time later that they were able to make out a long sandy beach, back of which was a huge area of green, the forest ringing it in a huge circle.

When they were opposite the stretch of golden sand, they swung the ship around to face it, and then lowered a small boat they had hung on the stern of the ship for going ashore when the water was too shallow for the main vessel.

Brent and three others hastened down a rope ladder and into the little boat, two of the men energetically rowing for the beach and wondering what might greet them.

With the boat safely pulled up above water level, they went up the sloping beach, two archers in front with bows primed, not knowing what they might find waiting for them.

As they reached the top of the huge sand bar, they looked down on a roughly circular area of green, about two kilometres across and slightly dish shaped, like a very shallow bowl. This was fringed by the forest in a clear cut line, as if the trees did not dare encroach upon the lush green circle. Asking the others to stay well back, Brent slowly walked down to the edge of the green circle, stooped for a moment, and then returned with something in his hands.

'These are seed heads of grasses like ours, but larger and with much bigger heads for grinding into flour. We'll collect the ripe ones and take them back to see if they'll grow.'

'There must be a settlement near by.' one of the men said quietly, looking around nervously for the owner of the crop.

'I don't think so,' Brent replied confidently, 'just look at the size of it, a settlement twice our size couldn't till and tend a crop that big. Maybe there's something in the ground which the trees don't like, but the food grasses don't mind, just like our forest where it joins the barren lands. No, I think it's a freak of nature, not man made.' They collected some more of the ripe seed heads, using a shirt as a bag, and returned to the ship.

It was just as well they did not stay too long at the corn field, the radiation which had poisoned the ground for the trees, and mutated the corn to its new giant form still lingered, ever ready to do its deadly work.

Underway again, the ship continued to sail south, hugging the coastline and still looking for the builders of the ship.

Brent's theory being that if they knew where the settlement was, they could steer well clear of it in future and so not evoke another attack, although he felt quite confident they could win any fight the others might offer.

Just before they dropped anchor for the night, the lookout called again, saying he had seen something sparkling in the middle of the lake. Brent was up the ladder almost before the lookout's voice had died away.

Using the magnifier he could just make out what he thought might be an island, but could not tell for sure because of haze on the horizon. Something was reflecting the rays from the slowly sinking sun, sending out bright flashes of light as the ship moved up and down in the gentle swell.

'Now that's something to look at tomorrow.' he said cheerfully, regaining the deck and telling the rest of the crew what he had seen.

This time they anchored further out in the lake in order to put some distance between themselves and the raucous din expected from the forest at nightfall, and the evening meal was prepared and consumed amid much optimism of what the morrow would bring. Even as the darkness of night dropped on them like an all encompassing velvet blanket, the faint flashes of light from the island still persisted, drawing ever more bizarre speculations from the enthralled watchers of what it might be .

An early start was inevitable after the excitement of the previous evening, and as the bright yellow sails creaked their way up the masts, they took on an orange glow as the sun heaved itself over the distant horizon.

As they headed out from the mainland towards the distant island, they caught the full force of the wind for the first time, and the ship came alive as the sails billowed and strained against their holdings.

'This is more like it.' Brent shouted, as he stood in the bows dashed with spray. 'She goes a damned sight faster than anything we had before.'

The Island was a little further away than they had first thought, distance over water always being difficult to judge, but by midday, details of buildings could clearly be seen, and a silver tower which had sparkled so much in the setting sun the previous evening. Their main fear now was that some others had found it first.

They dropped anchor some two hundred metres offshore. There had been no sign of life as they approached, but in case any incumbents were waiting in ambush, Brent still thought it prudent to wait a while, hoping that sooner or later, someone would move and it could be seen with the magnifier, but what they would do then, he was not sure.

Macie broke the tense silence which had befallen the crew,

'I don't see any landing place for ships.' he whispered.

'Nor do I,' Brent replied, 'and there's no reason to whisper, they couldn't hear you from this distance.'

'Perhaps if we go around the island some way we might find one.' he suggested, this time in a more normal voice.

The anchor was pulled up, and the sails set. Tacking around a promontory all they could see were more buildings, some right down to the waters edge, and one half submerged.

Once more they were running with the wind, and the ship soon left behind any trace of habitation. Now there was just grassland with a few trees dotted about that ran right down to the waters edge.

Later, and further inland, they could see a small mountain range with white tips to its peaks, and a thick green forest below. A small river flowing into the lake surprised them, indicating that what they were seeing was either part of the mainland, or a very big island indeed.

By evening, they had circumnavigated the island, and arrived back at the point where they had first dropped anchor earlier, confirming that it was not part of the mainland.

'Still no one about,' Brent commented, scanning the shore line with the magnifier, 'I think if anyone was there, we would have seen them by now. We'll anchor here, keep a watch in case anyone tries to catch us unawares during darkness, and then go ashore in the morning.'

For once the night was silent, Macie thought perhaps there were no large creatures on the island, and small ones would not make enough noise to be heard from where they were.

'Nice idea Macie,' Brent said with a grin, 'we'll find out tomorrow. You can go ashore first, and if we hear a yell, we'll stay here.' Macie was not amused, and showed it.

After a very hasty morning meal the small boat was lowered, and Brent, Macie and four others crammed into it, jostling to find a comfortable position in the tiny craft, which threatened to have them all in the water.

With only two working the oars and the boat low in the water, it took quite a time to cover the two hundred metres to shore, and then nearly tipped it over when climbing out.

The first building was about three hundred metres away from where they landed, the intervening ground being covered with short grass and the odd patch of sand.

'These dwellings are almost whole,' said Brent quietly,

'Only the tops of the tall ones have been torn away.'

The blast wave from the nearest fusion flare had ripped off the top of most tall buildings, but those in their shelter had survived almost intact, except for their windows, and a few of those still remained where they had been protected from the direct blast. For some reason, only known to the higher powers, this small area had escaped the ravages of the ancient robot wars, one of the very few places to have done so.

The first building they came to had lost all its windows and the main glass entrance door. The reception hall was full of blown sand, leaves, and general debris, making it difficult to access. As the doorway faced due north, the wind had driven in anything which was mobile.

'No point in trying to clamber over that mess,' said Brent dismissively, 'let's try another one.'

The further they went into the mass of ruins, the more clogged the streets were with debris blown in over the years.

Small trees had taken root where there was sufficient light to enable them to flourish, but by the rotting trunks of dead trees and shrubs, they had been preceded by many more.

As there had been no sign of life, not even that of an animal, they moved around with a little less caution, and their voices had returned to their normal excited level.

'If these are trading stores, I'm damned if I can see what they were trading in,' said one of the men, peering in through a shattered first floor window, 'it's just a tangle of rubbish and bits of metal.'

'Don't forget, our stores were underground, and protected from the elements,' Brent said, surprised at the man's lack of understanding, 'and they may not be trading stores, anyway.'

One small building seemed to have escaped the general holocaust. Tucked away in a back street and shielded by its taller neighbours, its windows were still intact, and a metal door had protected its contents from the inflow of detritus most other building had suffered. As the door gave way to the persistent attack from Brent and his determined followers, they entered the gloom of the first undisturbed building on the island they had found.

Only objects made from metal and other non perishable materials had survived, the others had succumbed to the general breakdown which time demands, and marked their presence with little piles of dust or crumbling flakes of that which had been.

And then they found their first skeleton. What had once been bleached white bones had now taken on a pale brown colour, but still lay where their previous owner had fallen when the neutron wave had struck, whisking away the life of all those in its deadly path.

They stood there, a frozen tableau, gazing in wonder and a little apprehensive at the sad remains of one of the ancients, who had created so much, and lost it all.

'It looks as if they were bigger than us,' said Macie in hushed tones, 'that's if you can imagine those bones fleshed out and standing upright. Wonder why we didn't see any bones at the underground stores?' he asked as an afterthought. Brent had wondered that too, then he realized why.

'If the disaster had happened at night, then everyone would have been in their own dwellings, and as they would have been on the surface, they would have been destroyed.'

They went from room to room, finding a few more skeletons in different poses, and a lot of machinery which made little sense to them. Apart from the remains of the composition rollers and the piles of disintegrated paper, the printing works was in very good condition. The workers were somewhat less so.

The large self service food store was unrecognisable for what it once was, as the glass front had been blown in and decay had altered everything except the stainless steel shelves. A small gas service station was still in reasonable condition, and caused a great deal of excitement when they found one of the valves still in working order, and released a quantity of gas from the large underground storage tank.

'Let's go back and get the others,' Brent said, 'they ought to see some of this.' And so they made their way back to the ship, stopping every now and again to stand in awe at some wonder created by the ancients, and trying to guess what they had been used for.

Back on board the ship, they told the rest of the crew what they had seen while they had a meal, after which, they brought the ship in as close as possible to the shore so that they would not have to row so far when they returned to the island, but several trips would have to be made as the little boat only held four safely.

Macie felt nervous at leaving the ship unmanned, but as they had seen no one during their exploration, Brent felt it was quite safe to do so, especially, as he pointed out, it took an experienced sailor to handle her, and it was most unlikely one of those was on the island.

From the shore they could just see the tip of the silver tower which had drawn them to the island in the first place, and decided to make their way there to see what it was, checking out anything interesting on the way.

To save time climbing over rubble filled streets, they circled around the main mass of buildings and went in from an easterly direction, finding many more seemingly undamaged buildings on the way.

The door of a gun shop finally gave way to Brent's persistent coaxing, and before long they had figured out what the displayed stock was meant for. Constant fiddling with a rifle exposed the loading slot, and moments later they had a shell in the breach. Time had decomposed the explosive, so nothing happened when the trigger was pulled.

Some all metal crossbows still worked, and when they found the bolts, they realized the power of the weapon.

'We had better be careful with these,' Brent said, as he fondled the bow, 'they probably have a greater range than our ordinary bows, and therefore anyone else's.'

The silver tower was finally reached, but no way in could be found despite a very careful search. It was some thirty metres in diameter and completely featureless, its clean metal surface giving a hollow ring when struck hard enough, which Brent did frequently in his frustration.

'Perhaps you get into it from underneath.' he said, standing back a few paces, and then, giving it one final whack, they left the disguised missile launcher to its own devices.

Six:
New lands beckon

SOME STREETS HAD less rubble than others, and they chose these to travel on as they made their way across the city to its outer limits, where ornamental parks had once graced the landscape. Sadly, only the outline of various structures gave a clue as to the beauty which had once been.

Graceful walkways of synthetic stone, and statues of people who merited remembrance were sensitively intermingled with water features, most of which had long ago silted up, but some still sported a trickle of water giving a suggestion of what the overall effect might have been.

'I think I'd liked to have lived in these times,' commented Macie, looking around at what once had been the pride of the city's landscape designers, 'they had a sense of grace sadly lacking in our world.'

'Maybe they did,' Brent conceded begrudgingly, 'but look what happened to them, it all looks a bit of a mess now. Anyway, we don't have the time or materials to spend on such unproductive things, or had you forgotten the water shortage of the metalworkers?' Brent was a little short on aesthetics, although he could appreciate the subtleties of a good mechanical design.

Beyond the recreational gardens of the city stretched the growing fields, not that any of the original crops had survived, but the road networks and general layout indicated what the area had been used for. Slowly an idea began to form in Brent's mind, but it was too bold to mention yet.

They left the old cultivated area and began to climb the foot hills of the mountain range, although it could hardly be called a range in the true sense of the word. Three mighty peaks thrust up defiantly into the clear blue sky, their tops crowned with a cap of glistening white snow.

'Why are we going up here?' asked one of the climbers, out of breath from the unusual exertion of climbing.

'So that we can get a general view of this part of the island. It might give us an idea why this settlement was spared the devastation the rest of our world suffered.' replied Brent, as they stopped to look back over the gently undulating agricultural area, and the ruined city below. 'I don't think this was always an island because there are no harbours for ships to dock in, so that means the lake has come about after whatever happened to them.'

As they crested the brow of the next hill in a seemingly endless series leading up to the higher peaks, the wooded area began. Not the super tall giants of their forest, but of a more modest type, tall and straight, and well spread out.

There was an absence of the usual tangle of undergrowth which plagued their forest fringes, and as they walked beneath their shady branches, they enjoyed the cool gentle perfumed breeze which drifted up from the plains below.

'What's happened to the wind?' asked Macie, looking around as if in so doing he would find it lurking somewhere.

'Don't know,' replied Brent, puzzled, 'come to think of it, I didn't notice it when we left the settlement down below.'

'You don't think it's another of those light flashing storms brewing up, do you?' asked a worried looking Macie, remembering the last one in the barren lands.

'No, I don't think so,' said Brent hesitantly, not sure if it was or not, 'but perhaps we had better be getting down again, just in case. We've a long way to go.'

When they had retraced their steps to the lake it was nearly dark, and the first aboard the ship lit a lamp to guide the others as they were ferried in turn across the inky waters, total darkness falling as the last one clambered aboard.

'What do we do now?' someone asked, as they sat down for their evening meal, 'they'll be getting worried about us back at the settlement, won't they?'

'Probably,' replied Brent, his mouth full of food, 'but there's one more thing I want to do before we go back, and that's look for an underground link. I'm sure all these places are connected somehow.'

'How would that help us?' Macie wanted to know, 'the tracks our end are broken by the funnel pit, and we can't reach the other one in the cliffs, or do you intend to build a bridge across the pit?' he added, a touch of sarcasm in his voice. Brent failed to answer, he was too busy eating.

After a short while discussing what they had found, and how they could use it to their advantage, they retired for the night, exhausted from a very long day's work.

Only two set out for the island next day, Brent and Gappy, (not being his real name, but one acquired in his youth due to a missing front tooth.) The boat had a rope attached so that it could be pulled back to the ship for the others to go ashore later to gather fruit, as the supply was getting low.

Brent had noticed a low squat building the previous day, and going by his instincts, headed for it with a ruthless determination, his companion struggling to keep up.

'Thought this might be it,' he exclaimed, as they forced one of the doors open, 'it didn't look like a store somehow, so I thought it might be the rail terminal.'

The rail link's walls were lined with glass cases, most of which were intact, their contents still as they had been left countless ages ago. Gappy ran from one to another in youthful excitement until Brent reminded him curtly of the purpose of their visit, and headed off down a flight of dusty stairs, his oil lamp throwing ghostly shadows on the walls.

Gappy raced after him, terrified of being left behind in the dank darkness of the emergency stairway, the only means of reaching the platform below as the lifts had long ceased to work. Several passages led off the main stairs on the way down, but were ignored for the time being as Brent fully intended to visit the place again in the not too distant future.

The platform, when they reached it, was just like the others they had seen, with a tunnel at each end inviting the intrepid Brent to enter.

'Where do you think they go?' asked the multiple echoes,

'On to other settlements, I expect.' Brent replied, holding his lamp up high to see if there was a plate showing the rail system and terminals, but in the feeble light he was unable to find it.

They were just about to leave the station when there was a deep rumbling sound followed by the squeal of metal wheels on hard steel. They froze where they stood as the underground transport carriage slowly crept into the station and stopped opposite them. Brent knew instinctively there would be no passengers on board, but had to look anyway, much to his companion's dismay as he had no intention of being left in the darkness.

They were unable to open the doors, and had to be content with peering through the dust coated windows. In the poor light from the lamp they were unable to see if anyone had been in the carriage when it had stopped at the top of the incline so very long ago.

'Better get back and give the others a hand.' Brent said, taking one last look around in case he had missed something important. Gappy gave a sigh of relief, he found going beneath ground claustrophobic and threatening in some indefinable way, treading on Brent's heels as they left.

Leaving the rail link terminal, they had to wait a few moments for their eyes to get used to the brilliant glare of the sun, before heading for the gun shop. It took them a little longer to find it than they thought, Brent being diverted several times by other interesting looking buildings on the way. Armed with three crossbows apiece, and a box of cartridges, they made their way back to the ship, only to find the little boat on the shore and no one in sight.

Brent called out repeatedly, but there was no reply, so he assumed the rest of them were still out gathering fruit.

They took the crossbows on board, and then returned to the island, sitting on a block of stone and talking about the ancient's settlement while they waited for the others.

Concern was now growing, as Brent had expected the rest of the crew to have returned by this time, as there was no sign of them having come back to the ship with a load of fruit and then gone back for more.

'We'd better go look for them,' he said to Gappy. 'Go back and bring a couple of crossbows and some arrows, we may need 'em.'

A nervous Gappy returned with the weapons, and after some fiddling about they managed to get the bows cocked and a bolt in place. Bent gave one last call before they set off, and a faint answer came back from deep within the buildings. They both headed in the general direction of the distant voices, calling out every so often to make sure they were still on course, and eventually the others came in sight, carrying one of their members between them.

'What happened?' asked Brent anxiously, as they laid the injured party down.

'We were on our way back with the fruit when we saw this store on the edge of the settlement, and went in.'

'It was a strange place, like nothing we've seen before. We had a good look around so we could tell you about it when we returned, in case you wished to visit it. It was full of odd looking tools, at least we think that's what they were. We've brought a few back for you,' and so saying he undid his shirt which had been used as a carry bag, and a collection of wood and metal working tools tumbled out onto the ground. 'These look like wood cutting things, but we don't know what the others are for.' The high speed drill bits and a small number of miniature circular saw blades lay glittering on the ground, as pristine as the day they had been made.

'You did well,' said Brent, 'these will be most useful additions to our workshops. Later we'll go back for some more. What happened to our friend here?' The man lay on the ground, holding his foot and softly groaning.

'He went up some stairs to the room above.' said the self appointed spokesman. 'All of a sudden there was a big crash and he came down along with a whole lot of metal boxes, and one of them landed on his foot, do you think it's broken?' he asked anxiously.

Brent bent down to examine the man's foot, and despite ear splitting yells from the unfortunate, wriggled his foot this way and that to ascertain the degree of damage.

'I think it's just badly bruised, there's a cut which we must clean up, but apart from that he should be all right after a few days.' And he dropped the foot to the ground soliciting yet another ear piercing shriek.

With the injured man supported between his friends, they made their way back to the ship. A few more yelps of pain accompanied the loading of the unfortunate fellow into the little boat, and then they were back on board for a well earned meal and a rest.

Anchoring off shore at night, as Brent thought navigating in the dark would prove too hazardous, it took them three days to get back to the settlement, and a very angry but relieved Eslie, the two Elders and a few others were waiting on the jetty as the ship glided in.

'The lookout on the ledge saw you coming through the magnifier,' one of the Elders said, 'we had almost given you up for lost. May we suggest you give more details of your intentions in future so as not to cause unnecessary worry to those left behind.' Brent felt suitably reprimanded for his lack of thought for others, and apologized profusely for the omission, promising to be more explicit in future.

Meanwhile Macie, wondering if he would ever be let off the leash again in the foreseeable future, was being told off and hugged to death simultaneously by a tearful Eslie.

Once things had calmed down a little, and the trophies they had brought back put on display and demonstrated where possible, the more mundane chores of the settlement were attended to. The water situation of the metalworkers was getting steadily worse, as they used quite a lot in manufacturing their goods and the water table had fallen even further. With two sail trains of drinking water per day, they were able to sustain life, but that was just about all.

The glassworkers were politely reluctant to accept an influx of people, as they too were concerned about their water supply, and could foresee future problems if the population increased to any great extent.

Brent's home settlement could safely house a small number by extending out into the barren lands a little, but this was no permanent solution to the problem. Brent had an idea in mind, but felt he needed to do some ground work first before suggesting it.

The microscope they had found in the underground store was sent over to Kelt, who could hardly believe his luck, and set about duplicating it. The lack of precision lens grinding equipment precluded a perfect copy with the magnification of the original, but he was pleased with the result being a practical man and understanding his limitations.

Along with the microscope, they had found a telescope, and when mounted up on the ledge, it had a regular stream of visitors viewing the creatures of the forest top in detail.

This frightened some and made others swear they would never go into the forest again, failing to realize that what they had seen belonged to the highest tree tops, and would never be found on the ground anyway.

Brent and a small band of helpers, one of which had come over from the metalworkers, spent some considerable time building an all terrain vehicle powered by the oil engine.

A small trailer had been made to hitch on the back of the main traction unit, and amid copious clouds of blue smoke, four of them set off to explore the local barren lands, Brent and Macie taking it in turns to drive, with two others in the trailer along with food and water in case of breakdown.

Once the engine had reached full working temperature, the smoke lessened somewhat, and the occupants of the trailer ceased to cough. They all enjoyed the experience as they chugged along at just a little more than a fast walking pace, which, considering the terrain, was quite fast enough.

They were about to turn around and follow their tracks back home when they came across a funnel pit. As pits go, this was only a small one, and Brent thought it might have only just started. They stopped a few metres away from the mysterious hole in the ground, leaving the engine on tick over, not really trusting the automatic starter fully.

Picking up one of the few large stones to be found in the area, Brent approached the pit and threw it into the middle, listening carefully for it to hit something. It didn't.

'There must be a bottom to the damned thing somewhere,' he said, looking around for another stone, 'if we could find one with a known bottom, we could go down on a rope to see what's causing it to grow.'

'You've got to be joking!' Macie said in astonishment.

'No one's asking you to go down, I'll do it, if we can find one which isn't bottomless.' Macie remained silent.

'If we got a piece of highly polished metal,' Brent continued, 'and fixed it to a long pole, we could hold it over the hole and use it as a mirror, and then maybe see what's down there.' Macie still didn't say anything, and the other two were off looking for large stones.

They threw in some more, slid some down the sides from the very edge of the funnel, and then a huge chunk of ground gave way next to them with a roar which made them all jump as it slid to oblivion down the insatiable throat of the funnel pit. It at least drove home the point that any part of the edge could give way at any time, and they all respectfully stepped back a few metres.

Having challenged the funnel pit, and lost, but proved the capabilities of the new oil powered truck, there was little else to do but return to the settlement. They all climbed aboard, Brent suggesting one of the others try the controls, and they took their seats for the journey home.

The new driver pulled the power lever too quickly, the engine coughed a couple of times, and died on them. The ensuing silence almost crashed in on their ears.

'Try the starter.' Brent said, trying to hide the shake in his voice. There was a loud hiss, a cough, and it fired.

'Like to get my hands on that big unit which drove the scavenger,' Brent said, as they bumped along, 'could make a real transporter out of that!'

'Do you want to take the whole settlement out in the barren lands for a joy ride then?' asked Macie, who had now recovered from the double shock he had received earlier.

'Or are you thinking of a really luxurious traveller for a few invited guests?'

'You really are a prat sometimes,' Brent replied, 'I'm thinking of a true explorer, equipped with a workshop for repairs, a big supply of food and water, and enough fuel to take us out for days at a time. I want to see if the rest of the world is in the same state as our little bit.

It's just possible it's a lot better, and then we could move there.' Macie wasn't keen to move anywhere, so he kept his mouth shut, hoping Brent could be diverted onto something a little less challenging, and a lot closer to home.

A bright flash of light behind the truck made them all jump, and when the bang came, they jumped again.

'Looks like another of those storms brewing up,' Brent said, increasing the speed of the truck so that they all bounced about like stones in a sieve, 'they seem to be getting more frequent and nearer to home.' The others didn't say much, they were too busy holding on to the sides of the trucks as they raced for the settlement.

A thick oppressive haze spread across the sky, dulling the normally bright sunlight, and the lightning strikes came closer as the wind dropped to a mere whimper of its normal strength. Their hair stood on end and the air crackled, just before a brilliant blue white flash struck the ground right in front of the trucks, Brent instinctively swerved and both trucks tipped over onto their sides, spilling everyone out.

Fortunately no one was seriously hurt, just a few cuts and bruises, and plenty of bad language as they righted the trucks, the one with the oil engine proving the most difficult.

'I think we need to widen the wheel base.' Brent said as they piled back in and he pulled the self starter lever. There were a few ribald comments about speed freaks, lack of consideration for others, and general bad driving, but these were fortunately drowned out as the engine coughed into life, and they were on their way again, trying to out run the storm.

By the time they reached the outskirts of the settlement, the sky had darkened to that of late evening, and the windows of several dwellings twinkled like yellow stars as the occupants lit their lamps against the early gloom.

The storm spent its fury on the barren land just short of the settlement, fusing the sand into glassy lumps as the immense electrical discharges ripped into the ground, the thunderclaps reminiscent of the very much earlier catastrophe which had devastated their world.

With the trucks back in the shed, the crew joined the rest of the inhabitants as they watched the electrical storm move over the forest area, huge columns of smoke and sparks rising up to join the already blackened sky as large tracts of the woodland caught fire.

The normally calm waters of the lake had taken on a menacing dirty grey colour as waves began to lash up against the jetty and shore line, threatening to dash the ship against the rocks if the anchor line should give way.

'What's that?' someone shouted above the noise of the storm, pointing out over the lake. The dark grey funnel of a water spout swung around the headland, heading straight for the settlement.

No one knew what to do, and so just stood there, paralysed, as the roaring column of water drew nearer, growing in volume all the time as it sucked up the waters of the lake in a swirling dance of destruction.

At the last moment it swung inland, clipping the edge of the forest and uprooting huge trees which had stood their ground against all for aeons of time.

For the first time in their lives they were drenched in rain from the fall out spray of the spout as it passed them by, and then headed out with its shrieking winds into the barren lands. Everyone was beginning to relax a little as they began discussing the horrific storm, and then the ground shook beneath their feet.

The monstrous column of water, no longer being spun by the winds of the weather front which had created it, collapsed, dropping countless thousands of tonnes of water onto the barren lands below. Apart from gouging out a huge depression in the landscape, the torrent of water tried to find its own level, and that was a gully which ran back towards the lake between the forest and the settlement.

They heard it coming long before the twenty metre high foam topped wave came crashing through, ripping out the ground beneath its turbulent swirling waters, and colouring the lake a dirty brown for several hundred metres in all directions. It had missed the settlement, but now there was a deep gorge riven between the settlement and their main food supply in the forest, which was used to supplement the grain and vegetables they grew in the limited space available.

As the storm and haze moved away, it grew a little lighter, but the sun was about to dip below the horizon for the night, hiding the damaged earth under its all concealing cloak.

The two Elders had joined Brent and his men as they watched the last of the storm fade into the distance.

'Do you think we will be able to cross the new gully created by the storm?' one of them asked, looking concerned, 'if not, it could compromise our food supplies.'

'By the time we get there to see how deep it is, it'll be too dark to see clearly,' Brent said calmly, wishing he felt that way, 'so we'll have a look first thing in the morning, and let you know.'

The main topic of conversation that evening was the storm, its consequential threat to their way of life, and if they would see more of them in the future. Even the Elders, or those of them who were left after the massacre, were unable to give any advice, except by making consoling noises, as this was something well beyond their understanding.

At first light, Brent, Macie and a few followers, tramped across the water torn ground to the new divide which lay between them and the forest. The deep vee shaped channel the storm had cut was rough and steep. It could have been traversed by single climbers, but they would have been unable to carry a useful load while so doing. A bridge of some sort was the only answer to the problem, and that would entail getting across to the forest for the wood in the first place. The water, in its frantic rush to the lake, had ripped out anything moveable, leaving a jagged jumble of rocks which looked less than inviting.

Macie thought they could use the ship, landing further along the coast to pick up their supplies. The difficulty about that was getting ashore from the ship, as the forest edge, in most places, had a sheer rock face dividing it from the water.

A bridge seemed the only answer so far, and Brent went to tell the Elders about their conclusions on the matter.

After looking at all the possibilities with the two sympathetic Elders, and the bridge being the only one which was really feasible, it was agreed to send a team across the new ravine to fell timber and begin construction.

This proved easier said than done, as the bottom of the ravine was strewn with rough boulders and twisted metal from something left over from the age of the ancients, although it was impossible to tell what it had been.

By evening, a small but serviceable bridge had been assembled, which allowed the construction crew easier access to the trees on the other side, and acted as a work platform for the construction of the main bridge. There was some concern that another storm could sweep the whole thing down into the lake, but there was no real alternative.

Fate, luck, or just pure chance, depending upon how you look at it, then took a hand in deciding the outcome of the settlements, precipitating the idea Brent had had on the island into a necessary action, although he had not worked out all the details as yet, and was thus not keen to discuss it with the Elders.

Word had come through from the metalworkers that their water supply had finally failed, only a trickle of dirty water was now obtainable from the deepest well, and they had to recycle whatever possible to keep the workshops supplied.

The glassworkers reported storms of equal ferocity to those which had recently visited the other two settlements, and they were occurring more frequently as time went by.

One flash of lightning had set fire to one of their huge piles of flame rocks, and there was nothing they could do to put out the flames, as they too, had to drag their water up from deep underground. The stockpile of coal was left to burn itself out, smothering everything in black smoke.

The Elders, realizing that something positive had to be done to ensure the survival of them all, arranged a meeting with Brent and his friend, and representatives of the other two settlements, to be held by the lake.

Word had come through that the slender bridge over the ravine between the metalworker's and the glassworker's settlements had been damaged by a storm, and without repairs, was no longer considered strong enough to take the weight of a truck. While repair work was being implemented, only single foot traffic was allowed across. While information was being shuffled to and fro, the meeting was delayed until all pertinent persons could assemble.

The wooden bridge across to the forest was completed, and food gathering recommenced, along with a good stock of timber in case the bridge had to be repaired or even rebuilt if there was another devastating storm.

Eslie had forgiven, but not forgotten Brent for his lack of consideration with regard to the island project, and normal relations resumed, with him taking most of his main meals with the family, and spending the evenings with them.

Another electrical storm spent its fury in the nearby barren lands, but fortunately not near enough to the settlement to affect them, except for the explosion. In the middle of the storm, the earth shuddered violently, a vivid flash of searing light left most who saw it blinded for several minutes with ringing ears, and the whole area was covered in a fine dust next day.

Speculation as to what had happened ran riot, with explanations running from the amusing and light hearted to things which did not bear thinking about, so everyone was relieved when all the Elders assembled for the great meeting which would solve all their troubles.

The meeting took place in the great hall, which had not been used since Brent's outburst with the Elders long ago.

Brent's co-operative Elder opened the meeting, as was customary for the host, outlining the problems of the settlement to date, and enlarging on the difficulty of accepting immigrants from other settlements, although not refusing to do so in as many words.

The metalworker's representative did a sterling job of describing how the lack of water was affecting them, to the point of refreshments being called for in desperation to stop him, while thanking them at the same time for the trucks of drinking water supplied and gratefully received.

The glassworkers had no earth shattering disasters to speak of, but the loss of their stock of flame rocks and the drop in level of their underground lake did not bode well for the future, and expansion was well out of the question.

As all three groups had difficulties which precluded offering practical help to the others, an impasse was reached, which was about the only thing they could all agree upon.

Brent had broadly outlined his idea of using the newly found island to his friendly Elders the day before, but only in very general terms and in an off hand manner, not wishing to generate any resistance at this early stage of his plans.

He was therefore surprised when called upon to voice his ideas by one Elder, who spoke of him in glowing terms which caused even more embarrassment, the hot red glow showing through his sun burnt face. Brent arose to his feet in total silence, all eyes looking with surprise in his direction.

'Gentlemen, I have an idea which will solve all our problems in one fell swoop, and secure our future for a very long time to come. Each settlement may think it will lose its individuality, but that's better than losing everything.'

'It can't have escaped your notice that things are changing. Water levels are dropping, the weather is getting violent and causing damage, something we have never had before. Because of our new discoveries, production has gone up and therefore population will follow, but there is little habitable space to expand into. A new homeland is required, and we've found it.' He paused for breath, and to see what effect his revelation had had on his audience. They sat in stunned silence for a moment, and then someone plucked up the courage to ask where this new land had been found.

'Some of you may have noticed the new sailing ship we have in the harbour. With it, we have been able to explore the lake for a great distance, which was impossible with the smaller boats, and we have found an island, and what an island!' he added with enthusiasm to emphasize the point.

'It is in what we think is the middle of the lake, and as no other land can be seen from its shores, it should be free of the storms we now have to endure, for they are created by the over heated land mass. It is a very large island, it took us all day to sail around it, and it has hills and forests and good soil to grow crops. There are plenty of fruit trees, like our own, and more timber than we could ever use.' Brent reached for a beaker of drink, his throat was burning from the effort of talking so loudly for so long. He looked around him, no one had moved or said a word since he had begun.

'There is one other thing this island has which makes it an ideal place to live, and that's the remains of one of the ancient's settlements. There are many dwellings which are still reasonably intact, and we could live in them. There are many stores, like the one we found in the forest, and vast amounts of metal and other materials.' he was not sure what they were, being carried away by his own enthusiasm.

'Anyone have any questions?' he asked, worried at the lack of response to his revelations. A long silence followed, and Brent began to wonder what he should do next.

'Just supposing everyone agreed to go to this island, how would we get there?' one of the Elders asked, a little hesitantly, as if asking the question would commit him to the move.

'We have the new sailing boat, and we could take about fifty people at a time. The round journey would be about five days, or maybe less, once we get organized.'

After the first question, the others came thick and fast, Brent thinking on his feet as he tried to answer questions he hadn't even thought of. As the meeting drew to a close, everyone was exhausted, either from talking or trying to get their heads around the concept of the three settlements all moving, and becoming one.

'I think we should take these ideas to our people, see what they want to do, and report back here in a few days, does everyone agree?' A chorus of concordance shook the roof timbers, and Brent sank back in his seat, the seeds of his dream had been planted, he would now have to nurture them carefully if he wanted them to grow, and finally bloom.

'Well you certainly convinced me,' his friendly Elder said, as the meeting broke up, 'I'll go pack up my things!' he added, jokingly.

A few days later, nature for want of a better word, took a hand with two more storms close by the metal and glass workers settlements. It was very noisy, although little damage was done to the actual settlements. This helped those of doubtful mind to rapidly come to the conclusion that all was not as well as it could be, and the thought of a sailing trip and a new home seemed quite attractive.

Four days after the meeting, a representative from each of the other two settlements arrived to seek an audience with Brent's group, as they thought of it. As they were few in number, the meeting took place in the dwelling house of one of the Elders, a sumptuous spread of refreshments being laid on at short notice, surprising them all.

'Is this how you live normally?' asked one of the visitors, the edge of a fruit laden flat cake threatening to escape his bulging cheeks.

'Most of the time,' replied Brent nonchalantly, 'except for celebration days, when we put on a bit of a do.' The visitor looked suitably impressed.

The upshot of the meeting was that most people in the two settlements thought the idea of moving to the island was a good one, with only a few dissenters wishing to struggle on against all odds. They were given the option of joining the move later if they found it too difficult to stay.

The repair work on the spindly ravine bridge had been completed, and normal traffic resumed. The Elder from the glassworker's only concern was getting people over the bridge, as he found the crossing quite traumatic, his face going several shades paler as he spoke.

Brent was quite surprised at the sudden turn of events, and as he had given little thought to the logistics of the operation, he now had to play for time in order to do so.

It was agreed that the migration would commence in ten days time, the majority of the metal workers being the first to move as their situation was deteriorating the fastest, the others following every five days in batches of fifty. The scheduling of the transportation trucks Brent left for others to work out, as he wanted to concentrate on getting the island ready for the huge influx which was to follow.

The following morning Brent and about thirty others set off for the island with the intention of clearing a few of the still usable buildings ready for the first batch of immigrants, who once established, would do the same for those to follow.

His plan was that they would occupy the outer fringes of the town, trying to restore whatever they could, and as the population grew, work their way inwards until the whole thing became a viable living unit as the generations passed.

It was hard work, but they had cleared enough space to house the first batch and a few more, the extra space being for carpenters from Brent's settlement to manufacture furniture as it was required.

It was while they were sitting on deck enjoying their evening meal, that Macie noticed three stars in a line which seemed to hang in the sky over where they thought their home settlement lay.

'If we kept the ship in line with those stars, we could safely sail at night, and so save a lot of time bringing the people out here.' he said, astounded at his own brilliant observation.

Brent reluctantly agreed to try it instead of waiting until morning before returning home, his main reservation being that if they got into trouble in the middle of the lake, they would be unable to anchor ship as the cable was not long enough, and sailing towards the shore for shallower water in the dark held its own particular perils.

They waited until it was pitch dark, the three stars then showing up unmistakably, and word was given to hoist sails.

Taking it in shifts lessened the burden for most, but either Brent or Macie had to be on watch to ensure the safety of the ship, and by morning they had had enough of night sailing. Late afternoon saw the ship glide up to the jetty.

After two more trips to the island over the next few days, and travelling back at night to save time, the accommodation was deemed ready to receive the first party of metal workers who had been accumulating at Brent's settlement.

The woodworkers had already made their home on the island, and would be employed for some time making the necessary furniture and other items required by the exodus of all three settlements to their new home.

As the numbers on the island began to grow, the clearing of the rubble from the old streets, and repair work to the damaged buildings which had been occupied, added to the feeling that this was a real settlement, something the ancients might have been proud of.

Eventually the metalworker's settlement became just an empty collection of buildings used only as an en route dormitory by the glassworkers swiftly evacuating their own settlement, as the straight through journey was too long for them to accomplish in one day.

As the artisans took their skills and tools with them, nothing was lost through the move. The island provided a plentiful supply of wood and metal, and the glass from the shattered windows of the old buildings could be collected and stockpiled for future use.

Brent had taken it upon himself to organize the operation of the exodus, and it naturally followed on that he would take control of developing the island's resources, and everyone seemed quite happy for him to do so as they indicated by their total co-operation.

By carefully choosing the brightest among the growing population, and putting them in charge of various work gangs, he together with Macie and a small band of followers, was left free to explore the old works of the ancients.

With the old metal and glass workers settlements now empty, and only a few left at the northern end of the lake, the move had almost been completed. There had been no storms on or near the island, although a few had been seen through the ancient's telescopes tearing into the top of the forest on the mainland, but this was only a spectacle to watch, not worry about.

As Brent and his crew explored deeper into the ancient's city, great treasures came to light, but not all of them were understood or would prove useful for some time to come.

Near the eastern outskirts, a large factory complex was discovered, and huge stocks of mineral oil in underground tanks had survived. They had no way of knowing how much oil was present, but resolved to use it wisely until something could be found to replace it.

There was no shortage of tools from the stores and derelict factories, and this spurred on those who could use them to even greater skills. Before long, sheet glass production began, mainly to replace that missing from those buildings they wished to inhabit, although they were unable to manufacture the huge sheets of the ancients, and so had to put in multiple sheets in wooden frames.

Both of the oil engines salvaged from the machine which had nearly demolished the old settlement of the metalworkers had been brought across, but the big one proved too heavy to transport over the rail link, also even the thought of getting it onto the ship put paid to that idea, for the time being, that is. Brent said he would get it over one day.

The ground outside the settlement produced better crops than they had ever experienced before, and the new wheat ears collected from the strange green circle on the mainland passed all their expectations.

Although no books had survived in readable form, there were plenty of printed words on other things.

Brent was determined to crack the code of the ancients as he thought it would lead to a much greater understanding of them, and their ways. Anything containing text was faithfully copied down, and its location and on what it was found recorded. This approach eventually proved to be helpful when exploring new buildings, and finding things they did not recognize, at least giving a clue as to their use.

Several unsuccessful assaults had been made on the silver tower, until it became a joke among those so employed. As Brent failed to see the funny side of it, and usually remained a bit grumpy for a while afterwards, the others kept their humour to themselves as best they could, but it sometimes leaked out as suppression only made the situation funnier.

At long last coal, or flame rocks as they called it, was found as an outcrop by a team scouring the foothills of the triple peaked mountain for anything useful. It only took a short while for them to follow the seam into the hillside, much to the delight of the metal and glass workers, as they only had charcoal from the forest to work with, and it lacked the intense heat of coke.

A various assortment of minerals were found as they dug and probed the rich hillsides, but they didn't know what to do with them except admire the pretty colours, but sooner or later, someone would stumble across their use, and another useful product would be added to their ever growing collection of materials. While all this was going on, Macie, or more accurately, Eslie, produced two more children, much to Brent's delight. Although he felt no inclination to take a partner himself, and there were many offers, he enjoyed the company of the youngsters.

All that remained of his old settlement by the lake were two hermit families who spurned the modern developments of the island, except when they were in trouble, and then help was generously given by a bemused group who had taken on their welfare as a sort of duty.

Several expeditions sailed across the intervening waters to visit the forest, but there was nothing of any use to be gained from such excursions, except the adventure itself, and that never died while there were 'Brents' around.

Finally the silver tower gave up its horrible secret. Brent and two others had been exploring some underground passageways beneath a small lone building which served no useful purpose that they could understand. They found a very heavy metal door with elaborate locking devices on it, and the door looked as if the locks had been withdrawn and the door opened the tiniest amount, and then left for some reason.

Using metal bars, they managed to prise the door open and enter a small room crammed with control consoles and other unfathomable gadgets. From the diagrams above the control units together with the words they had associated meanings to, they came to the conclusion that the purpose of the room and its contents was to fire something similar to their flame thrower, but on a very much bigger scale.

And then Brent realized the silver tower was the flame thrower, and this was probably one of the mighty weapons which had destroyed the world of the ancients so long ago.

They left the control room in sombre mood, jamming the door shut as best as they could, and wishing they had never found the dreadful weapon in the first place. Somehow the sun seemed less bright when they emerged from underground and the air a little less sweet.

Over the years, the settlement continued to expand into the ruins of the old city, buildings being restored, road ways cleared, and a few artistic improvements made here and there to suit the aesthetic desires of the people.

A proper harbour was constructed to accommodate the old sailing ship and an even bigger version designed by Macie.

Between them, they plied the waters of the lake, eventually reaching the southernmost shores, several days sailing away. Apart from a small section of the coast from the old settlement under the cliffs to half way to the island, the edge of the lake was fringed with continuous forest, the southern end containing trees even taller than those of their old home forest, and with an even more diverse range of wildlife.

Using a telescope they could see creatures normally only encountered in nightmares roaming the shoreline, gargantuan hulks of bone and flesh with hideous wrinkled hides, looking for something a little smaller to eat.

At one point, a dark shadow had passed over the ship causing them all to look up. A lizard like body supported by ten metre wings had glided overhead, its beady black eyes glaring longingly at the tasty little morsels below, but unable to land because of the masts and tangle of rigging which festooned the ship.

Any inclination to land and explore was promptly extinguished having seen what might greet them if they did, so they just contented themselves by marvelling at nature's attempt to repopulate the planet with the greatest diversity of creatures possible, in the hope that some good might come of it in time.

On one occasion, they had encountered a race of small people covered in a fine pale brown down like hair, but they were simple folk and completely naked.

What little language they had was indecipherable by the crew, and they expressed little interest in their visitors despite the offer of simple gifts. Brent was quite certain that they could not have been responsible for the original sailing ship, and they never did find out who built it.

Occasionally they came across odd bits of ruins on the shores of the lake, but these were usually only fragments of what had been, and after exploring the first few and gleaning no artefacts or information from them, they were ignored.

The occasional forum was held to resolve any problems the settlement had, and at one of these relaxed meetings the possibility of others like themselves cropped up.

Brent maintained that it was most unlikely that they were the only ones to have survived the ancient's holocaust, as there had been three separate settlements at one time, and they had developed independently until the time of the tracks.

Their old settlement had been hemmed in by the forest on one side and the lake and the barren lands on the others. The idea of forging a path through the forest was a non starter, and the barren lands would need some form of powered vehicle to carry them and their supplies. There seemed no possibility of that, as the only two engines they possessed were too small for a long haul across the wastes.

Realizing that the island was going to be their home for the foreseeable future, a greater effort was put into making it as comfortable as possible. Remembering the small electric motor Kelt had shown him, Brent and his team sought out the largest motor they could find in the industrial section of the old city. A large windmill was constructed on a promontory jutting out into the lake where it would catch the full force of the wind, and using salvaged gears, the motor was linked to the main drive shaft of the mill.

After much trial and error, and quite copious amounts of bad language, they managed to produce electricity, but not before several of them experienced the bite of touching bare conductors. The fluorescent lights of the ancients were stripped from those buildings they had no use for at the present, and installed in their new homes, once the mysteries of wiring and switches had been solved.

During the day there was little need for power, and so a line was run out to the workshops, enabling the electric power tools to be used, once they understood what they were for and how to use them. This new addition to their skills enabled their manufacturing abilities to soar to new heights, and the new industrial age arrived.

One of the small oil engines was mounted in a specially designed boat and fitted with two paddle wheels. Apart from the smell and noise, this was a much preferred method of moving around the lake and greatly enjoyed by any youngsters who were fortunate enough to be invited aboard.

As the settlement was now so much larger, instead of the old system of Elders, a new approach to a governing body was tried. Brent had been asked to head up this new body, but he refused the post as it held little interest for him. He did suggest a system that would be fair and efficient, whereby the inhabited area of the new settlement would be broken up into ten arbitrary sections, and each section elect one person to represent them on any matters which would affect them all. Once the concept that everyone's voice counted for something, the idea caught on, and there were very few absenters on matters of importance.

A system of tracks had been built linking the growing fields and the forest in the foothills to the new town, the other oil engine acting as a traction unit, pulling six trucks.

There was sufficient metal in the old ruins for them to make rails from, but it meant developing new methods of metal forging to utilize it. Old habits die hard, and as there was plenty of the extra hard wood available in the nearby forest, they chose to use it for their new track system.

Although the years were catching up on Brent, he still felt young at heart, but somewhat frustrated as younger men surpassed him in physical prowess, and now mental agility.

His sense of adventure had never wavered, but apart from the forest on the mainland and the barren lands, there was nowhere else to go except the triple headed mountain and the southern shores of the vast lake.

He had often argued with Macie about the constant water level of the lake, as all the streams and rivers they had seen emptied into it, and none left acting as an overflow, so how come the lake always remained at the same level?

Macie thought evaporation was responsible for the disappearance of the excess, but Brent would have none of it, stating there must be an exit somewhere for the level to be held so constant.

After many discussions among the elected council of what to do to satiate Brent's hunger for something interesting to get his teeth into, it was decided to back his request for a sailing ship to explore the rest of the lake. Although not as large as the one captured so long ago from their attackers at the cliff site, it would be equipped with two sails and the oil engine from the paddle boat, but this time powering a propeller, the idea copied from an electric fan of the ancients.

Brent was overjoyed at the announcement, and showed it, which was not normally expected of one with such a taciturn nature. Building began a few days later, once the design had been approved by a now very impatient Brent.

Despite the many willing hands which had volunteered their services in recompense for all that Brent had done for the settlement over the years, the ship was slow to grow, at least according to the very impatient Brent.

The fitting of the oil engine proved troublesome, as did the casting of a suitable propeller to drive the ship, but eventually all problems were solved, and she floated at the newly constructed dockside with her masts tall and proud, a testament to many hours of devoted skill and labour from an ever grateful community.

Macie had automatically assumed that he would be included in the crew of the *Explorer*, as she was to be called, but the years had caught up with him in an unkind way. His joints refused to flex as they once had, and any form of stress brought on a 'nervous bowel' condition much to his consternation and the dismay of those around him at the time.

Brent and Eslie managed to talk him out of the idea of joining the impending expedition, and he gave in as gracefully as he could, realizing that he would be more of a hindrance to the rest of them than an asset.

The ship was fully stocked with everything it was thought they would need on an extended exploration, and the day finally arrived for departure with the whole community turning out to cheer them on their way.

Brent stood proudly in the bows of the brightly painted ship, and after waving goodbye to all his well-wishers on the shore, gave the order to hoist sail.

Eager hands hauled on ropes, and the twin sails of the *Explorer* slowly ascended the gleaming masts to catch the ever constant wind, filling out with a series of cracks like pistol shots in the clear morning air.

Straining at her moorings with her sails full, the ship creaked as she heeled slightly over to one side, and then Brent gave the word to 'cast off'.

They had to cut the two moorings which held her to the quay side, as the tension in the ropes was far too great for them to overcome, despite the many eager hands which heaved and strained.

The *Explorer* surged forward, throwing Brent off balance and causing him to stagger about in a most undignified manner for a few moments, and then they were underway.

A thunderous series of cheers and hand clapping gradually died away as the ship cleaved her way out into deeper waters and then all was silent, except for the creaking of the rigging and the constant slap slap of the waters on her bow.

Many a silent tear was shed that day by those left behind, for they were losing a strong leader and very dear friend to the unknown waters of the lake.

Despite his somewhat irritable nature at times, and a level of sarcasm which had made some wince, he had pulled all three settlements together and given them a much better standard of living than they would have had if he had not existed. His dogged determination and ability to overcome bureaucratic claptrap had earned him the respect of all, except perhaps some of those on the receiving end of one of his more devastating tongue lashings.

At times, when all had seemed lost, he had come up with a solution, and then hammered it into existence, brooking no compromise or resistance, and his stabilizing influence would be sorely missed in years to come.

Life got back to near normal for the settlement after a while, but it seemed a little subdued, a bright and sometimes controversial light had gone out, and they missed it.

The island with its gleaming tower soon disappeared over the horizon as the ship ploughed on in a southerly direction, and then they were surrounded by water, all traces of land having been left far behind them.

By early evening there had been no sight of anything but the never ending water, not even the giant forest which fringed the lake for so long was visible anymore, so it was decided to drop anchor for the night and travel on next morning. The anchor failed to reach the bottom of the lake despite adding another length of rope to the already long line, so they let the ship drift where it would, a watch being kept just in case anything untoward happened during the hours of darkness.

Fishing lines were thrown over the side, and soon they had a wholesome meal of fish, bread and fruit, washed down with a weak wine-like fruit juice which was a recent development of some enterprising member of the group.

Copious amounts of fruit in varying degrees of ripeness had been stored well below the water line where it was cool, the thought being that it would last them for some while, so delaying the time when they would have to go ashore to replenish their stocks.

Lanterns were lit as the sun finally dipped below the horizon, the waters turning a deep blood red before they eventually turned black, the lights from the ship reflecting from the dancing wavelets like so many sparkling fish.

Surprisingly, everyone slept well that night, except the watch keepers, and they dozed at their posts as no one had thought to appoint an overseer of the watch.

Next morning the sails were hauled aloft before a meal was taken, and the ship soon gathered momentum as the stiff breeze filled the billowing yellow canvas.

Around midday land was sighted, and the ship turned towards the shore in the hope of finding a suitable landing place. As usual, the shoreline either had dense undergrowth right down to the waterline or sheer rock faces, offering no easy access to the forest behind.

'It looks like this is a long finger of land sticking out from the main mass,' Brent said hopefully, 'so let's go around it and follow the shoreline for a while, there may be a landing place somewhere.'

As soon as they had rounded the peninsular, the land mass shielded them from the main force of the wind, and the ship consequently slowed down. They had only gone a few kilometres when figures could be seen running along the top of the short cliff above.

Brent called out, expecting to get a favourable reply, but his greeting was met by a hail of arrows, most of which fortunately fell short of the ship, although one did manage to embed itself in the bows.

'Not very friendly,' he commented, as the ship pulled away from the hostile natives, 'probably been visited by the same lot who attacked us.' They were disappointed at the reception they had received, and realizing that they probably did not have a common language between them, decided it was pointless to show they meant no harm.

As they pulled away from the shore the wind picked up as did the speed of the ship, and they followed the peninsular until it merged in with the mainland some ten kilometres ahead. There were no more sightings of natives, friendly or otherwise, but a sandy beach came into view, very much like the tiny one at the foot of the cliffs in their old settlement, but much larger. Brent was determined to make landfall, and so the small rowing boat was lowered.

Brent and two others jumped into the tiny boat, one of the men manning the oars as if he had done it all his life, which left Brent suitably impressed at the man's abilities.

'Let's sit in the boat awhile,' Brent said, as the boat ploughed a small furrow in the soft yellow sand, 'we want to be sure we don't get skewered by jumpy natives. The first sign of trouble, spin the boat around, and row like hell.'

There was no hail of arrows, or anything else. A strange looking flying creature swooped down from a nearby tree, took a second look at the three in the boat and decided they were just a little too big to take on, and left, still hungry.

'Looks safe enough,' Brent said after a while, 'so let's quietly take a look at what's behind the beach.'

They clambered out of the rowing boat, dragging it a short distance up the beach and then headed for the dense greenery at the top of the sandy slope. They had failed to notice the disturbance in the sand as they hurried along, which was just as well, as hungry mouths were only a few centimetres below the surface and had sensed a meal was at hand.

The shrubs were not as dense as they had first thought and so they were able to push their way through with little effort, reaching a clearing some fifty metres ahead. And there they stopped, open mouthed at the sight before them.

A lone tree stood in a small grassy clearing, and firmly bound to its trunk a struggling human figure had been tightly bound. The trio stopped, looking around for those who had done this cruel thing, but there were no sounds to indicate others present, just the background noises of the forest life and the soft rustling of the struggling man and his occasional moan of despair. His completely naked body was tanned a deep nut brown and covered in a fine fuzz of hair which was only noticeable when they moved close up.

At last the bound figure saw the approaching trio and stopped his struggles, his face frozen in fear and his mouth wide open. As they drew near they could see the grass around the base of the tree had been worn away and the ground disturbed as if sharp claws had dug into it.

'Cut him free,' Brent quietly said to one of the men, 'we'll keep a lookout for anything approaching, and shoot to kill.' he said to the other man. Although armed with their crossbows, they would be no match for a large number of adversaries.

The bound figure whimpered with fear and closed his eyes as one of the men drew his knife and moved towards him.

A few quick slashes with the razor sharp knife and the unfortunate creature slumped to the ground in a dead faint.

'Pick him up, and let's get the hell out of here,' Brent said, swinging his crossbow around to cover as much of the surrounding bush as possible, 'the others might come back to see how he's doing.'

The two men grabbed an arm each and ran for the boat, while Brent brought up the rear of the rescue party, occasionally stopping to point his crossbow as menacingly as possible at anything which might be following.

When he reached the boat, the other two had dragged it into the water and slung the still unconscious fuzzy man in the bottom. As he clambered aboard, the other two already had the oars in the water and were pulling with all their strength. There was still no sign of pursuit from the forest.

'That was a nasty do.' Brent commented, as they made their way back to the ship. 'I think that poor chap had been left there for the forest animals to eat, maybe as a punishment or sacrifice. We can find out when he comes to.' he added, failing to realize the probable language difficulties.

Eager hands pulled the party aboard, expressing surprise at the extra passenger and the fact that he was naked. Brent quickly explained what had happened, and at that point the fuzzy man decided to rejoin the land of the living.

A string of gibberish issued forth from the shaking figure on the deck, and they all stood back a little just in case he became violent. Someone thoughtfully brought a beaker of water and held it out to the terrified creature, but he seemed unable to understand what it was for. A little water was poured from the breaker just in front of the unfortunate, and then he grasped the significance of the beaker. A few moments later, and he was greedily drinking from the proffered beaker and indicating he wanted more.

Try as they might, they were unable to make any sense of the strange sounds the man emitted, and Brent suggested the only way they were going to understand him was to rebuild his language word by word, and a volunteer was asked for to accomplish the formidable task.

'Might as well get underway.' Brent said, as the fuzzy man was gently led away to the cool of a cabin below.

'There's nothing for us in this area unless anyone fancies having a go at the tree game.'

With the sails full and straining on the masts, the *Explorer* headed out into deeper waters and stronger winds, soon leaving the sandy beach and its lone tree in the clearing to those who enjoyed its macabre significance.

Several days later, 'Fuzzy' as the rescued man had been named, had learnt several words of their language and was able to hold a very limited conversation, backed up with signs and gesticulations which brought much mirth to the rest of the crew who had now joined in the act, so speeding up the learning process.

It was many days later when they managed to get the full story of the tree binding out of him, and then they realized what had been going on.

The group in which he had the misfortune to be born had the notion that if they made the odd sacrifice to the forest creatures, then the majority of them would be left alone to live their lives out to the full. Not that the sacrifice made one jot of difference in reality, but they feared if they didn't do it, then things could get a lot worse. They seemed to be a very primitive tribe of people, using few tools and indulging in copious amounts of mysticism and folk lore.

The task of 'civilizing' the new member to their group took a while, the notion of clothing being quite abhorrent to him, although he accepted it quite readily on others.

The ship ploughed on through the waters of the vast lake, stopping here and there to inspect the land where there was easy access, which occurred less frequently than they would have liked.

A large river emptied itself into the lake at one point, and Brent decided to go up stream a short way to see if there was anything new to be discovered. Although the river's flow was quite gentle, it was not wide enough for them to easily tack the *Explorer* from bank to bank, so they resorted to using the oil engine for the first time.

The steady chug chug of the engine echoed back from the forest, sending the various life forms scurrying deeper into the tangled undergrowth for cover, and giving them an idea of what they might come across if they tried to land.

About four kilometres up stream the river narrowed considerably, consequently the speed of the flow increased and as the *Explorer*'s engine was not powerful enough to push the vessel against the racing waters, they dropped anchor.

As it was late afternoon and the sun was already close to the horizon, it was decided to spend the night in the middle of the river and go ashore early next morning if all seemed well. A double watch system was set up to make sure they were not taken by surprise by inquisitive night visitors, and a very pleasant and relaxed evening was had by all.

As this was the first time they had spent a night so close to the forest, they were not prepared for the hideous cacophony of screams and yells which began a few hours after the sun had dipped below the horizon. In the inky blackness, feathers flew, flesh was torn and bones crunched, accompanied by the howls of protest from those unfortunate enough to be on the menu. Sleep didn't come easily to the crew of the *Explorer* that night, and they were a rather bleary eyed bunch who gathered for an early morning breakfast, the night music of the forest having been cut off as if by a switch as the first rays of sun splashed across the tree tops.

'After all that noise last night, I'm not so sure I want to go ashore.' one of the crew said, chewing his grain bun.

'And anyway, the forest is all the same wherever you go, so what's the point?' There was no reply to his comment as they were all too busy eating.

In the light of early dawn, the forest didn't look so menacing as it had sounded the night before. A large grassy area ran from the river bank for about half a kilometre before the forest proper began, and then it didn't sport the giant trees they were so used to.

Ten volunteers were called for to explore the region, all of which would be heavily armed with crossbows and a portable flame gun, which had now been modified to use a fine mist of oil instead of the flame rock powder as this was more powerful and easier to handle.

The little rowing boat made several trips before all ten were assembled on the river bank, and they set off in high spirits in the knowledge that they were well able to defend themselves against most things.

They encountered virtually no life forms as they crossed the grassy area, remaining blissfully ignorant of what lay beneath their hurrying feet or what was watching from the cover of the distant forest. The grass eventually gave way to sand and gravel, and up ahead a pass between two low tree covered hills was the only way forward.

Brent called a halt so that the rest of the expedition could voice their opinions as to whether they should go on or return to the ship, and after a short discussion, the general consensus was to see what lay on the other side of the pass and then return.

The climb up the pass proved more exhausting than they had expected, but they were rewarded for their efforts when they reached the top. Before them lay a flat area of barren ground, and in the distance a tree topped cliff of immense height blocked all else from view. Scattered about on the plain were clumps of what looked like rock, but they somehow looked too angular and well defined to be like any rocks they had seen before.

It was too much for Brent's curiosity, and they set off down the slope and onto the gravel plain. The rock formations revealed their secret as they drew near the first one.

'It's like the machine we found at the metal workers place,' exclaimed Brent, 'except something has given it a right bashing, just look at all that twisted metal.' The little group stood in wonder, as few of them had heard of the scavenger, let alone seen it. They moved on to the next clump of twisted metal, little realizing what had happened.

All the other 'rock' formations turned out to be destroyed robot machines from a bygone age. As the explorers had no knowledge of the robot wars which had taken place as man had finally relinquished control to automatics, they were at a loss as to what had happened and why everything had been destroyed.

'Just look at that cliff face,' one of the men commented, 'it's been ripped into by something very powerful by the look of it, there's no way we could do damage like that, even with our mining tools.'

The cliff had been under sustained attack from explosive shells for some time, and when these had failed to penetrate the solid basalt rock sufficiently to reach the factory caverns behind, the 'liquid flame' machine had fought its way across the heavily defended plain and pumped a liquid explosive straight into the main entrance.

The ensuing blast had destroyed the entire complex along with the machine which had delivered the death blow, all that remained was a series of mangled heaps of distorted metal, a fitting and lasting tribute to man's extreme folly.

The largest pile of ripped and twisted metal was blocking a large hole in the cliff face, and although they could have wriggled through its mangled mass of beams and bent plates, they feared to do so in case it shifted while they were inside the tunnel, and their escape was blocked.

They wandered from crumpled heap to crumpled heap, trying to work out the purpose for which each had initially been constructed, but failed to do so because of the extensive damage and a lack of engineering skills.

It was Brent, after considerable thought and pondering who came up with the reason for the total destruction of all they could see, although he could barely comprehend it.

'I think there has been a massive conflict here, not between humans and machines, but between the machines themselves. Nothing a human could do would cause so much damage, so it must have been two lots of powerful machines attacking each other.' he paused for a moment, deep in thought. 'I wonder why the ancients didn't stop it? It's a terrible waste of materials, and look at the work that must have gone into making these things.'

The others, not quite able to grasp the concept, just nodded, hoping enlightenment would somehow bless them at a later date.

There was little sign of anything trying to grow on the gravel plain or the ruptured cliff face, leaving the scene almost as it must have been at the end of the mechanical conflict. Except for a little corrosion on the twisted metal work of the robotic war machines, there was no clue as to how long ago it had all taken place.

'The metalworkers would have a lovely time collecting this lot up,' Brent mused, as they wandered back to the tunnel entrance, 'except it wouldn't be worth the enormous effort of taking it all the way back to the island.'

They hung around the remains of the monstrous machine which was blocking the entrance to the tunnel complex and the workshops beyond, but still thought it too risky to try and force a way in.

'There's nothing more for us here.' Brent said, sounding almost sad at having to leave an area which contained so much mystery and information of how things had been.

'We'd best be getting back to the ship, or the others will be getting worried.' The journey back took no time at all as they chatted among themselves about what they had seen and what it all meant, some getting very close to the truth.

Arriving back at the river bank they were in for a surprise. A long bodied four legged creature with an evil looking head and teeth to match lay studded with crossbow bolts on the now blood stained sands opposite the ship. Several men stood around it, one posing with his foot nonchalantly resting on the now still flanks.

'Glad you're back,' said one of the men, 'we thought we'd better kill it once we'd seen its teeth, this thing has never eaten grass and we thought you would be due back soon.'

'Well done,' Brent replied, 'I doubt we'd have been able to kill it before a few of us had been dismembered. I think you'd better recover the crossbow bolts soon in case something else comes along to eat it, and ruins the bolts.'

With the bolts recovered, washed and returned to their holders, and a light meal taken, it was decided to return to the lake and continue their exploration.

Shortly after they had up anchored and begun making their way down river, something long, thick and slimy came down stream, heaved itself up onto the bank and swallowed the three metre carcass whole, and then slipped back into the water leaving only the blood stained sand to mark the spot.

Back on the main lake, the ship cruised along the southern shores for three days with no sign of a suitable landing place, not that many of the crew were any too keen to make land again after dispatching the horror on the river bank.

Two more immense rivers poured their tumbling waters into the vast lake, reinforcing Brent's theory that there must be an exit somewhere, it was only a matter of finding it.

A few days later, and the mystery was solved. A break in the forest clad sheer cliffs was spotted by the lookout high up on one of the masts, and everyone rushed up on deck to see what all the fuss was about.

It was as though a giant celestial spade had taken a huge clean cut out of the impenetrable cliffs nearly a half kilometre wide, and down this the excess waters of the lake poured in a smooth majestic slide with hardly a ripple on its glass-like surface.

'There you are,' Brent yelled triumphantly, 'told you we'd find it.

Better run the engine up, we don't know how strong the current might be and the wind is blowing directly down it.' With the sails down, the only sound was the soft chug chug of the little oil engine and the soft lapping of the waters against the bows, the crew being shocked into silence at the amazing scene before them.

'Do we go down it?' someone asked, 'and if we do, how do we get back?'

Before Brent could answer, the decision was taken out of their hands as the engine's steady rhythm faltered, spluttered, coughed twice and then went silent.

'She's out of oil!' someone shouted. The man in charge of the engine sprinted for the hatch and disappeared down the hole like a frightened rabbit. Long before he could recharge the oil tank and get the engine started again, fate, or something else had taken its inexorable hand in the matter, and the *Explorer* gracefully slid towards the huge curving lip of the overspill, gently assisted by the wind.

There was nothing they could do as the ship dipped its bow over the edge of the spill and then accelerated down the smooth slope of water without a sound, except for the collective gasp of the combined crew.

Within seconds the ship was at the bottom of the slope, bobbing up and down in the now turbulent waters at the bottom of the huge slide, its crew still paralysed with the shock of what had happened.

The engine coughed back into life at last, and Brent suggested they try to go back up the water slide, knowing in his heart that it was quite impossible with the limited amount of power they could get from their tiny engine. But it had to be tried, if only for the sake of those of the crew who didn't understand such things.

The engine was now running at full throttle, its vibrations causing anything loose on board to rattle and shake in sympathy, but it was to no avail. The mighty flow of the water was far too much for the little engine to overcome, and Brent ordered the ship to be turned around and head down the boiling waters of the turbulent river until they could find a place to safely moor up and decide what to do.

Gradually, the river calmed down in its headlong rush south and they were able to raise the sails to speed them on their way, as there had been no mooring places to offer them sanctuary so far.

The lookout again heralded the next change in the saga.

'Another lake ahead,' he called out hesitatingly, 'at least I can't see any more land.'

The river mouth opened into a vast expanse of grey water which stretched out to the horizon, the coast swinging around on either side, still clad in its green mantle but this time with the occasional sandy beach to break up the monotony of the sheer cliffs.

Someone slipped a container on a rope over the side of the ship to obtain a fresh supply of drinking water. His expletive on taking the first mouthful is unprintable as he had never tasted sea water before.

This posed a new problem for the ship's company, and a hasty retreat to the fresh waters of the river was undertaken to fill all available containers with drinkable water.

That evening they anchored just off the coast in shallow water, and during a rather sombre meal discussed their options, which didn't amount to many.

'How do we get back home?' one of the youngest members of the crew asked, a slight tremble in his voice.

'The short answer to that is, we don't,' Brent announced rather brutally, 'we can't get the ship back up the water slide as we don't have enough power. There is little point in abandoning the ship and trying to walk home as the distance is far too great, and the local wild life would enjoy it far more than we would. There is no way home. As far as we are concerned, home is where we choose to make it.

'We may find some other tribes which might prove a little more friendly than the last lot, and if so, we could join them and maybe even take mates, for those of you who are young enough.' A nervous titter ran through the assembled crew as they realized the enormity of their plight.

'Let's sleep on it, and see what the morrow will bring.' Brent said, trying to be as cheerful as possible, and not really succeeding.

The following morning saw a somewhat despondent crew going about their duties in a desolate manner, until someone spotted another sail on the horizon.

Brent was called for, the oil fired cannon in the bows made ready, just in case, and they headed off towards the distant sail, hearts a thumping and adrenaline running high at the start of a new venture, but that's another story...

The End

**More from sci-fi-cafe.com
by David Reynolds-Moreton**

Anthology of Futures
Anthology of Possibilities
Divergence
Enslavement
Exchange Rate
Extreme Difference
Flight of the Tristan
Fully Guaranteed
Greenways
Inheritance
Light Quest
The Martian Enigma
The Power Seeds
The Seed Garden
The Single Twin
The Sweepers
The Tribe
Transplant
Of Wood, Metal and Glass